A Mosaic in Time

Who will survive?
The girl, the boy, the woman, the aliens?

Author & Publisher

Susan Allen

03/28/17

A big THANK YOU to all my friendly volunteer readers, editors and IT advisers; and to my Father – for keeping his photos.

To Margerie & Peter,
Lovely to meet you & enjoy your company. Hope you have fun reading my words, borne from a vivid imagination :)
Susan - x
7th October, 2020.

Pre-Amble

2010

The mosaic twinkled in the starlight. Shadows fell across the scene - negatives of statues built in memory of those souls sacrificed for freedom many years ago. How could something so beautiful commemorate such awful times?

Jennifer had given up work - retiring at 60 years of age. She now had time to sit and think; to walk and ponder; to stop and remember. Being Matron of the Hope & Charity boarding school in Tokyo had presented her with many challenges - and a few grey hairs - but it had kept her alive and focused; able to put aside those other memories; the childhood nightmares, the sense of loss and helplessness, the unspoken, lurking fear.

Only 3 people had managed to escape and live to tell the tale of their incarceration by the Invaders. Theirs was a harrowing tale - more fantastical than any computer game and one that could not be re-played - if you failed to succeed the first time. Jennifer gulped silently as the images pierced her mind.

Maybe she should write her story.

Table of Contents

Susan Allen

Chapter 1 – A Japanese Island in 1953

On the beach

The 3 year old was barely decipherable as a living child let alone a beloved, bright and, currently terrified, grand-daughter. She wore every layer of clothing her grandma could squeeze on her. The grandmother's reasoning was twofold, to protect the infant from the night time drop in temperature and, at the same time, to carry as much of her once lavish wardrobe as possible. The matriarch was dressed in a similar fashion. Over the past week Georgina Hayes had changed from a self-assured and elegant, mature socialite into a bruised and hungry alpha female; she had to be strong and wily if this precious child was to survive.

George Maynard, Skipper of an Australian merchant ship, had deliberately detoured to this remote island, part of the Japanese archipelago. He made a habit of calling in from time to time with much loved Western treats for the islanders and, in return, he and his crew would take some well earned R&R in the little known hot springs haven. But this visit proved to be no mini holiday. His stomach had churned at the islanders' plight and he desperately wanted to help. His vessel had restricted space and he could only take those who were fit and healthy enough to endure 20 days at sea and cope with limited rations and crowded quarters. Some would be able to sleep below decks but many would have to find what shelter they could beneath makeshift canvas bivouacs strung between cargo containers. The islanders were not seasoned blue water sailors; in addition their recent deprivations and emotional trauma had sapped their strength and vitality. He would do his best for them but there was no doubt in his mind that it would challenge their battered resilience even further.

Everywhere was in the turmoil of recovery and rebuild after the 2nd World War. Captain Maynard was fully aware the farming equipment and machinery he carried on board were essential commodities Down Under - if normal service was to be resumed. He had to complete his delivery but could not sail away and leave these people to a protracted and gruesome fate. It was horrific enough that the majority of the island's small population of less than 200 individuals had already been singled out for 'special treatment' by the Invaders. He was mortified he'd arrived too late to save them; however there was a chance he could help these bereft older individuals who were reduced to sleeping rough on the narrow black sand beach. George Maynard's innate compassion compelled him to put himself, his crew and precious cargo at risk. After all they'd been through who knew what the future held in store for any of them.

The experimental abuse practiced by the Invaders on the younger men, women and children was keeping them entertained on the other side of the island. Thank goodness that aging Scotsman had remembered his Morse code and been able to send out a distress call - which George, in turn, responded to. Under the guidance of a retired radio operator, willing volunteers converted old blankets and the fire keeping them warm on the shoreline, into a signal. George hoped the Invaders considered these people too old and frail to be worth bothering with but, he tried to suppress the thought, maybe they were being saved for later. Most were at least 70 years old, only the fair haired woman and her grand-daughter were younger. Whilst the woman certainly looked haggard and distressed George doubted she was any older than him. In fact she was actually English but had managed to disguise this, along with her age, by wearing traditional Japanese attire and make-up, otherwise – he shuddered - in all probability, she too would have been retained to undergo potentially fatal research methods. He registered he had yet to find out exactly how the child escaped detection and capture.

Chit chat

'Stink, stink, these manOids stink' ...Wil decried.

Fee responded...'Stench, stench, pervading stench. The keePers hose, hose to tolerate. Twice, twice a day. Skin, skin is useless. They cover, cover with fabric. No protect from weather, weather. Ugly, ugly, cover up. Crude and dirty, dirty. Agree, agree?'

'Yes, yes, primitive race.' Wil shrivelled his nostrils into his head to emphasise his disgust - causing his masQ to move. 'MasQ, masQ essential. Must, must avoid germs. Noxious, noxious breath. Watch, long, long distance. Use worM, worMcamRas.'

Their brief conversation over Wil and Fee turned away from the scene and briefly, almost imperceptibly, brushed shoulders.

Wil was taking part in his first eXploratory miSSion to find alternative life forms and environs which might provide opportunities for breedin and groWth. So far he and the other kaRRak citiXens on board were disillusioned at how under-developed these early manOid creatures remained. Every one of the beings they'd thrown from the tree tops had failed to fly, whether manOid or femanOid, young or old, they crashed to the ground, splattering their innards all over the place. Thankfully, with a little prodding, the other specimens were able to clear up the mess; none of his comrades could stomach the task. The scans and vivisections the knowAlls subsequently carried out, in their sterile lab, revealed the organ, bone and muscle mechanics of this particular manOid species to be mundanely perfunctory and uninspiring; except, curiously, they seemed to carry around with them far more brainBox than they used; hardly an effective and efficient use of resources.

He soon became bored with observing the water tests. Some of the manOids dropped in the sea flailed about and managed to keep afloat; others just splashed, screamed, then sank - not to be seen again - until they washed up on the shore, battered and lifeless. Those that could swim on the surface were taken down below in stages. Again, they were very limited in their abilities. A couple made successful attempts to swim to the surface but none enjoyed the experience or took advantage of their underwater world. When keePers held them below the surface the specimens drowned, their lungs filling up with water. Yet further confirmation of the lesser beings they were. In the end the knowAlls had resorted to inserting a fisHPop into two samplings- both having survived the initial tests, one juvenile manOid and one adult femanOid. To see if there was potential for improvement.

DWellers, back home, always wanted more. No matter how comfortable they were they could not be satisfied. They wanted groWth. They wanted to expand their influence into other worlds - which was shorthand for taking what they wanted and leaving a mixture of cross-fertilised beings to develop as they could. The usual process was for a miSSion to return a few generations later to see if the improved off-spring could be of used in kaRRak as worKers, breeDers, labRats or foDDer. KaRRak citiXens were so convinced of their own superiority that they never considered these improvements unwarranted or their interference intrusive and unnecessary.

Thankfully, on this occasion, the mediCTeam had also been able to implant a lingOPop into the brain of a few samplings so at least they were now able to communicate with them and they could carry out basic instructions. The knowAlls only talKed-up four 'Oids as it was not economical to use too many pellets. These specimens were capable of communicating with each other and therefore could pass on whatever orders they were given. The leader of the miSSion, Fee, and the other knowAlls in the group were keen to stay a while longer. They felt, given time, they could devise a method to ensure these sub-creatures advanced (to the benefit of dWellers) – but first they needed to carry out more tests and observations. So far most experiments proved fatal but this didn't put them off; they were convinced it was only a matter of time before they had a breakthrough. Wil, a senior teCHno, wasn't so sure - whilst he didn't want the miSSion to fail he would be glad when it moved on to more fertile territory.

The phYto-knowAlls were in the process of examining local flora. Dissection of the stomachs of the manOids and other indigenous species revealed part digested vegetation. So far the results had proved inconclusive as many species also ate the flesh of other species, as well as their own, and some even had more than one stomach to process the huge amounts of vegetation they consumed. What they couldn't understand was why the samplings also ingested poisons to damage their systems. It would appear the manOids used chemicals to prevent insects from damaging their crops. Totally at variance to kaRRak people who grew vegetation to encourage insects; a great source of protein and a pleasure to watch go about their business. Another oddity was that most of these creatures also suckled on a plant based substance they set light to.... a substance which appeared to create a black sticky residue on their breathing organs; it was as if they were deliberately harming themselves; as if they set no value on their bodies. The miSSion's knowAlls were intrigued. They tied down breathing manOids and slit them open. Then they worked on each organ in turn... cutting through the protective tissues and fat; testing to see which parts of the body function they affected. With practice they could keep a specimen alive for nearly half a mooNRing whilst they conducted their analysis but, despite the screams which gradually lulled to a whimper, and the blood spewing continually over their aprons and instruments, they could not determine the physiological and pathological genre of a species which deliberately chose to mutilate its organs and ability to function.

As far as Wil was concerned, as each 'Oid took its last breath, it was good riddance. He missed home and his pet cocKRoach, Bud. Always there to greet him and guaranteed to clear up crumbs dropped on the floor. His antennae going off in different directions were a constant source of amusement, especially as they gave a reliable indication as to his mood ... once you got to know him. CocKRoaches were graded as social insects and they interacted with each other by chemical signals, identifying group feeding troughs and shelter zones. By smearing pheromones, produced by sCent-knowAlls to mimic those emitted by cockroaches, it was possible to convince a young cocKRoach that you were his best friend - his buddy. The fact a pet cocKRoach could forage for itself made it an extremely popular pet among eXplorers & miSSionaries. No matter how long a citiXen was gone from home the intrepid cocKRoach would take care of itself and be there, twitching its feelers and keen to greet you, when you returned. Wil smiled at the thought of home.

Leftover manOids

'Ok mates. Who knows what we're gonna find......'

Having seen the SOS signal George realised there might not be the usual good humoured welcome. They dropped anchor just off the spit, beyond easy reach of the jetty.

'Andy, you stay on board with the others, I'll take this motley band,' he pointed to the three crew members already preparing to lower the tender.

'If you don't hear from us in 4 hours, up anchor and away – get help.'

'Maybe I should go ashore and you stay back ... after all, you're the Skipper.' Andy felt sick at the idea he might have to leave his crewmates and skipper behind.

'No, definitely not ... I can't ask you,' George swept his bronzed arm in an arc, encompassing all of them; 'to go instead of me ... you and this vessel are my responsibility. We'll find out what this Mayday signal is all about and be back in touch. With any luck it will be kids messing about.'

George knew this was the least likely option – and so did his crew. He left his First Mate on board with the other half of the crew. Instinct told the captain not to use the outboard motor, to row ashore as quietly and unobtrusively as possible. The small, dormant radio in his back pack was intended for emergency use only - there had to be some reason why the islanders signalled by firelight rather than radio calls - every fibre of his being prickled the need to proceed with extreme caution. His hand checked for the torch, the loaded revolver and flare-gun in his vest.

What they found was almost beyond belief. Elderly friends and acquaintances, folk he'd laughed and joked with on previous trips, shrunken and huddled together with their backs against the sheer, tectonic cliff side. The faces that turned towards him mirrored fear and horror, others were fixed, staring emotionless out to sea, lost behind drained eyes. Tatami mats had been thrown over the volcanic deposits beneath their feet in an attempt to provide somewhere to sleep but there was little comfort to be had in this bleak location. These people must have been at their wits end to seek sanctuary in such an inhospitable place. Thank goodness they thought to bring emergency chocolate and water rations ashore with them. Leaving his 3 crew to administer what comfort and first aid they could to the beleaguered islanders George sought out the message sender – Ian Campbell - and followed the agile pensioner up the steep pathway - which was no mean task.

It was a narrow, rocky track, difficult to negotiate in flickering moonlight. The vertical ascent challenged George Maynard's legs and lungs, especially after weeks at sea. The Skipper's admiration for his guide grew with each demanding step he took. He'd listened to the islanders' explanations of why they were camped on the shale and he was understandably incredulous whilst, at the same time, intrigued. What he subsequently witnessed brought steel to his eyes and tears to his heart.

Choices

The logistics of getting the 'leftover' people off the beach embarked and away from their island paradise turned hell-hole, was almost overwhelming. He could not take everyone yet didn't want to play God and make the decision as to who to take and who to condemn. Fortunately the valiant souls camped on the shoreline made that decision for him... they knew there was nothing they could do for those already 'taken' but several courageously volunteered to stay so that the others had the best possible chance of escape - it would be their last altruistic act before preparing for death. At least it would be a demise at their individual instigation - carried out with love and kindness - not for amusement or clinical research. Within his cargo Captain Maynard carried a supply of a new antibiotic drug recently trialled for use with cattle and sheep. In tests it proved an effective and reliable treatment for respiratory infections affecting farmed livestock. However, there was a caveat - it could also be exceptionally toxic to the cardiovascular system of humans and swine. Unfortunately, during field tests, the accidental injection of this drug into a human had caused his death and, as yet, there was no known antidote. Needless to say the medication now carried a large scarlet and yellow warning sticker as well as instructions to wear protective clothing when injecting infected animals. He explained all this to the islanders who elected to remain and to be left a small supply, including syringes, for their personal use. Captain Maynard tipped his hat to the two island women, two island men and retired naval radio operator.

Chief Petty Officer Campbell knew he could have made the trip. At 78 he was physically strong and sound of limb and mind but, since his lifelong sweetheart and wife of nearly 50 years died 2 years ago, the drive to go on at all costs had left him. He'd had a good innings. Ian and Lorna Campbell had made a wonderful team and partnership. During the war both Ian and Lorna had taken on land-based duties… too old in years to undertake active service and too young in mind to sit back and do nothing. After the war they had talked through their options. They were financially secure, in good health, and wanted to help others who were less fortunate. Many communities had been devastated by the years of fighting.

'Well, what do you think?' Ian paused, allowing his beloved wife time to respond. He did not want to push her into doing something she would rather not.

'It would be a big step.' Lorna's soft Highland accent was music to his ears.

'It would indeed, and it will no doubt be somewhat primitive,' Ian chewed his words as he gazed on Lorna curled into her favourite armchair by the fire.

'But probably with no more mend and make do than we've had these last few years…. just in a warmer climate.' Lorna smiled, watching her husband pace the floor, waiting for her nod of agreement. She knew him so well. He had to be doing.

When they were offered the opportunity to join an education mission, organised through their church, on Papua New Guinea, they were instantly tempted but the gentle caution that comes with maturity prompted them to research the reality of such a mission and set time aside to mull it over before making a final decision. This in fact had been their way throughout their married life. Having no children or dependent relatives they were totally reliant on each other for support; that is, each other and their faith. It was this faith that had cradled them through two miscarriages and a cot death. They were committed Christians, in the broadest sense of the word; there was nothing small-minded or paltry about this couple. And so, at a time in life when most people were settling down to a cosy retirement, at the end of 1946, Lorna and Ian made their decision to uproot and go to work with both adults and children in an extraordinary land where segregated communities had escaped Western civilization, if not the ravages of the war, Papua New Guinea. The rawness almost swamped them initially but, given time, the simplicity of their life revealed its own reward. Unfortunately, three years into their mission Lorna contracted malaria and, from then on, was susceptible to intermittent bouts of the disease. Ian brought her to the sanctuary of this Japanese island, a place he had discovered in his naval days; a place where the natural spa baths were purported to help its inhabitant live long and active lives. They relished their new environment and getting to grips with yet another culture and language. Lorna helped teach English in the sole classroom and Ian busied himself wherever needed. Heartbreakingly, an intense, protracted malarial flare-up brought about Lorna's demise barely eighteen months after they established themselves on the quiet island paradise. Ian accepted Lorna's death without anger or resentment; they had both lived their lives as they'd wanted, serving others - together - but her going created an all pervading sadness within him. Nothing could fill the void she left and, lately, he had sensed her, hovering in the background, waiting for him. He looked forward to joining her soon but not just yet - no, not quite yet - his God had another task for him.

Ian Campbell no longer viewed God as an omnipotent being responsible for and benevolent to all whom believed in Him. These days God represented much more than that to Ian. God was the label for an ever-surprising power, greater than his own or anything he could imagine; the muscle of nature, the law of the universe. It wasn't just karma in the way that some mystics claimed; it wasn't just what goes around comes around; God was a word, a tag, for something more subtle and all encompassing. It represented that which was most spiritual to each individual, the force that is both inside and outside of each of us; that unseen energy that connects all humanity. No matter how many times in his life he'd felt completely overwhelmed, whether by a decision that needed to be made, an endemic of world catastrophes or the loss of a longed for child - if he sat with it, listening with his whole being – at some point hope and a chance of resolution would present itself. He truly believed in the inner good within all sentient beings, no matter how ignorant or damaged they were. Throughout his life he'd endeavoured to tap into this goodness. Mind you, he also acknowledged that all beings were capable of evil, of irrational thoughts, of behaviour and actions that shocked and horrified others. He'd learnt to accept life and all it brought with it, including death.

Ian had taken life. He'd killed as directed, long distance from ship to ship, ship to shore, ship to air. Hand to hand. War was ugly. The need to protect and make a stand sometimes left little choice. He'd killed to eat, to survive, to feed his family and community. He'd never killed for pleasure, for entertainment, for sport - but he'd seen others do so. Lorna, bless her, had stopped eating meat when they lived with the Papua New Guinean natives. She occasionally ate a little fish but generally preferred to stick to pulses, fruit, vegetables and eggs - from the chickens they kept. He believed that years of eating produce from their own vegetable plots along with Lorna's penchant for simple home-cooked meals had contributed to his well-being: that and the love she poured over him and put into everything she did. He missed her every morning, every evening - he knew he could have a silent chat with her whenever he wanted but he couldn't reach out and touch her as he used to. He stroked the scarf around his neck, it was hers; he'd grabbed it when they fled their homes as the Invaders swept through the village. Was it his imagination? Was there a hint of her soap still lingering on it? It was enough to comfort and strengthen him for the job to be done.

Chapter 2 - Rescued

Hope & Charity

Georgina held Jenny close. The trip on the tender to the ship was slow and perilous as the sailors negotiated the swelling waves and troughs. They daren't use the outboard motor in case they alerted the Invaders; no, for better or worse, the bedraggled refugees were dependent upon their rescuers' rowing and navigational skills to traverse the fast currents and hidden rocks along this shoreline. The merchant ship never seemed to loom closer no matter how many strokes the four sailors bent their backs into. Georgina felt for them. She and the child were on the first boat load of refugees - the sailors would have another 4 trips to make. Thank goodness they would be taking it in turn to row back and forth. The weather was already starting to worsen, so much so that, despite the fact she hadn't eaten for 2 days, she felt like retching. The combination of fear and rollercoaster was churning her insides out. Luckily Jenny had fallen asleep from sheer exhaustion – so at least she didn't have to worry about her crying out. Georgina held her even closer, as much to comfort herself as the child. She was trying not to think of her daughter and son-in-law. She wished them dead despite her love for them; she did not wish them to be tortured, to undergo endless trials and ordeals, as the Invaders sought fresh information and discoveries. Neither did she wish her grand-daughter to be an orphan but she felt it was unrealistic to hold out false hope that anyone could survive being treated as a lab rat and come through the experience whole. Where had these Invaders come from? No-one saw them arrive. There was no warning over the radio. She shuddered; her arms around Jenny subconsciously gripping tighter still. The infant's eyelashes fluttered, she let out a soft moan, found her thumb, and buried her face in her grandmother's breast.

At last, the sides of the ship were visible from the crest of a wave; the next wave revealed her name – The Hope & Charity - an unusual name but totally appropriate - considering her new cargo.

Captain George Maynard took Jenny from her grandmother and carried the child up the ladder, handing her to one of the sailors on board. He then came back down and gently encouraged Georgina to put her first tentative foot onto the wet, slippery wooden slats. He stood behind her prompting each weary step until she made the top rung. Hands reached out to welcome her aboard and Jenny was placed back in her arms. A pair of wide green sightless eyes met hers. The child was awake but stunned into silence by the experience. Georgina cooed and stroked the toddler's face, forcing herself out of the insidious despondency which threatened to render her helpless; she had to keep going ... for the sake of her grandchild. She was under no illusion. If Jenny had been taken along with her parents Georgina would have stayed ashore with Ian and the others. For the second time, strong, weathered male arms took Jenny from her and Georgina allowed herself to be led down below, into the galley, where hot drinks and broth were awaiting them.

It was just as well they didn't all come on board at the same time; it was steamy and cramped below decks. The crew who came aboard with them gulped on mugs of strong tea whilst encouraging the islanders to do the same. Four fresh seamen were already on board the rescue boat – rowing back to shore. Over the next two hours the lower deck filled up with its bedraggled human cargo. Blankets, mats and bedding materials were distributed. The refugees busied themselves making up as many bunks as possible. It was patently obvious that eating and sleeping would need to be taken in rotation. This was not a problem to the elderly islanders; they were immensely appreciative of their rescue and keen to not be a burden to anyone. They each stoically carried their own burden; they were still alive.

There was little need for conversation; the islanders just shared looks, weak smiles and a few tears. Everyone ate and drank what was on offer - the sustenance was sorely needed. They'd snatched sleep on that narrow shale beach under the jetty for six long, weary nights and, as Skip and his crew quietly steered them away from their island home, their drained bodies were rocked to sleep where they sat or lay.

After they had been separated from the younger members of the island community, discounted by the Invaders and left to their own devices, Ian Campbell had encouraged them to take everything they could carry and camp near the jetty, their only possible escape route. Ian worked hard to rummage for bedding and supplies from deserted homes but, inevitably, their shared scavenged supplies had run out - other than a couple of tins he saved for the child. That was 2 days ago. The sailors had wanted to leave some vittles ashore for those who remained but these were politely refused. The Elders left behind declined to accept anything other than the chocolate and water they took initially. They knew the crew would need everything they could scrape together to keep the ship's expanded cargo alive.

Five older people had volunteered to stay behind - including Ian Campbell. George and his crew managed to ferry 40 islanders to the Hope & Charity, including the sole infant escapee. She had been hidden from the Invaders, secreted under her grandmother's long skirt and kimono, to avoid detection. The rest of the population, or more correctly, any who were still alive from the 142 islanders taken, were held by the Invaders. The aliens, or whatever they were, had been in occupation for nearly 7 days. George knew of no other island in the area that had reported problems. At sea, the regular weather and news broadcasts from the mainland were considered a stalwart source of information, avidly absorbed by the Captain and crew. There had been no warnings broadcast or reports of unusual sightings. Where could these creatures have come from?

The voyage across the Phillipine Sea, along the edge of the Pacific Ocean and then across the smaller Ceram and Arafura Seas to the Coral Sea off the North East coast of Australia, whilst arduous, was relatively event free. It was a route the Skipper knew well; he and his crew managed the vessel, adapting to the sea and weather changes in a seamless fashion. George, his sailors, and the Hope & Charity worked well together. The refugees, although shell-shocked, were ever polite and considerate of each others'needs. They took it in turns to share the limited bunks and sleep, either under canvas or down below, and they rallied round, cooking and cleaning - performing miracles.

'Excuse me, Captain Maynard, would you like one of these?' Georgina gingerly offered up a plate of what looked like rock cakes.

'Skip, call me Skip please – that's my official name on board ship.' George smiled at the woman. 'How's your grand-daughter doing? And you? This must be very difficult for you.' He was trying to make conversation and put her at her ease; to maybe even see a little of the pain lift from her eyes. Georgina struggled.

'Oh ... Jenny's down below ... learning how to wash up ... she's curious about everything ... now she's stopped being sea-sick. It pays to keep busy.'

It was like the story from the bible about 5 loaves and 3 fishes. The food just kept on coming. The islanders and sailors threw makeshift nets over the sides of the boat, trawling for fish and floating seaweed. Everyone got a bowl of hot food each day - which they ate in shifts to allow for the limited crockery and cutlery on board, and, amazingly, there was a different type of bread every morning for breakfast and cake, yes cake, each afternoon - only a little mind, but what a boost it gave all on board. Shared 'afternoon tea' was the highlight of the day, everyone took part. This newly formed ritual took place on the deck of the Hope & Charity at 15:00 hours each day, whatever the weather - that way those on watch could also join in. Word games became a firm favourite; they entertained and distracted those on board, lightening the mood for an hour or so and helped to break down language barriers.

The only commodity they really struggled with was toilet paper. The stores of the Hope & Charity were intended to support the sanitary needs of 8 male crew and not 40 passengers! With a little lateral thinking and a modicum of good humour, they made-do. Working in pairs they took it in turns to methodically tear up every strip of old wrapping paper and newspaper they could find, even dog-eared copies of the Readers Digest were re-cycled! Fortunately the passengers soon adapted to one of the key lessons of using the 'heads'; used paper goes into the bin, not the bowl, and if one chose the outdoor latrine (the bucket and chuck-it option) it was wise to make sure the wind was blowing out to sea.

Sixteen days later George radioed ahead details of his additional human freight and the invasion that appeared to be happening on the remote Japanese island. He'd calculated it was best to wait until he was nearly at his destination before sharing this information. Something warned him not to risk letting the Invaders know they were escaping until there was a great deal of ocean between them and their aggressors. The Australian authorities were sceptical. They weren't sure if they were dealing with crackpots or genuine refugees. They kept the vessel and its occupants at sea a day longer than necessary whilst they decided what to do.

In the end they were allowed into the Port of Brisbane where the Hope and Charity and its cargo was thoroughly checked before the island refugees and sailors were taken to an immigrant hostel beneath Story Bridge. They were to be kept in isolation, questioned individually and physically examined. Two reconnaissance Jindivik drones were launched to bring back pictures and information to ASIS (the Australian Secret Intelligence Service) which had entered into direct communication with the newly established Japanese Public Security Intelligence Agency and the CIA (the United States Central Intelligence Agency) as soon as they received the radio call from Captain Maynard. The use of the drones needed to be sanctioned by the US and Japan; the US still occupied Okinawa and was key to the defence of Japan. And so it came to be that the USA, Australia and Japan shared their

resources and pooled their knowledge. All hands on deck –
as it were - old grievances put to one side.

In the Hostel

George perched on the edge of a metal and canvas
chair, elbows on the equally perfunctory dining table. He
sat staring out of the hostel window; not really seeing the
swallow butterflies dancing through the tropical shrubs and
trees, or hearing the peewees' singing their duet to protect
their territory; he was deep in thought. His work-
toughened hands clenched into fists supported his freshly
shaven square jaw which, at that moment in time,
concealed grinding teeth. Lips, generally quick to smile,
were compressed tight. A flop of grey fringe fell forward
but he didn't notice; narrowed blue eyes saw nothing other
than what his brain brought to mind. He wondered what
had happened to the others - to Ian Campbell and co. He
wondered what the Invaders were up to, how far had they
progressed? Were they on any other islands? Had they
reached the mainland? Although he purposefully had not
kept in touch to avoid detection as they sailed away, he had
continued to listen to the daily VHF marine broadcasts.
There had been no mention of an invasion or mass
genocide. His wide shoulders slowly rose, circled and
dropped as he let out an inward sigh. He had done what
had to be done. Appreciating whatever was happening was
beyond his control he had purposefully concentrated on a
job he could undertake – and that was to keep his human
cargo safe and deliver them, and their story, to the
authorities. He shifted position slightly, attempting to
relieve the tension held in his neck and across his forehead.
His thoughts now turned to his exiled passengers and how
they might be faring. They had bravely thrown their
depleted energies into the journey, making it work for

themselves and the crew. Thankfully this had afforded a brief interlude when they were able to temporarily detach and recoup from the trauma of their experience. Unfortunately, since arriving at the hostel, they were forced to re-live their ordeal over and over again; the soul-shattering horrors they had heard and seen; the losses that broke their hearts and fed into their sense of impotence; the feelings of guilt at their own survival. And, if that wasn't enough, on top of all this anguish, they were plagued with worry about their futures and the future of this world. Everything hung in the balance, the unpredictable, unknown and uncontrollable future. George felt for them and the whole human race. He sought out the Officer in Charge.

'Look, I'm not an aggressive individual but these delays are enough to test the patience of a saint!' protested George Maynard, totally exasperated.

'I understand this must be difficult for you but at least we have some good news,' the Senior Officer smiled, trying to defuse the tension. 'The Docs have given everyone a clean bill of health, no nasty diseases to worry about.'

'Of course not! They escaped because their lives were at risk from alien creatures, not because they have the plague!'

George spat out the sarcasm. He needed to calm down. He swallowed.

'I realise the authorities need to interrogate and examine everyone but what hitherto untold information can a one year old girl provide you with? Keeping her here is only damaging her further.'

It was a simple but true statement. The child was utterly traumatised and needed to be nurtured and coddled, given the opportunity to enjoy nature and childhood again -

not to answer questions or be observed in contrived play schemes.

'Obviously we are concerned. We are also aware that everyone's nerves are stretched,' the Officer gave George a meaningful look; 'Those who are willing to undergo the experience are being offered a new-fangled talking therapy after their de-briefing sessions.'

The Officer was not sure he approved. His experience was that one had a stiff drink and got on with the job ... and life.

'Yes, I've read about counselling, in the Readers Digest.' George's face softened as he remembered the makeshift toilet paper. 'I don't doubt we'll all need it. This constant interrogation and observation leaves you questioning your own recollections, your own mind; you almost wish you really were making the whole thing up, particularly as your account is met with such incredulous faces and comments.'

'Yes, uh hum,' the Officer was uncomfortable with this tack to the conversation, 'well we're all doing our best and, hopefully you'll be out of here soon.'

The Officer made a quick exit - leaving George alone to manage his agitated thoughts and feelings.

'It doesn't help that no-one saw the Invaders arrive.' George's mind would not shut down. The voice in his head was relentless. He knew how difficult it was to approach the island by sea and there was no runway. Whilst a small helicopter could land on the plateau - if the wind was right and there was no fog - the noise of it would alert the whole island. The one time this had happened, bearing in mind the helicopter was a relatively new piece of equipment to the American Forces, it had been a complete novelty to the islanders and considered such an exciting event that the entire isolated community, without exception, came out to greet the whirring, ear-splitting machine from the sky. No, the only way he could think alien creatures could reach the island unobserved, was underground. He knew the geysers were extremely hot but wondered if these aliens had found a way to produce heat resistant materials that could protect them as they navigated the vast underwater caverns and hot springs prevalent in volcanic areas such as those in Japan. Maybe they had simultaneously landed in Iceland – that area was also remote and had geysers. Had they found a way to travel around the world underground? And he didn't mean by subway. The thought made him jolt upright. Initially he believed the idea would fit better into a comic book but, on reflection, it was no more ludicrous than encircling Earth in a spaceship from another planet and using tele-transportation to reach the island - which seemed the only alternative explanation!

The authorities were reticent about sharing any information they'd gleaned from the drones and landing party with Skip or the refugees. They were desperately trying to keep the press out of it because they wanted to avoid a mass panic. Also they were having trouble accepting the refugees' stories. Mind you, they didn't need to be convinced that those arriving on the Hope & Charity had left their homes in a hurry; they had very few belongings with them and all reported having undergone the same segregation process at the hands of the supposed aliens.

Their Story

It had been towards the end of an ordinary day, when the islanders were settling down for the night, that the onslaught started. They were rounded up and divided according to age, size and gender. Those who appeared too old for the invaders' needs were thrust aside and the only child to escape had done so because, according to the reports, she had been well hidden beneath the long skirt of her grandmother's kimono. Two of the older Japanese women had helped dress her grandmother in an effort to conceal the little girl. Fortunately Georgina was an excellent actress and with the aid of eye-liner, a Sugegasa (conical hat) and reshaped padded body, she passed for an old woman - hunched over her walking stick, struggling to get around. Georgina Hayes used her guise to support her grand-daughter, Jenny Dean, to stand on her feet and hold tightly to her legs; the ruse was successful. They'd escaped the aliens' clutches – for now.

Yes, but what do they look like?

The description of the aliens was always incomplete because they were only ever seen wearing black face masks. According to what the refugees told the investigators, their attackers had two black eyes bulging over their masks, each with a single yellow spot rotating in different directions, reminiscent of a chameleon. They had narrow hips and large barrel shaped chests, walked upright and had four muscular limbs, much the same as humans. But there were also differences. They didn't seem to grow much above 5ft tall and their upper limbs had wing type skin growing from the underside, attaching to their torso with strengthening bones visible at regular intervals. Their feet were long with extensive webbing between the toes and appeared able to bend and curve as though made of rubber. These beings came across as extremely flexible and supple. In fact survivors reported it was hard to tell which way they were looking or likely to go next. No-one ever caught sight of a nose or mouth and the general consensus was that they heard everything through invisible ears. Their bodies were covered in a mixture of hair, skin and feathers; more hair than humans but less than apes covered the front of their torso and legs. The colour varied, ranging through all the shades of blonde, brown, auburn, black and red that humans displayed although it was always toned to match the vibrantly coloured feathers which lay flat against their backs and bat-like wings; the overall effect evocative of parrot plumage. Their actual skin, where it was visible, was dark, a grey/brown blend which was only exposed when they fanned out their upper limbs and stretched their necks. There was no obvious indication as to whether they had different genders although some had gaudier feathers than others with a Mohican type comb streaking through the hair on their heads; this comb lifted and dropped as though reflecting a mood change or degree of inquisitiveness. Drawings produced by the more artistic refugees and the Australian security artists, brought in for the purpose, revealed a series of what could be construed as science fiction characters. Beings which looked as if they could possibly fly like birds, swim like dolphins and walk like humans; creatures with a certain degree of attractiveness and allure, magnetism in fact. Could it be these were humans of the future? And, if so, were they a gross mutation … or a refined improvement?

Life moves on

In her presence he was on high alert, his senses heightened. The hairs on his arms and back of his hands stood out as if anticipating sensual pleasure. His eyes were drawn constantly to her face yet he avoided eye contact. It was as though his body wasn't quite ready to reveal all that was going on within - to her - or to him. He couldn't remember at which point he could recognise her step, her scent, her breath, but he always knew when she was around, even when she was behind him or out of sight. Did she notice his nervousness and slight stammer when talking within her earshot; or his propensity to smile, like a mischievous schoolboy, in his attempts to please her? He wasn't sure these were appealing attributes in a 58 year old craggy sea captain but that's the way it was, he couldn't seem to stop himself. He'd been around the world a few times and he enjoyed women, their femininity and their differences to the male genus. He'd always considered himself a well-adjusted, emotionally stable, heterosexual male who had simply never felt the need to settle down; the sea was his mistress.

She wondered if he'd noticed. She didn't mean to be snappy. Generally her good upbringing guaranteed she remained ladylike in the most bizarre of circumstances. Admittedly these circumstances were more than bizarre, they were mind altering, spirit draining and soul swamping; yet, despite all this, she questioned the curtness that she seemed to reserve solely for her interactions with him. Her breathing tightened whenever she heard his voice, the Australian drawl that she'd always found grating now warmed her deep inside. A flame that she thought had been extinguished many years ago, when she had premature widowhood thrust upon her, had been rekindled - she was not overly happy about this turn in events, potentially it could bring complications and more loss in her life which, until now, she had deliberately avoided. Was it this that fuelled her short fuse? And was it the life threatening situation they found themselves in that caused her barriers to drop? The fact she was compelled to mourn the loss of her daughter, Gloria, and son-in-law, John Dean, whilst at the same time trying to protect and provide for her treasured grandchild? There were days when she wanted to disappear under her sheet and stay there. Already in this lifetime she'd had to overcome exhaustion and desolation to bring up her daughter alone, now she was going to need to do the same again for her grand-daughter. Whatever it was, she was in turmoil, zipping between girlish nervousness, womanly heat, human suspicion, resistance to change and anxiety driven fear, all of which resulted in abrupt responses to even the most innocuous dialogue with the Skipper of the Hope & Charity.

The old style iron hospital beds in the hostel were comfortable enough, the cotton linen - white and crisp beneath mosquito nets; you didn't need anything more in the humidity and heat. Her skin was accustomed to mosquito attack, Jenny's was more vulnerable. She queued each evening for the mosquito coils offered at the hostel. The fragrance and soft glow were strangely re-assuring in the middle of the night when sleep resisted her, or terror awoke her. Tending to Jennifer's needs helped her keep sane in these insane times. Knowing they were being closely and constantly observed yet not knowing what was going on beyond the walls of the hostel was playing havoc with her imagination. The persistent questioning by the Australian authorities sapped her resolve.

Suddenly her heart was pumping loudly, she had to swallow hard; her limbs felt as though they were dissolving to jelly. A thought crossed her mind, what a silly analogy, jelly hardened not dissolved, anyway whatever it was it couldn't be happening to her, 'that' only happened in fiction, in Mills & Boons books, not here, in a hostel under the Story Bridge, but happening to her it was. She missed him. She had tried to deny it to herself but the uncomplicated chortle of his laughter had triggered this reaction. He was in the building, just around the corner chatting to one of the Japanese refugees. Would she get to see him? Talk to him? Fear and delight flooded through her simultaneously. Delight won out when there he was, stuttering 'Hello' in her direction. She dropped her eyes, inspecting the tanned big toes poking through his sandals, then she looked at him; a

33

slow smile melted her lips, a broad grin flooded his face, a tentative twinkle reflected in two pairs of eyes.

Jenny had no reason for any such reservation; this was Skipper George, her saviour. The man who carried her on board when she was so scared; the man who gently held her hand as he took her on a tour of his ship, introducing her to his home and her sanctuary, the Hope & Charity. She grabbed his hands, ready to be picked up and hugged. She felt safe with him. She felt safe with Grandma. A tear trickled. How had she lost her Mum & Dad? She didn't mean to lose them. Where was Heaven? Skip squeezed her to him. Grandma's hanky wiped her cheek.

'Grandma, look what I got at school today!'

Jenny was excited. She ran through the sun-faded back door brandishing her spelling test with a gold star radiating from it. It was the first time she'd managed to get all 10 spellings correct. She was certainly a Trier and her enthusiasm and brightness were starting to shine through again. Georgina breathed an inward sigh of relief and smiled as she shared in the youngster's elation. Both she and Jenny were beginning to feel safe enough to allow joy back into their lives. They were the lucky ones. Georgina tried not to dwell on the fate of those chosen. She was so grateful for this fresh opportunity presented to them both, together.

George was to thank for that. George and Ian, the old radio operator, and those left behind on the island, all those who helped save them that night 4 years ago.

Was it really just 4 years ago? It felt like aeons. Sometimes Georgina visualised she must have been on another planet or in a parallel universe; only the fact she was here, now, with Jenny, stopped her believing she was actually mad. There were moments when she was convinced she was insane and her mind was caught in a recurring nightmare - sent to taunt her; a terrifying sleep induced world from which she would awaken to discover her body was not her own. When the nights were at their darkest her body lay covered in lava, rivulets of sweat pooling between her breasts; her tongue, a coarse piece of sandpaper, scraping at the roof of her mouth and, her once lithe limbs, rendered rigid and motionless by terror. Try as she might to send a message from her brain to her legs and arms, they did not move. Only her eyes could move and they darted this way and that, inside her head, waiting for death to reach her. She could not run away. She could not fight back. She could not save her beloved daughter and family. Then, just when she felt she would implode with despair and frustration, her cry of anguish pierced through that blackened world and kick-started her body, forcing her back to the present time. Sometimes, on the journey back to reality, she saw bleached skeletons waving from branches in the moonlight, fluttering pathetically until they fragmented and fell into the undergrowth beneath. Once an arm waved; an arm with a gold watch about its wrist - the same gold watch she'd given her daughter for her 21st birthday. Was it merely a dream? Her gagging and tears were real enough.

Chapter 3 – Ian, George and Grandma

What Skip saw

Ian led George up the steep, crumbling track. Ian knew the route well - he often ran this way and had done so with impunity over the past 2 years. He no longer had to worry about making Lorna anxious. The thought brought a wistful flicker to his face, softening the ingrained lines that came with age and were currently accentuated by anger and fear. Lorna used to worry when he went out on his morning runs. Okay, he'd had a few slips, scrapes and sprains, but it was the constant changing environment that called to him... sunshine brought small flower faces out to pave his way - he made a point of hopping over these; it also painted the most awe inspiring palettes; vivid blues and greens, contrasting golds and reds ... he tried to capture these in his artwork - as he also did the wet weather tones muted by cloud and rain - that same hazy film making magical and mystical the spectrum of different textured greys, faded greens, softened purple and blues.

The ever changing landscape of sea against sky presented a constantly perfect panorama which he tried to snapshot in his artist's eye, over and over again.

Where had the last fifteen minutes gone? Amazing how time disappeared when your mind wandered into the realms of reflection. Meditation was sheer release, an essential part of his daily routine, it helped calm his wayward thoughts and disquieted body. Usually it also helped remind him to work with the adage his Lorna advocated 'Let my first response be Love'. However, he was struggling to find loving compassion for these Invaders with their merciless menace. The two men continued their journey in silence. Ian signalled to George to watch out for overhead branches and slip hazards. The thorns on the Locust tree could be spiteful, ripping skin and clothes; in exquisite contrast the fragrance of the Jasmine and vibrating song of the cicadas appeased one's senses – they could lull him into an entrancing rhythm of movement and breath. They spent another 25 minutes walking through this surreal setting; pass deserted homes where life stood still; no human occupants or domestic animals - just the occasional foraging rat or quivering in the undergrowth as frogs and geckos went about their evening business, searching for insects. Beetles, cockroaches and centipedes, all creepy crawlies were noticeably absent. They were being tempted into honey traps set by the strange beings currently controlling the island - as Ian and George were about to find out.

Then they materialised - the Invaders, humans and lured bugs, all together - visible on a plateau above the escarpment which led down to the volcanic crater; each easily discernible in the lilac glow of the moon.

The honey traps were the dissected corpses of fellow islanders, those friends and neighbours who hadn't survived the trials set for them by the Invaders. Their callous assassins were now squatting or standing around the trees where the post mortem bodies hung; pierced through by thorns holding them to the trunks and branches of Locust trees. The cadavers were being stripped of their flesh by avaricious insects. Good-humoured birdlike monsters watched and cheered on the diners, as though it was a great sporting event. George clasped a hand over his mouth to suppress the cry of horror that wanted to explode out of him. Ian stood mouthing a silent prayer. They saw blood smeared bones held together with remnants of sinew dancing a ghoulish jig in the gentle breeze to the chorus of the cicadas and the hooting, honking, whooping song of the spectators. Every time a bone dropped to join the macabre piles mounting up beneath the leafy canopies it was as if a race had been won and the cries of the race-goers escalated in synchronised harmony. George and Ian could only stomach this scene for a few minutes but it might as well have been a life-time the imprint was so deeply entrenched in their minds.

Keeping down-wind to avoid detection and treading as carefully and silently as possible the two men circumvented the scene looking for signs of living human beings. They saw indications that those taken had probably been held below ground. Footsteps had worn away the grass leading into fissures in the escarpment, fissures that hadn't been there a week ago. There was no light or noise emitting from these subterranean prisons. They looked at each other. No words were spoken. No emotion shown. Holding their breath, their sorrow and their despair in check, they walked away. Gently, deferentially … they sensed they were leaving the last living and resting place of 142 people; family people; once joyful, warm people, people who had welcomed them into their homes, their community. Jennifer's parents had been among them, last seen corralled like livestock into secure invisible paddocks. Ian had already explained to Captain Maynard that when they were first detained anyone who stepped out of line was brought to their knees with a repulsing shock to their nervous system. There was no visible wire only a slight humming of sound waves. The aliens had no need for fixed fencing.

2010, again

Jennifer sat on. The beauty of the dolphins playing in the ocean with the brilliantly arrayed parrots flying escort overhead mesmerised her, as it did the sun-baked families watching from the seashore - such an unusual yet spell-binding theme for a tiled mosaic. It was dark now and the moon and stars twinkled movement into the ceramic creatures – as if they were all characters in an old-fashioned silent motion picture. Five stationary figures stood watching benignly from their stone pedestals. They watched both the picture show and the solitary movie-goer. Jennifer too was motionless, deep in thought. She knew the outside world was waiting for her but wasn't sure she was ready to face it. She had managed to lose herself in the safe haven of education for nearly 30 years.

The school had been her idea. A school focused on learning and acceptance; on emotional well-being as well as skills and abilities. It worked on the principle that a balanced approach to life helped a budding adult appreciate the logic and satisfaction of meaningful work and, at the same time, enjoy the wonder and benefit of a creative mind. She wanted to equip young people with the resilience and understanding to absorb loss and hardship, to accept disappointment, which, whilst inevitable, need not be a death-blow. Life was an opportunity to grow with charity and hope. She was ever grateful to George & Gina Maynard. Their memory brought a warm flush to her lips, eyes and heart. Their wedding had marked a turning point in many people's lives; especially hers.

Reflecting on 1955

She had never been a bridesmaid before and remembered twirling all day in her pale blue sateen dress, the skirt permanently splayed by a petticoat of white netting sprinkled with daisies. She wore blue lace gloves and blue shoes to match, a head-dress made of the same blue sateen with daisies and even her white ankle socks had daisies sewn on. Her grandmother looked absolutely beautiful, like a guardian angel. Georgina had an athletic figure which lent itself to simple dress designs; the dolman sleeves, fishtail skirt and matching wide belt in ivory silk accentuated her gracefulness. Although a mature bride, she was stunning. Her radiant oval face with its wide sea green eyes, lightly freckled nose and full coral lips presented alluring features which needed little make up, especially as they were framed and complimented by soft blonde curls; curls which, in a previous life-time had been constrained by a French pleat but were now allowed to fall more freely. Since meeting Skip her hair could not help but express the new bounce in her step and her rekindled openness to life. Neither Jenny nor Skip saw the salt and pepper shades within the curls, nor the faint lines at the corners of Georgina's eyes and mouth; no, they both saw a beautiful angel, beaming at them with endless love. Jenny was too young to understand then, when, as a blossoming 5 year old, she'd pirouetted and paraded her princess's dress to the assembled guests but when she was in her late teens and looking critically at herself in the mirror, a pastime that seems to be an inherent part of teenage-hood, she registered she had inherited her grandmother's looks, poise and energy, although she wasn't sure that poise was such a great quality in a university student. Reflecting on these moments erased the line from her brow as she sat before the mosaic. Jennifer mused on, lost in time and the magic of her memory.

Little Jenny didn't know how or when their romance blossomed, she was too young to recognise the tell-tale signs; all she knew was that from the moment they landed in Brisbane there was hope ... and there was Grandma ... and there was Skip.

When they eventually moved to Holland Park (a suburb to the south of Brisbane) Jenny felt cosseted with love and knew she had a family about her again. They lived in a split-level chamferboard dwelling built into the hillside. It perched on concrete stilts to keep it cool and relatively bug-free and the ground fell away at the rear into a sub-tropical Eden. The oranges from the two trees at the end of the garden were the sweetest and juiciest she ever tasted and the mulberry trees next to them towered way over her head, high enough to be in line with the roof; the large dark red berries tantalisingly out of reach to human hand but not to the fruit bats that came to roost at night. She and Grandma always knew when they'd been there, feasting on mulberries; the back of the house was bombed with purple droppings as the night time foragers took off before daybreak. Skip would laugh and accept the job of re-painting the burgundy splattered green paintwork at the end of each spring with good grace. He later told her it was because he was so pleased the annual event helped her overcome her fear of bat-like creatures.

The home the Maynards created always had open doors. It wasn't that they went out of their way to take in waifs and strays but they seemed to attract individuals with a whisper of a warm heart just waiting to be nourished. They were guaranteed to receive a genuine smile and a hand up from Gina and George. Jenny flourished in this environment. Skip and Grandma nurtured her totally, feeding her a daily diet of tender loving care peppered with patient understanding and empowering guidance

Jenny's new family wasn't always together in Brisbane, there were times when Skip was away at sea and she and Grandma were there on their own. Then they would work on a special album she and Grandma were putting together about her parents; their lives as children, their wedding and their sheer joy at having a daughter, a baby girl they called Jennifer. Grandma and Jenny sometimes cried when working on this album and Grandma said that was just fine, it was perfectly okay and natural to cry over both sad and happy times, especially when remembering loved ones who had died. There were other occasions, during the school holidays, when they were all together, all aboard the Hope & Charity, helping with cargo deliveries. These were the best times, with nothing but happy memories, when there was love and laughter and no tears. Skip had that effect on Grandma and Jenny; the retreat to the sea and days spent basking in Skip's love seemed to release them both from unspoken anxiety. For Jenny that anxiety stemmed from an emotion she could not name, let alone speak about ... that was until Grandma took her aside one day.

'Come here Jenny, I need to talk to you about something.' It was midmorning and Grandma usually stopped for coffee and a biscuit about this time; Jenny had milk.

'Coming Grandma; here I am; are you alright?'

'Sometimes I am ... and sometimes I'm not, Jenny. It's hard to explain.'

Jenny slipped her small hand between the hands her grandmother clasped in her lap. 'I feel like that sometimes too. Sometimes it makes me very sad.'

'That's it exactly Jenny. Sometimes I'm so happy to be living here with you and Skip and then I remember your parents and all those other people who died on the island and I feel guilty.'

'Guilty, Grandma? How does that feel?'

'As though my stomach is in knots and there's a pain around my heart, and that I wish I had died and your Mother and Father had lived.' Georgina hoped she hadn't said too much to this child who had already been through such heartache but she needed to help Jenny understand the emotions she could see were piercing her brow.

'Me too, Grandma, I try and try to remember Mum and Dad's voices and faces, but can't, unless I look at the photos. That's when I get that knotty feeling, like you, and cry myself to sleep.'

'Shall I tell you what I do when I get that sad?'

Jenny nodded.

'I remind myself that we cannot change what happened we can only enjoy today; that is the greatest gift we can give your parents.'

Jenny thought about this and asked, 'Is that because they would be happy to know we are alive?'

'Exactly. Now let me give you a big hug and a kiss, as your parents would want me to do. And as I want to!'

'And I'll kiss and hug you too, because they would like that too.' The woman wept silently above the child's head.

Jenny harboured guilt; guilt that she couldn't really remember her parents no matter how hard she stared at their photos or helped with the album. She cried because she could not remember.

Georgina felt guilty because she had not only survived her daughter and son-in-law but also, for the first time in many years, she felt fully alive; dazzlingly animated by the thrill of love. Each day she woke she smelt fresh, sweet air; she heard the glorious sound of birdsong, even the chortling kookaburra sounded good to her. She relished the taste of the cold milk and hot buttered toast shared with her delightful grand-daughter. She loved Jenny dearly, exchanging hugs and cuddles on a daily basis, but these moments often brought inner tears of sorrow as well as pleasure. The warmth of the bond she shared with her grand-daughter was marred by the thought that this tie should have existed between Jenny and Gloria, Georgina's daughter. Then there was the thrill of love, of a love she hadn't sought, the love between a man and woman, the love that brings such ecstasy and elation it heightens all one's senses and experiences. In her darkest moments Georgina felt almost crushed by such a huge weight of guilt; she wept for the loss of her daughter and son-in-law and for the gift of a new life in Brisbane with George and Jenny. She discovered meditation helped at these times. Georgina had learnt about meditation during her time in Japan. It was practiced by Japanese Buddhists who had been happy to explain the process and help guide others with their initial attempts. By sitting with her sense of guilt and observing the tormented thoughts that led to it she was able to extend love and understanding to herself and to acknowledge that her guilt was just a reaction to loss; it was not a fact. As the years went by Georgina gently tried to share this coping skill with her young grand-daughter. She must have been successful because, by the time Jenny was approaching senior school, she had grown into a kind, considerate, unpretentious youngster who had the confidence to mix with both her peers and adults; the ability to apply herself to her studies; and to know what kept her safe.

For Jenny safety was the loving presence of her family enhanced by the freedom to explore her surroundings and flex her muscles with the children next door, Luke and Jason; as well the knowledge that she could always have quiet times. Quiet times were a natural part of her life when she would mull over her days and thoughts and notice how her body and breathing reacted. This way she could recognise any pain or angst and talk it through with Grandma. Often the best quiet times were when she was swimming; the flow of the water around her body as she swam cocooned her in her own sensual, hushed world, where problems were solved and anxieties shrunk into insignificance. Skip said she was a water baby, it was in her blood. The child knew no different, she felt as if she had always swum, it was as elemental as walking and breathing.

Jenny might not remember her parents but she did soak up the stories she was told and gleaned from snatches of conversation she overheard between the aging islanders when they recalled their memories and experiences of that horrible time. The survivors regularly talked to each other over afternoon tea; the habit, developed on board, had evolved into a reassuring custom among the refugees. It provided them with breathing space to freely voice their recollections, to support and succour each other. As she grew up Skip and Grandma were very careful to tell her only as much as they felt she could process at any one time; they didn't want any setbacks just as she was coming out of her shell. Jenny however had other ideas - her nightmares drove her to delve deeper. As she learnt to read she avidly scoured every newspaper or magazine article, consuming the words and piecing together their story. Once she even saw her parents' picture in the Courier Mail. The article said they had been on the island as part of a diplomatic exchange. Her father, John Dean, aged 32, was a senior administrator to the British Consulate in Tokyo and he'd agreed to go to the island, with his wife, child and mother-in-law, for a 6 month long exchange with the eldest son of the leading family on the island. It was isolated from Honshu (mainland Japan) and virtually inaccessible in bad weather. The population of approximately 180 residents was relatively self-sufficient with shared small holdings and farmed seaweed and shellfish. The intention of the exchange was to foster a greater understanding of how different cultures functioned, not only from country to country but also from island to island, in disparate communities such as those that had developed in the extensive archipelago of Japan. Everyone was working towards more 'entente cordiale' and less fear of the unknown. No one wanted a third World War. That was at the end of 1952 and most families still grieved for young men who would never return home. It was a shame the family was wiped out when plague hit the island ... that's what the papers said.

Living on the edge of a volcanic crater, on an island serviced by monthly boat deliveries, with a single school, teacher and nurse (all housed in the same building) was certainly different and challenging. Her grandma revealed in later years that she had travelled with Jenny and her family, not only for the adventure but to ensure her daughter had someone to talk to and to maintain contact with her grand-daughter at a significant developmental stage of her life. Jenny wasn't aware of this at the time, she was too young. Grandma always seemed to have a very busy social life of her own - they certainly didn't live in each others' laps. The indigenous inhabitants were most welcoming to their visitors, viewing them both as a curiosity and source of entertainment. The lifestyle, diet and social life on the island was completely different to that encountered in an English village; it was even at variance to that of Tokyo where Georgina had lived for some years, between wars, when her husband was alive.

There was no church; people practiced their own versions of Shinto & Buddhism. In the traditional home where they stayed there was a small alter in a cupboard off the living space with various offerings and symbols to revere the Gods and Buddha. There had also been an urn containing the ashes of a deceased relative when her father first visited the occupants but this had been taken to the cemetery by the owners just before they left and the 'Deans from England' took up residence. Jennifer was brought up always knowing to remove her shoes in the Genkan (porch) when entering someone's home, so as not to bring the dirt of the outside world inside. In Tokyo she'd seen monks and nuns going about their business in bright saffron and burgundy robes - however it was many years later before she had a true understanding of what 'The Awakened One' taught.

When her parents were pronounced 'lost, assumed dead' there were no bodies to bury but there was a secret Remembrance Ceremony for all those lost to the Invaders and her grandma always kept an ornate box, containing the few keepsakes she'd managed to retain, on her dressing table. Jennifer now kept that ornate box on her own small shrine - alongside an exquisite opal box, purchased for her graduation, which now harboured mementos of Skip and Grandma. It gave her immense pleasure and comfort to bow in reverence to all of them; she willingly acknowledged and accepted the need within her to express her undying gratitude, respect and love - her reverence of her loved ones.

Enough of Reminiscing

Where to now? What to do? The Southern Hemisphere had provided Jennifer with a home and livelihood for almost 59 years. She had never been to England, or at least, not in her living memory. Obviously she must have been there once because she was born there, at her mother's family home in the small Parish of Binfield, 8 miles south-west of Reading. John and Gloria Dean, with baby Jennifer, had left for Tokyo in 1951, just after her first birthday. Jennifer had kept in touch with her cousin, Edward Anderson. He was the son of her mother's brother, Peter; it was Peter Anderson who had made the journey down under to give his sister, Georgina, away in 1955, and celebrate their new chance at life. Her paternal grandfather and grandmother had died before she was born and had no other children. Edward was her only living male relative; he and his wife, Patricia, had produced 3 girls all with different talents and interests taking them as far afield as the United States, Europe and India, but not, as yet, to Japan or Australia.

England 2010

These days Edward and Patricia found themselves rattling around in a large 6 bedroom cottage with 2 dogs and 3 cats. They were keen to have Jennifer join them, even offering to make a few alterations to their home so she could have her own annexe. The suggestion was tempting. But would she like it? Would they like each other, in the flesh, so to speak? What would she do in Blighty? What if she wanted to leave, she didn't want them to make significant changes to their property and then she couldn't settle. They seemed to have no qualms about this. As far as they were concerned the improvements would only add to the value of their property and could eventually provide separate accommodation for one of their daughters - should any of them decide to stop globe-trotting at some point in the future. In fact they wondered why they hadn't thought of it before.

There were no geyser fields that Jennifer knew of in the UK ... but there were thermal springs. Those at Bath, Buxton and Harrogate didn't worry her too much because they were highly populated, commercial spa towns, indeed Bath was a City; but the one in Wales was another matter. It was in an old mining area with many underground caverns and derelict shafts. An inward shudder travelled from her heart to her feet as she forced her head to concentrate on being realistic.

Where was her home? Tokyo? Brisbane? England? It was probably time she found out; she would start with her roots.

Chapter 4 – On the island in 1953

Left behind

Ian decided to sit with it. He had not been able to take any comfort from nature on the hike back from the plateau. The sweet fragrance of Jasmine had been replaced by the sickly, infusing, cloying smell of rotting flesh; it permeated his nostrils, his skin and clothes. He needed to gag, to be sick, but felt he would choke if he opened his mouth or inhaled deeply. He was desperate to shower, to scrub the smell and vision away but that was not an option as they stumbled back to the shoreline and, despondently, he doubted it would have worked. He thought of Lorna and the way her nose wrinkled as they passed butchers' shops in Aberdeen. She'd hold her breath until they were well away. He doubted he'd have an appetite for meat again. She'd be glad that he'd finally seen the light but absolutely distraught if she knew the reason why. For the first time he was grateful she was no longer of this world.

They didn't actually talk about what they'd seen until they reached the top of the cliff; then they exchanged knowing glances realising that they had to decide how much to tell the others and what it all tangibly meant. George and Ian tacitly agreed that, although they could not be certain there was no-one left alive, they doubted it. They were however certain that these creatures were more powerful than either of them or those congregated at the base of the cliff; they surmised the most sensible approach was to manage a mass exodus and take the information to the authorities to decide. A mass exodus, that was a joke, 45 individuals were seemingly all that were left of the island's population and 4 of those were too frail to travel. Camping on the shoreline for the last week had brought even the hardiest to the point of exhaustion. Ian was the exception. He wasn't frail but chose not to escape. He was currently incensed into action. George Maynard and Ian Campbell were of one mind and opted to keep their account factual, not to mention the smell of decaying human flesh or the sound of thousands of insects munching through skin, organs, muscles and ligaments; bugs that were camouflaged red from their gorging expedition through blood and brain and presented as a bubbling claret gauntlet fondling once human bodies –disjointed and pinned to the spikes of the Locust Tree. Neither of the men believed in heaven and hell but, that evening, both went to Hades and back.

They finished recounting their observations to the small encampment of adults who stayed the course and continued to listen. Some had drawn back, unable to take anymore of the gruesome details on board. Others had already heard the cries of family and friends as they were taken away, thrown from a tree or tossed into the sea…. Enough was enough.

When they'd first caught sight of the aliens they were fascinated, enthralled at their shape and colours, eager to establish a means of communication with them, until they realised that for these Invaders that meant holding what looked like a futuristic handgun to their heads and firing a pellet into the left side of their brain above their ears. Whilst this pellet meant the recipients could understand the aliens it dramatically took away their ability to see – a side-effect which seemed of no concern to the shooters. It didn't take long for the islanders to realise these were not friendly beings from a philanthropic universe beyond the sun's solar system but potentially deadly, detached explorers who did not care about the vulnerabilities of the human species on planet Earth. They showed no remorse or concern about the blood they spilled or the death and devastation they reaped on the island's population. They did however appear fascinated and excited by the island's large and aggressive creepy-crawlies …its insect population … predominantly the cockroaches, praying mantis, stag beetles and centipedes. The islanders now knew that the spent remains of their pets and domestic animals were being fed, as a matter of course, to the insect population, along with the flesh of dead family, friends and colleagues. The implication being that the aliens considered all the animals, humans including, living on the island too inferior to be of interest or use to them beyond their initial function as pseudo laboratory specimens - they would all eventually be recycled as a food source. No islander actually witnessed the aliens consuming human flesh but by the time Ian and George had finished their de-briefing many perceived it a distinct possibility.

Everyone sat quietly with their own thoughts and fears. Silence seemed to be the only fitting response to what they knew. Hushed tears fell on blood drained cheeks. Sleep brought no release; it only served to let in the blackest of dreams which, in turn, only wakefulness could keep at bay.

Ian sat away from the others, his back against the cliff, cross legged on a tatami with a blanket wrapped about him. His eyes were closed and his hands rested in his lap, fingertips gently touching. He looked at peace - but it was an illusion, he was no such thing. He was watching his thoughts, his emotions, his reflections and deductions … where they took him. A Spanish Bullfight of all places! He'd been taken to one in his naval days, not with Lorna - she would never have countenanced such entertainment - but with his fellow sailors when they were harboured off Gibraltar. The then Commodore thought such an experience would be good for their morale and provided a chance to socialise with the locals. That was when he'd first been really exposed to a blood sport. To the smell and sight of hot blood spurting from sweating, thundering animals; to the amplified noise and hullabaloo of the spectators every time a picador's lance hit home or the matador finished off the confused, angry, fearful beast that had been revered, tormented and tortured for man's pleasure. To the climatic roaring cascade of approval and applause as the bull met a courageous death and the Matador exhibited his honed killing skills. The whole procedure was steeped with ritual and could be traced back over 200 years. He'd read somewhere that the largest bull-ring, in Mexico City, could seat 48,000 people. He registered the link this flashback exhibited. The aliens' enthusiasm and exclamations whilst watching the insects escalate the decomposition of male, female and children's body parts were much the same as the reactions of the humans watching the bullfight. Excited spectators egged on the participants to satisfy their need for entertainment. In fact, he reflected, it might well have been the same in Roman circuses. Gladiators pitched against gladiators, barbarians and wild beasts. Wild beasts let loose on sacrificial Christians. Or, in today's world, boxing rings. All intended to amuse and win over the populace and to feed an inherent blood-lust. Contemplating further he recalled that throughout history and, even now in some countries, corporal and capital punishment was carried out as public events; fascinating and repulsing onlookers at the same time. For many years in England public executions and floggings were treated as an excuse to party - to eat drink and make merry. In Paris the crowds flocked to see 40,000 die at the drop of Madame Guillotine, some even felt short-changed complaining it was all over too quickly ... preferring the hit and miss action of the Axe man!

Identifying this commonality with the Invaders helped Ian. It helped him find a degree of compassion for them, the bull-ring spectators, the Parisians, the Romans and Britons of old; all those mis-guided souls who found escape in a blood thirsty and theatrical world; the stylised spectacle of others suffering, the smell of their life blood oozing away, the brutally silenced cries of their anguish.

He was not of that ilk. He anticipated no high due to hedonistic escapism or thrill of delight from what he had a mind to do. The action he was considering was being driven by altruism, a desire to put a stop to this invasion and save humanity - so people could go on to learn from their own mistakes. He had until dawn to formulate his plan, by then the Hope & Charity would have left it's anchorage with the island refugees on board. George Maynard had promised to leave enough syringes and toxin for the five individuals left behind so they could determine their own demise, if they wanted. The final choice was theirs' alone. They were the fortunate ones, they had a choice. Ian was going to suggest a hitherto unconsidered course of action to the four Elders.

The Invaders' Prisoners

They turned their backs on the hoses …. As used as they were to the procedure by now it still hurt, luckily this was the 2nd and therefore final time for that day. That is if it was still today. Down here in the bowels of the earth it was impossible to tell night from day, or the number of days they'd been confined, herded together in crates. They started off over ten to a crate but now they were down to a maximum of five. The youngsters had been the first to go … for whatever reason the aliens thought they would be the easiest to test, possibly because they were smaller and lighter to manoeuvre. Out of the 12 children only 6 returned after the first series of trials, and they were in gut-wrenching distress; crying and garbling that their friends had been dropped from the sky by huge flying birds that spoke the same tongue as the aliens. Yes, they could understand the aliens. Two of them had been shot in the head, above their ears - the initial pain was excruciating, taking their breath away and making them faint. Fortunately it didn't last long but it tipped them into darkness, unable to see so they were dependent upon their school friends to guide them. Only one of these blind youngsters came back and he complained his aural powers were bewildering, much more acute and that this unsought capability corrupted his senses. He didn't know what to make of it, not seeing, yet picking up every conversation and movement going on within extended earshot. The single pellet was lodged deep inside his head; the skin puncture left behind had closed within seconds, just a dark bruise remained. Eventually, if he concentrated hard enough, he was able to differentiate the conundrum and clamour of noise going on in his head and could let his parents and relatives know when the aliens were coming, when they were walking above on the soft grass, or when there was the swish and flap of wings pulsating for take-off. The next day the water tests started and Ryuu, the youngest lad came back with his aunt, Atsuko, and said he could almost breathe under water; he'd been given a 2nd shot, this time in the back of his neck. He'd always been the best swimmer of his generation and had excelled at diving, exploring the underwater ridges and caves that jig-sawed around the coastline - looking for tasty sea food and daydreaming about finding hidden treasure. He now felt odd, as though he had a sixth sense - he could see and hear things without using his eyes or ears – the adults thought he was confused and ranting. It was two days before the children were take out again and that time only Ryuu returned to cower in his crate, unable to say a word, vomiting and weeping at the loss of his school-friends. This was a tightly knit community - all of the children were brought up together, like siblings. The remaining adults were mortified. Two of them were taken to one side to receive the language shot; they were left where they fell, to come round and call out for help in their blinded state. Atsuko, a very young looking 20, escaped the language pellet but was given the swimming pellet. She said she felt her lungs expand, pressing against her rib cage and it was as though there were flaps of skin in her ears and nose... whatever had happened she could definitely breathe longer and deeper underwater and had a greater sense of her surroundings.

Their captors were feeding them once a day, or so it seemed, after the day's tests; but the food was not the islander's' usual fare. It tended to consist of 3 different items each day, each designed to test the recipients chewing powers and digestive systems…. taste was not deemed important. There were seeds, insects, grubs, plants and molluscs, plus a little meat from unidentifiable animals. Sometimes it was served raw, sometimes lightly steamed in

the thermal geysers. When one of them indicated they
needed to toilet they were presented with a labelled bag
that, once used, was taken away so the contents could be
analysed. For a fastidious and scrupulously clean race of
people this was inordinately torturous. Initially the men
had shielded each other, and the women had done the same,
so each could carry out their ablutions with a degree of
dignity - attempting to protect each other from the aliens'
scrutiny but in a matter of days there just were not enough
islanders left to be able to offer an effective screen. Those
returning to the crates each day had little appetite but if
they didn't eat what was on offer they had tubes thrust
down their throats ... it was better to try to eat something.
Having sufficient water was never a problem; they were
always left with a trough-full after the final hosing down of
the day. They found solace huddled together for warmth
and comfort on the fresh fronds provided each evening by
their captors to cover the floor of their crates. Sleep came
through sheer exhaustion - no matter how frightened they
were. It was hard to know which was scarier; the thought
of going to sleep and not waking up, or the realisation that
one had woken up to face another day.

Ryuu was taken out with 4 men the following day,
one of them his father, Daiki; the others were Sho, Kin and
Takao (now blind from the language pellet). Five women,
including Ryuu's mother and aunt, were taken in the
opposite direction, one of them also blind and able to
understand the foreign tongue. The aliens wanted to test if
Ryuu's aquatic aptitude came from his family genes or was
predominantly a male attribute. His father was also a
strong swimmer, as were Kin and Sho, but Takao had never
mastered swimming, his skill was gardening. They
assumed he'd been kept alive by the aliens because he was
a designated interpreter. It became apparent that whilst
Takao and Ryuu and others given the language shot had a
basic understanding of these creatures' language (they

could respond to simple instructions and questions with appropriate words - albeit their tongues struggled to make the necessary sounds) the creatures could not understand or speak to them in Japanese. This oversight presented a unique opportunity. They watched and listened for a chance to escape, whispering and signalling to each other. Ryuu's sharpened hearing proved invaluable. He suddenly gestured that they were on their own; their captors had gone to eat; they too appeared to eat once a day, generally late morning, on what seemed to be a mixture of grubs, seeds and insects, although Sho had noticed they couldn't resist a tasty snack of Madai, red sea bream, especially if a school swam by as they were testing their captives' diving abilities.

The boy and 4 men had been left unattended on a narrow strip of land at the edge of a thermal spring. The hot water created a screen of mist and at the same time diluted their human odour. Quickly they dunked themselves in the adjacent spa before heading for a stream used to feed the still-water pond which formed the basis of the island's much loved reflection and meditation garden. The five males strung out, hand to hand, silently; wading shin deep through gently running water, guiding their two blind comrades between them. It felt as though it took hours to cover what would normally be a 10 minute journey. Fortunately, on this occasion, nature was with them. The flow of the natural rill worked in their favour; their steps blending with the babble of water over boulders and pebbles. Kin knew this route well, his job had been to help maintain the island's garden and water features. He was familiar with its secrets and concentrated on leading this breathless, desperate band to one of them.

The red bridge arched poetically across the stream to a man-made island. A miniature island covered in strategically placed symbolic ornaments, rocks, flowers and

Acers. There was a flow of graded stone spiralling around the time-honoured Buddha rupa but these rocks were not there just as an allegory they had a secondary purpose. They concealed controlled air vents and an emergency doorway to the filter and pump room facilities below. As natural and serene as this garden was intended to be it needed filters, pumps and hidden services to keep it looking so peaceful and tranquil.

There was a harsh decision to be made. The large rock needed to be moved and would require at least two men to shift it, it would also take two men to put it back in place and meld it into the landscape once more. Although there were five of them, the four adults unanimously agreed that Ryuu had to go into the filter room, the men were determined to try and save the child; Daiki was willing to be a rock mover in order to safeguard his son; Takao believing his blindness would hinder the others likelihood of survival, opted to be a rock mover, Ryuu could hear and understand the aliens as well, if not better, than him. This left Sho and Kin to accompany Ryuu; to take on the challenge to outwit the Invaders and to survive – to live to tell their tale. They all worked together to heave the rock to one side and reveal the hatch below. Takao and Daiki hurried their friends down the steps and out of sight, time was short, there was a brief goodbye between father and son. Daiki put both hands on his son's shoulders, squeezed gently and guided him to the steps. Ryuu heard the tears spill from his father's eyes. He did as he was bid, turned and staggered backwards down the steps inching his way below guided by Kin's hands on his feet. Time was ever more critical and the two rock movers worked hard. It felt as though they acquired super human powers and strength in this auspicious setting. They managed to move the rock back into position then, grabbing handfuls of foliage, raked and swept the sand back into place. Finally they blew on the sand so it looked slightly weathered and blended back in situ, completing the original helix. They allowed themselves a brief moment to stand in the pond to survey their crucial task and wash their bodies down. They wanted to leave no trace of human scent or footsteps. With a bow to the Buddha they headed for the cliffs - taking the broken, used foliage with them to cover their tracks. As they travelled further away they bothered less about obscuring their direction with the same degree of diligence. At this stage they wanted the aliens to follow them – but not to catch them. They dragged greenery behind them, deliberately disguising their footprints. It was important their pursuers didn't know there were just two of them but believed they were following a trail, unwittingly left by them all which eventually finished where the perceived inept humans perished. Blind Takao followed Daiki along the track until they came to the cliff top; there they formally bowed to each other and smiled before they held hands, leapt and soared… soared into nothingness and oblivion, with a glimmer of hope.

The Aliens make a decision

The conversation bubbled around the forum. Excitement and amazement expressed from all quarters – squeaks and squirts abounding.

Fee and Wil sat side by side; they had an underSTanding, the fore-runner to a full blown coUPling in their society. It was a well thought through process, formatted after years of turmoil spent with many mal-adjusted breWren bred as a result of poor coUPling decisions and single unit parenting. Finally the coUNcil had stepped in, following the guidance recommended by soSHal knowAlls of that time, they had decreed that all citiXens had to undergo a mental health analysis following puberty to assess if they were sufficiently physically and emotionally balanced and were totally committed to the coMMon gOOd. If so they were decreed trustworthy and would be progressed to potentially produce breWren. When their body reached optimum development they undertook an aptitude test to gauge where their strengths and weaknesses lay and what attributes their perfect partner should possess. When they reached 25 they were presented with the details of 6 potential breedinPartners and met each, in turn, in courtiNChambers overseen by dOns. These dOns were acknowledged leaders in their field, able to detect a bad match from the body language and courtship gesticulations exhibited at introductory meetings. Once two citiXens had expressed their interest in each other, and the dOns had rubber stamped their approval, they were actively supported to explore their underSTanding before any final coUPling could take place. This underSTanding could take 3-5 years, rushed decisions were not acceptable. If a particular individual failed to progress to the coUPling stage after 4 underSTandings they were considered unmatchable and their breediNPermit withdrawn. It was quite usual for a breediNPair to be almost middle-aged (in human terms) before producing their first breWren.

Their homeland, kaRRak, no longer had unwanted, under nourished breWren; abused or deserted partners; and the young grew up in well-adjusted, supportive environments where, not only their brEEders, but the entire community contributed to their upbringing... all citiXens acknowledged that the young were the future of their soSHal order.

This exploratory miSSion was to find out if there were other beings with similar genetics which could enhance the skills and lives of citiXens. So far they had met with little success. This particular world was centuries behind their sophisticated kaRRak and, whilst of historical interest, it was painful to watch the misTakes the inhabitants made and the damage they caused not only to themselves but also the environment. Wil was glad he was breWn in his time and world.

The lively debate ongoing at the foRUm was about this particular world and its population. Until today they had thought them fairly mediocre examples of humankind, of little worth, but would you believe it – 5 of them had dared to run away and seemed to have disappeared. Neither the worMCamras nor flyTScouts could find them. A lone male body was seen warping over the rocks on the coastline but that was it. The question being considered was – is this an example of ill-considered migration, apropos lemmings, small earthly rodent creatures that risk drowning in their efforts to transmit to better feeding grounds, or is it a poorly thought through attempt at escape? And, if so, did it reveal a degree of inventiveness and logic they had not anticipated or examined in their tests. Or maybe it showed how mindless the manOids really were? Some of the knowAlls wanted to expand their assessments to explore each possibility with the remaining four specimens. Unfortunately the five femanOids they'd taken to the sea that day had failed miserably in their attempts to swim underwater and only one had survived; the one they had improved with a fisHPop. This meant they had one solitary female and three male samplings left to experiment with.

Wil was keeping quiet; he genuinely wanted to leave these inferior beings alone. They were woefully underdeveloped and the smell they emitted was playing havoc with his respiratory system. Plus he wanted to pursue the underSTanding between himself and Fee. They had been working on it for 3 years now and he felt the time had come to coUPle but they would not be allowed to do this until they had reported back to the dOns and obtained their sanction ... which, once received, would result in a public acclamation and celebration followed by the allocation of more spacious accommodation in the breedinKWarters.

Fee, as the leader of this miSSion, held the deciding vote as to what they should do. She too had mixed feelings. The knowAll in her wanted to find out more about these subjects, maybe they had a resilient core fuelling raw survival skills lost to kaRRak citiXens during their civilization. If so, it would be useful to gain a greater absorption of them in order to learn more about the evolutionary ladder that brought her species to where they were now. Or maybe these were just particularly stupid and rash manOid samplings. It was hard to tell without more tests; but more checks meant staying here longer and she knew that this created a great deal of hardship for her crew who daren't venture out of their pOd without face masQs to protect them from the smell and germs projected by the indigenous inhabitants. In the end she opted for a compromise; they would stay another 6 mooNRings - if they could find one of the escapees to examine within the next mooNRing. She doubted any escapee could survive longer than that without seeking succour from their kind or their homes.... All of which were being watched by worMCamras – an extremely useful hybrid developed by knowAlls to take on this miSSion. Worms with the photographic eye and lens of an eagle, able to move about undetected, transmitting images back through their synchronised nervous systems which were linked into the nerve centre of the mothRWorm kept in its own quarters attached to the pOd. The beauty of these worMCamras was not only that they could travel above and below ground unnoticed but they could also penetrate the human body, entering through any orifice that presented itself. A favourite method used by the keePers was to impregnate the food and water administered to the manOids. Whilst they couldn't actually receive back images when the worMCamras were within the bodies - because the pulsating blood interfered with their transmissions - they could interrogate the messages received by mothRWorm once they were emitted in the samplings' waste material. MothRWorm was the nickname the scientists had given to the receiving worKstat (RW) they had programmed to link up to their central mind unit. They proudly claimed that within five wingBeats of receiving any input the information could be deciphered and transmitted to eXplorers out in the field. And, yet again, the knowAlls had come up trumps, developing a grub that could hasten expulsion of faeces. Fortunately Wil didn't have to locate the worms in the samplings' faeces – that job fell to Ess, a particularly unusual citiXen who enjoyed dissecting and eXploring the primeval human body, despite the stench.

Wil had read Ess's biography; it was held on the central mind unit which he was expected to maintain as part of his teCHno's duties. It made for disturbing reading. Ess was different to most citiXens; he had no sense of smell, could fly a little but made no attempt to swim; his eyes were lazy, rarely looking in two directions at the same time and his feathers were un-preened, which meant they looked lack lustre and, instead of being bright blue with a yellow neck collar and comb as nature had intended, they had degenerated into an indistinguishable and unattractive mustardy hue that blended into the bacKGround. In fact the bacKGround was where Ess liked to spend his time. He lurked, unobserved, behind the others, watching and waiting – no one knew what he was watching and waiting for and neither were they tempted to ask; he was not the sort of citiXen you voluntarily struck up a conversation with. He was dubbed a noNer and the general consensus was that he chose not to mix with the rest of them and purposefully instigated the unseen barrier between him and his miSSion eXplorers.

Jealousy was not a term that held much meaning to most citiXens and why should it? Just look at them, chattering two to the dozen, twittering this way and that, all making their views known and certain they were being heard. Ess was not a happy citiXen; he was always side-lined. He'd given up even trying to fit in these days. His first attempts to join in group activities and discussions had resulted in humiliation and ridicule, he wasn't going there again. What this eXploration group did not realise was that he was actually brighter and more observant than any of them. He'd had to overcome a terrible start to life. His father had died on a miSSion when Ess was still in prep-sKool and from then on his mother had never bothered to look after herself or her breWn. He did his best to manage and look after both of them; when the foDDer in the lodge had run out he foraged in neighbours bins and broken into foDDer dispensers but Ess had no idea how to prepare a nutritious meal and his physical development was impaired as a result. By the time the coMMunity waRDens had picked up on this sad youngster living in filth with a mentally ill mother the damage was done. Whilst Ess's passion to survive had honed his mental faculties his limited diet had resulted in damage to his sense organs; he could no longer smell and his hearing was limited within a small range of sound so he had no echOSonar. In addition he had not been shown the correct way to preen at the recognised critical growing stage and, whilst he did eventually get training when taken to a coMMunal lodge, he never did acquire the habit of such a mundane and time consuming process. Fortunately whilst his impairments might have rendered him soCHally inadequate and therefore isolated, they did guarantee him work. He could take on the jobs that other citiXens refused; jobs that were made easier if you could not smell and did not feel the need for group activities and conversation. In reality Ess would have loved to twitter with someone else but he was so hard of hearing that it was embarrassing; if he kept asking citiXens to repeat themselves they became irritated and agitated, and if he just sat there, trying to follow the chit chat he was overwhelmed by too many voices going off at the same time and became distressed and disorientated. No, he was better off staying in the bacKGround, admiring Fee from a distance, imagining it was him and not that teCHno knowAll, Wil, who had the dOns' permission to progress an underSTanding and, if all went well, one day coUPle and breed with Fee.

Wil's mood lowered - if they could only find an escapee or its faeces they would have the answers to their questions. He could comprehend the development knowAlls clambering for more time but as a senior teCHno he felt none of their excitement, his paSSion was reserved for the smooth running of their craft and his forthcoming coUPling with Fee.

If any citiXen had bothered to look and take in the whole of the action at the foRUm they would have noticed that the invisible Ess looked noticeably different. His neglected comb was flattened hard against his skull, he stood alert; one eye was admiring Fee's gold and green plumage, the other was sending daggers in the direction of Wil, whose bright red neck collar was swelling and falling in time with the matching cock's comb he was displaying. A citiXen seeing Ess in this posture would have been stunned by the change in his demeanour, his eyes were no longer indolent, his chest convex rather than concave as, standing erect to his full height, he breathed slowly and intensely in time to the rhythm his fists drummed on his thighs. Jealousy was not an emotion that enhanced Ess's features and disposition but it could certainly spur him into action.

Chapter 5 – Brisbane Days

1955, Post wedding

Gina (she'd welcomed his pet name for her) had been an independent woman for many years. She didn't need a man to provide for her, or at least, not to provide financially, but George judged that the love and respect he poured over her fulfilled a void Gina hadn't owned existed until she met him. He knew he hadn't realised there was a void in his life either, but how fantastic it was that she'd agreed to fill it, to marry him.

George looked forward to each and every morning he was on land. Each morning he woke he marvelled that she was there next to him; her warm indentation in the bed called to him like a light to a moth. He resisted, he wanted to treasure the moment, the unique opportunity to wallow in her presence, to swamp her with unadulterated love and admiration, without her knowledge. It was sheer bliss to start each day with her, to share their lives. He never realised that joy could be obtained from making a cup of tea but it could; presenting her with a cup of tea in bed prompted a softly whispered 'thank you' from her velvet lips, her eyes still closed, her head cradled in her hands - a joy to hear and behold. He always responded, 'you're welcome' and taking his coffee to his side of the bed he'd sit and wait for her to stretch out. Her catlike movements held him spellbound. It was a marvel indeed; he'd married a 58 year old grandmother, with an adorable grand-daughter ... a ready-made family, for an ageing, converted bachelor, to cherish and adore. Not in a sickly sweet way but in a healthy, committed, fun way. He leant across to kiss her, she opened her eyes and moved closer, bringing her warmth to touch him, to arouse him ... he stroked her sides, her waist, her breasts ... he predicted Gina would be drinking cold tea that morning.

Gina embraced Aussie life with zeal; she was keen to make a home for the three of them which included subtly easing Jenny into her new, exciting, relatively safe environment. The mosquitoes no longer bothered the child and she loved their walks along the vast beaches, however she wasn't so keen on the woodland routes – the rustle of leaves made her shudder and the laugh of the kookaburra at twilight held sinister undertones triggering unspeakable memories. A breakthrough came when Luke and his family moved in next door. Luke was 8 years old and already attended the local primary school; his family had lived in the area for 3 generations and jumped at the chance to buy the spacious neighbouring property when it was offered for sale. His confidence and general acceptance of all that life presented rubbed off on Jenny. He took her under his wing and treated her like a little sister. He had a bossy older sibling, Jason, so it felt good to have someone who looked up to him as a surrogate big brother. Jenny learnt to play and have fun with other children, to appreciate a joke, to swim, play cricket and, as she got older, to support their local rugby team. There were a couple of summers when Luke even came with them on the Hope & Charity but, inevitably, in due course he was off to university. He went to study marine biology and, thankfully, Jenny found she could survive without him. Aged 15 she had her own girlfriends and was discovering her own interests. When it was her turn to consider a career and university, she opted to take a degree in clinical psychology. She wanted to help people manage their fears and anxieties. Personal experience had shown her that whilst they couldn't be ignored they could be managed.

1980 brings change

Jennifer had made the decision to start the boarding school after Skip & Gina had both died within 2 months of each other. She was glad they went that way but devastated at losing them. They had provided her with a loving, warm, secure home for so long that, when in turn they needed her support and care, it had been a privilege to be there for them; the last few years had deepened her love and gratitude to them, and theirs to her. Together, in this happy home they had reached a good age, most of it spent living life to the full, savouring each other, their environment and their friends. George Maynard had gone first, going to sleep one night and not waking up – he was almost 84 years old, wizened and slightly hunched but still with a twinkle in his blue eyes that refused to lessen with age. That was in the November. Gina Maynard continued to breathe for a further two months, but that was all it was, just breath, there was no real life left in her. She responded with feeble smiles and nods to Jennifer's enquiries as to what she would like for lunch or tea. She had no preference, she went through the motions of eating a little, washing, waking and sleeping just to please her grand-daughter but it was no good, at 82 she was ready to give up, to follow George and her daughter, to sink into the great unknown. Jennifer felt her precious grandmother ebb away with mixed sentiment, on the one hand willing Gina to keep living, even though she realised this was purely for selfish reasons to avoid more loss or pain, and on the other hand urging her to go quickly, to minimise the pain and deterioration that slow starvation would bring. Two months was too quick. Two months was too long. There was no right time to lose and mourn beloved parents.

Now she felt truly alone. Yes, she had girlfriends and male friends. She had a rewarding career as a Clinical Psychologist in the paediatric department of the local hospital... but it was not enough. The house in Holland Park was no longer a home. Jennifer, ever mindful of her spending, was financially secure; she could support herself easily and had more than enough money put away for a rainy day; on top of which the Maynards had bequeathed her a very tidy sum. They were not necessarily frugal by choice but their life-style choices, enjoying everything in moderation, meant they hadn't squandered the income earned through deliveries and, when George had retired, ever generous, they had put the money from the sale of the Hope & Charity into a trust fund for Jennifer. They were keen to ensure the orphaned 3 year old they cherished and considered their own, would always be provided for. On top of all this their home, the value of which had escalated with rising property prices over the past 30 years, now belonged to that little girl turned adult.

Jennifer paced around, her mug of tea clasped between both hands, hovered below her lips, never quite meeting them and she was too preoccupied to realise her thirst had not yet been quenched. She was lost in thought; her newly found wealth status obliged her to give a great deal of serious consideration as to what to do with her life. Without knowing how she'd got there she found herself stood in front of the house, her eyes drawn to the welcome sign that George had carved into a piece of driftwood and hung above the porch leading to their ever open front door. 'Take what you need and give what you can'.

Luke's parents had sold up once both of their fledglings had flown the nest. Luke never returned to live with his parents and nor did his brother. They both had careers that tempted them to wander further afield; it was the Aussie scourge or gift, depending on one's point of view and experience. The young felt driven to travel and regularly took off taking their learning, their inquisitiveness, their skills and their parents' love with them. These days communication was so easy to achieve and maintain it encouraged folk to move about; it didn't matter whether they stayed within Australia or went abroad; whether it was hundreds or even thousands of miles away today's young people had the security of knowing they could spread their wings whilst still keeping in touch with loved ones. Jennifer hadn't wanted to venture to pastures new; there had been little appeal in the notion of leaving home. She had however wanted to extend her knowledge and learning and to spread the care in her heart to all who suffered and needed a leg up. In pursuit of these aspirations she had gone to university, invariably eager to return home after each semester and, yes, she had occasionally travelled overseas for a holiday, but generally on the Hope & Charity, helping Grandma and Skip with a delivery. Jennifer insightfully owned that whilst she would avidly, almost obsessively in truth, keep abreast of what was going on in the outside world, she much preferred to stay where she was, where there were no volcanic craters or thermal geysers.

Once George and Gina Maynard had been given a happy and celebratory send-off Jennifer took their ashes to scatter in the sea. The new captain of the Hope & Charity was more than happy to take them and Jennifer on this one last trip. At the last moment Jennifer couldn't bear to part with George and Georgina entirely and she kept a little of each of their ashes which she put in a small plastic bag in the opal box they'd given her, so they could always be together. This final act of deference undertaken Jennifer was forced to stop and take stock of her situation, her thought processes and her dreams. She had choices to consider and make. How much to take and how much to give.

Chapter 6 – 1953 continued

Survivors

As a little girl growing up - confused and saddened by the loss of her parents, scared and bewildered by nightmares and memories she'd unsuccessfully tried to block - Jenny had been saved, not only by Grandma and Skip, but also by those five brave souls left on a little Japanese island all those years ago. At first the security services of all three countries investigating the stories told by the refugees had been sceptical. The experimental drones brought back aerial pictures showing no indication of life and no sign of material or environmental destruction. However the very fact there was no sign of any inhabitants aroused curiosity and set inert alarm bells ringing. So the drones were sent back to gain additional information and, this time, to obtain thermal infrared sensor readings.

The second drone expedition, as well as presenting the security services with a series of maps consisting of some unusual heat patterns, revealed a previously uncharted third crater. Disconcertingly this crater did not appear to have a geological heat source beneath it. The Australian Government offered to send in a ground party consisting of highly trained Tri-Service Unit personnel, who would escort elite Japanese scientists, experts in disaster field studies.

Following the end of World War Two Japan no longer had any real military power and was dependent upon the United States providing any defence forces deemed necessary. The U.S. authorities agreed to share the load in this instance with Australia. The co-operation between forces that fought together in War and, in particular, the experience and reputation gained by the Australian Army when it made up the majority of the Allied Forces engaged in combat in the south west Pacific, meant theirs' was a natural and welcome contribution. Furthermore the sincere and meticulous effort they were prepared to bestow to help address this problem now affecting their one time adversary spoke volumes as to their commitment to move forward, to offer support and friendship in the interest of world peace.

The Australians met with no resistance when they landed. They initially parachuted a scouting party onto the relatively small plateau between the two known volcanic craters. The scientists weren't trained for this so they and the rest of the unit were landed by sea two days later. Their landing, onto the jetty, meant they instantly perceived small signs of a deserted encampment beneath the wooden structure and against the bottom of the cliff; the odd piece of ripped matting, empty water bottles and tin cans, even a chocolate wrapper, all of which evidenced the sailors' accounts of what they'd found and endorsed the story of the refugees. The island was approximately a mile wide and two miles long and by the time the boat party disembarked the parachute scouts were there to meet them, having surveyed most of the island on foot. What they found was mind-blowing. The third crater appeared man-made or maybe even spaceman-made. It went into the earth and concealed a network of tunnels and crates; crates that held no prisoners or animals, just the remains of uneaten meal floating on water in what looked like feeding troughs. The tunnels leading away from this artificial crater were connected to underwater caverns. The scouts had left further exploration of these until their colleagues arrived and had provisionally posted guards. That was until they found something even more exciting, something that demanded their full attention and resources.

Three Japanese survivors, inhabitants of the island; all males, two adults and one juvenile; barely alive, traumatised and shit-scared but keen to mumble their tale and bewail the loss of their loved ones.

The young lad, called Ryuu, a slight but surprisingly athletic ten year old, was intriguing. He had kept the others alive with his fishing skills despite the fact he couldn't see. He explained initially he'd been shot above his left ear and then in the back of the neck by the invaders. After the 2nd bullet was inserted he could hold his breath for long periods of time and swim easily under water. The more he did it, the better he got. He reported that it felt as though there was new skin in his nostrils which he could open and shut to control his breath and that his lungs (or in his words) his chest could expand so that he seemed to have an almost endless supply of air. This meant he was able to swim underwater a lot longer and had total control of when he surfaced to breathe; also, although he had been blinded by the aliens' gunshot, he said he was now aware of a mind sense that told him where other beings were, their size and their shape; he could hear their vibrations and it didn't matter that he couldn't actually see them. This skill had naturally confused him at first and he'd felt quite disorientated but, after his first couple of catches, he realised he could trust this new found instinct. The scientists heard his account and thought what he might be explaining was bio-sonar, a mechanism used by dolphins and bats to locate and identify places and things, and to communicate with each other. They observed Ryuu invariably make almost imperceptible clicking noises when negotiating obstacles and routes. His blindness appeared no deterrent to his mobility.

The two adult survivors, Sho & Kin, didn't exhibit these skills nor were they permanently blind. However their eyes were light sensitive having been underground for over 3 weeks but, fortunately, they were gradually adjusting to daylight with the help of military issue sunglasses. They had nothing but praise for Ryuu and his bravery. It was Ryuu who listened intently for footsteps; who could recognise the approach and retreat of the Invaders. They knew they were being searched for and that the Invaders were confident in their hunting abilities but they had struck lucky with their choice of hiding place. It was a metal container that had undergone a cathodic protection process to limit its likelihood to corrode in the underground nest created for it in the soil next to the pond. This protection process involved creating an electromagnetic cell and it was this cell that protected the escapees hidden within the metal pump room. The electromagnetism jumbled the sonar signals received by their hunters, in fact it gave them a headache, which they put down to contamination wrought by the ignorant abuse of the environment with chemicals used by their manOid

76

prey. If these marauders had been less arrogant and more inquisitive they would have discovered the hidden trap door above the container and the water logged filter trap beneath it. But they weren't and they didn't. Instead Ryuu, who from the inside out didn't experience the same degree of headache and sense bedlam as the Invaders, learnt how to negotiate the filter trap, swimming underwater to catch unsuspecting Koi, the same ornamental fish which hitherto had been regularly fed by Kin but were now helping to keep the three of them alive. Raw Koi was an acquired taste but nutritious enough. The escapees had managed to eat and sleep in relative safety but the circumstance of their imprisonment and the mental anguish of living in the dark, underground for over four weeks (if you included the time they'd spent in the crates) had taken its toll on their mental and physical well-being. For all his bravery and efforts Ryuu had been unable to move the rock over the trap door in order to release the adults when he realised the Invaders had gone. Unfortunately Sho and Kin were also too large to negotiate the filter trap. They were snared in a prison of their own making - all he could do was keep them alive with fish and fresh water.

The three surviving males were whisked off by helicopter to a special military hospital where they underwent months of treatment and observation. The scientists, having x-rayed Ryuu, desperately wanted to remove the pellets implanted in his head and neck but, fortunately for him, they hesitated. They had no idea what affect removing the pellets would have on him and didn't want to impair him further after all he'd been through. In the end they opted to x-ray and observe him at regular intervals - until he died of natural causes - then they would undertake a full post-mortem examination and his remains could possibly become a great source of scientific advancement. Mind you, none of this could have been foreseen when they first found him and resisted the temptation to surgically remove the pellets.

In truth, the troops did not find Ryuu, he found them. He'd heard their footsteps as they skulked through the garden and could tell from their shape and weight that they were not Invaders; so he swam via the filter trap into the pond, not knowing it would be for the last time, and surfaced under the bridge where he could listen unobserved. What he heard were foreign voices, voices like some of the visitors who came to enjoy the small island oasis and relax in the thermal spa. Taking a deep breath he shouted out, before he had time to change his mind. His voice carried like a croaking frog, he was used to speaking in whispers to avoid detection and had not used his vocal chords properly since their incarceration. He'd experienced so much fear in his short life that it should have been automatic for him to imagine the worse, but something within him told him that these unknown strangers were his best chance of survival, certainly better than what he had at present.

Fortunately the Australians had a Japanese speaking soldier in their troop. He understood Ryuu's gesticulations and muddled account and was able to direct his colleagues to the trap door under the rock. They soon had it open and beneath were two pairs of deep brown eyes squinting at them from the nervous, pale and drawn faces of Sho and Kin. The smell emitted on the opening of the trap door was noxious causing the rescuers to take a step back. These poor entities, unwashed and unkempt, and had been living in an 8'x8' metal box for demoralising day after day. There was a mountain of faeces, urine and fish remains in one corner with worms threading it, leaving their castings. Makeshift bedding was scattered around the pump. The bedding was made from rags, the clothing they had once worn; by now all three males were naked. Strong, tanned

Aussie arms reached down; emaciated, trembling, spidery fingers reached up; as they were hauled into the daylight Kin and Sho cried out; partly from relief but also from fear and pain. They could see nothing. The shock of coarse hands on their flesh teamed with the instant blindness they experienced in reaction to sunlight was overwhelming. They were wrapped in military shirts and jackets the soldiers pulled from their own bodies; their eyes covered with the cleanest handkerchiefs the unit could find. The digger who spoke Japanese was doing his best to reassure them they were there to help and not to harm them; that their medics would soon arrive to look after them. Ryuu was also joining in the conversation, reiterating the soldier's words with a wide smile across his face that although invisible to his dazed fellow escapees could be heard in his voice, and they trusted his judgement. His new found 6th sense and instinct hadn't let them down so far.

Two members of the Tri-service Unit donned protective clothing and breathing apparatus and went down into the pump room, taking photos and reporting back to their comrades above what they saw. It was just as Ryuu had described, all except the drawings on the walls.

Sho later explained that he was the artist, using fish bones and blood he'd painted from memory all that he had experienced - in the hope that, if they died in that metal can, their story might eventually be told to the outside world. There were depictions of the aliens just as those in the hostel described and sketched. There were horrific images of beetles crawling all over dead bodies, bubbling up out of wounds, mouths and eyes; drawings of flies swarming over puddles of blood that seeped from faceless islanders, the beetles having already done their work. There were icons of huge bird like figures flying between trees and bombing their human cargo to the ground below. The pitiful cargo looked like children, their eyes and mouths wide open in fear, screaming in utter despair as they tried to break their fall by flailing their arms in wing-like gestures - to no avail. There were heads of gasping women, swamped by waves, as they fought for breath and tried to stay afloat. They could have been mistaken for harridans except it was sheer terror, not anger, which poured from their eyes. There were webbed footed, barrel-chested beings trailing boggle eyed islanders deep underwater - it was obvious from the few bubbles escaping their tight lips that these islanders were trying desperately to endure the dive and survive. The final painting was of bloated, crab nibbled, carcasses washing up and down on the black sand in time with the ebb and wane of the remorseless sea. The wonder was that this horrific and amazing mural was painted in virtual darkness. The only light available to the escapees was that from a small torch. The torch had been left hanging at the hatch entrance to the pump room by Kin in the course of his work. He always kept a small tool pouch on the hook. He'd been caught out in the past when visiting this place and found a Swiss army knife generally adapted to suit the occasion. The battery in the torch had run out 4 days ago. The knife had seen constant use.

How any human being could have survived the treatment these people had been put through was beyond the soldiers' imaginations and yet here were three who, despite having witnessed and endured such torture, had found the energy to escape and the resilience to hide in what was potentially a metal tomb for weeks, not knowing how, or if, they would be saved. The men of the prestigious Tri-Service Unit so wanted to find these inhuman Invaders, yet so dreaded doing so. Even with all their intense training, sophisticated armoury and elaborate preparation they doubted their combined force would be a match for creatures intelligent and complex enough to have the resources to travel from another world, to be adaptable enough to not only swim above and below rough seas but also to fly across tree tops, as well as walk and talk like man.

By the time the boat landed with the Japanese scientists on board the crack scouting unit had finished their initial patrol of the island - they found no other signs of human life but plenty of remnants of human death. There were piles of bleached bones beneath trees, where bodies once hung, pierced through, until there was no more sinew to hold them together. They found a rotting corpse wedged into rocks on the northern shoreline which Kin later confirmed was of Daiki (Ryuu's Father). Takao was nowhere to be seen. Also, surprisingly enough, there was no sign of the masses of insects they were told appeared to banquet on the remains of the islanders and their pets. And search as they might they could not find hide or hair of the 5 older residents reputedly left behind near the jetty when the Hope & Charity sailed away. However what they did notice was a predominance of worms, where-ever there were bones or houses, there were worms under foot, disappearing into the foliage and soft soil as each footstep approached then popping up again when it passed. Odd. They surmised that because the bird and frog population also appeared decimated that the worms were multiplying unconstrained by their natural predators.

Needless to say,, the scientists wanted to investigate the third crater and follow the caverns underground. The necessary diving equipment was air-lifted out immediately but the small exploratory sub had to come by ship and took almost 3 days because the seas around the island were so rough. It was obvious the refugees in Brisbane were extremely lucky the Hope & Charity reached the island on the day that it did; another day and they might well have met with harsher conditions which would have prevented anyone getting on or off the island. As the helicopters delivered the wetsuits, air tanks and diving paraphernalia so they picked up the 3 survivors and took them off to Tokyo from where, eventually, they were flown to another military hospital, this time in the USA. The Yanks were determined to manage the recuperation and interrogation of these recovered islanders. Japan was not in a position to put up much of a protest being dependent upon America for military defence. The Aussies were not about to argue. There was no denying that the US had far more resources at their finger-tips than their partners in this operation and, besides, the Aussies already had forty refugees, the skipper and crew from the Hope & Charity.

Reports of how the two men and the lad were getting on trickled back to the Australian Secret Intelligence Service and their Japanese counterparts. Whilst they all regained their physical strength and the two men their sight, all three had continual flashbacks and mood swings brought on by post-traumatic stress disorder. Not actually a new phenomenon, more a newly recognised condition that affected those caught up in combat and other gruesome life and death situations. American psychiatrists and psychologists were in the process of developing a variety of therapies and drugs to address this increasingly prevalent, affliction. Two world wars and numerous natural and man-made disasters were fuelling this malignant malady

Ten days earlier

The escape of the five male manOids shocked the entire miSSion, especially as they were never found. Fee took stock. She assumed the escapees had drowned when they jumped into the sea off the steep cliff at the southernmost point of the island. This miSSion was disappointing. It didn't look as though the manOid race inhabiting the area had any attributes or aptitudes to offer her people; except maybe their latent instinct to survive;

although even that was now debatable - it seemed for some that death by drowning was preferable to survival. She ordered the remaining solitary femanOid and three manOids they had in stock be brought into the pOd; she didn't want to risk any more losses. Her thinking was they might prove acceptable breedinStock to produce workers capable of adapting to the unforgiving climate outside of their citicAPsule. The steam and changing weather conditions of this land appeared to cause them no harm and they were oblivious to the most toxic odours.

　　The four remaining Japanese prisoners were kept in an isoblution unit within the pOd. Ess was given the job of feeding them and cleaning out the unit. He found that if he gave the prisoners the tools they were quite prepared to clear up after themselves; they actually wanted to achieve an exceptional standard of cleanliness. The femanOid related to the manOid and junior that escaped, was particularly intent on keeping herself and her fellow inmates comfortable. He wished she'd had the lingOShot so they could converse but she'd escaped that blinding bonus so he was reduced to using the age old system of pointing, miming and naming the things and actions he wanted her to understand. Fortunately she was quick on the uptake. She knew his name was Ess and he knew hers was Atsuko. She thanked him for the screen and water he provided so she could wash and toilet herself in private; the men too took advantage of it, but that was by the by. He found himself wanting to receive her polite and deferential - 'domo arigatou gozamaisu' (thank you very much) when he gave her their meal and then hear her softly murmur - 'oyasumi nasi' (good night) when he handed her clean bedding each evening. This was the first genuine validation of his existence and grateful acknowledgement of his contributions that he'd received from anyone this trip; indeed from anyone in his life since his father died. He had been elated when Fee brought them into the pOd and singled him out to attend to their internment. He'd instantly been determined to make a good job of the responsibility in order to impress her but now it was even more worthwhile. Each day he looked forward to the positive affirmation he received from the gently spoken gratitude the femanOid expressed in response to whatever minimal care and support he offered. He found himself drawn to her.

They knew they were being watched and every word or gesture monitored. They also knew the Invaders couldn't really understand their language, so they whispered in broken sentences to each other. The men were feeling particularly fearful and aggrieved. They were way out of their comfort zone in this alien environment with no link to the outside realms; night and day manufactured and the air they breathed recycled and piped back to them. The men became suspicious about the daily interactions between Atsuko and their jailer. However they were sensible enough to realise that the seemingly innocent, staccato conversations worked in their favour; they had crisp, clean robes; unsullied mats and bedding; a regular meal with fresh water and no more torturous experiments to endure. The aliens' research work seemed to grind to a halt when Kin, Sho, Daiki, Ryuu and Takao had run away. The men in the pod began to feel guilty at their own survival. Atsuko was philosophical, she was making the most of each moment, knowing it might be her last, and she didn't want to go with anger and hate in her heart. Her tentative friendship with Ess was revealing how vulnerable and tragic this creature was. Yes, she was hurting, she had watched her precious sister-in-law die in the last dive they were put through and now her beloved brother and nephew were missing. She herself had managed to adjust to the depth they were taken down to, how she did not know, it had felt as though her lungs would burst and her eyes would pop out of her head but somehow she had successfully controlled her breath long enough so that , once released by her captor, she could manage her swim to the surface. It had been sheer agony, her body contorted in pain from ascending too fast, but there was no other way. She realised the pellet they'd fired into the back of her neck had contributed to her enhanced breathing technique, although it didn't feel like much of a technique at the time, more like an enforced survival mechanism. Her sister-in-law didn't get the neck shot and hadn't surfaced alive. Atsuko was also noticing something else, a new sense? Possibly other infused traits assigned to her? She didn't have words to describe the new found instinct she was developing but she could tell the size, shape and whereabouts of aliens and objects without actually seeing them. She knew when Ess was approaching and had a good idea what, if anything, he was bringing with him. Sometimes there was just too much going on above them for her to differentiate individuals and their activities and, although she knew they were talking, she didn't understand what they were saying. One of the men had received the language shot; he was now tragically blind. If Atsuko listened intently enough and repeated what she heard in her clear, melodic voice, he could interpret some of what was being discussed. It was by doing this that she learned the fate of the rest of her family; the aliens surmised that having nowhere else to go, they had jumped off the cliff rather than be re-captured. Her sadness was immobilising, she just sat and cried dry tears, holding her breath for minutes at a time. The men watched in amazement, expecting her to turn blue and keel over - but she never did. When Ess came to deliver their meal he was concerned and, for the first time, actually touched her arm. He'd touched human flesh before, but it had always been cold, dead flesh. This was different. This woman's flesh was warm and tactile, silk-like as it rippled under his hand. He didn't want to pull away but he had to, he knew his movements were being watched in this room, along with the manOids.

He mumbled to the interpreter in the group, 'What, what matter?' and grumbled, much more loudly for the benefit of the watchers ... 'No, no nonsense. Speak, speak me!'

He was playing to two different audiences. Each was satisfied. The interpreter responded that Atsuko was sick and needed proper fresh air; the obserVAtion knowAlls determined that Ess was, understandably, on a short fuse - having to attend to the smelly manOids' needs. The interpreter stated he hoped that they might all be given daily walks in the fresh air to stop them becoming sick.

Within his nestBox in the sleeping quarters Ess pondered. He did not like to see Atsuko so unwell and considered his options. If he told Fee she would probably hand Atsuko over to the mediC knowAlls, and, where lower life forms were concerned, they had a reputation for cutting first and curing later. He didn't want that for his femanOid friend, he wanted her well and beholden to him. Maybe he could take her out on to the surface for a few minutes, on the pretext that he was using her to seek out and carry more bedding and mats from the deserted houses. The more he thought about this ruse the more it appealed to him; he would get to spend some time with her, unobserved (except for worMCamras), and she would recover, and talk to him again, expressing her gratitude in her polite and respectful manner, with her eyes cast downward, and her lips generating velvet chords that caressed his lonely core. Whilst Ess lusted after Fee he was unwittingly falling in love with a femanOid, a soft, gentle being that listened to him and saw his frailty without recoiling. Ess knew there was no hope for anything more than a few minutes spent together collecting detritus but he could dream. For the first time in his life he gave thanks that he could not smell and was able to take on tasks his fellow citiXens despised.

Ian Campbell plans

The time for thinking and plotting had passed, it was time for action; it was now or never. Ian spoke at length to his old neighbours and friends. He needed to call on their help and knowledge of the island if his plan was to stand any chance of success. They listened incredulously; it was a far-fetched scheme, the product of a lateral-thinking optimist who was prepared to die to achieve his goal. Ian aimed to kill every single Invader, to make sure that no other community suffered what they had suffered; total annihilation at the whim of an arrogant, ignorant, super race. It was a tall order for five elderly people who, until a few days ago, were placidly ending their lives in a sheltered, heavenly oasis; safe in the knowledge that they would be surrounded by loving family and friends to the end. Their lives - and deaths - had been turned upside down. They were keen to be of assistance to Ian and bring his plan to fruition.

Ian asked one of the men to go with him in search of the Sparrow Bees' nest; he heard them buzzing as he woke each morning. They took two blankets with them. He asked the other man to very quietly raid garden sheds until he found four hand-held crop sprayers. The two women, left under the jetty, were to carefully fill each syringe with 15ml of the potentially fatal animal antibiotic. All were spurred into action by the thought they might be able to make a difference. It was an implausible operation but, if all the facets came together, it could eradicate these Invaders forever; unfortunately whilst too late to save their friends it could go some way to protecting future generations and avenging the destruction of their paradise and loved ones.

As confident as he might sound, Ian was anxious. There were parts of this plan that were in the laps of the gods; he was relying on a wing and a prayer to appear at just the right moment. He felt Lorna fall into step with him as he went up the trail looking for the hornets' nest. She prompted them to turn left, when he would have gone straight on; the route she chose for them was through gravel drainage ditches, away from the more direct dirt track he had in mind to wend a way to his garden.

The men heard them before they saw them, flying in and out of their nest in a tree at the back of Ian's garden, Giant Japanese Hornets - locally known as Sparrow Bees. These were an essential part of Ian's plan. He grabbed a tool box from his shed and emptied the contents onto the bench; he wouldn't need all of his tools, just the mole grips and Stanley knife, oh, and the tool box. He looked for a jar of honey he hoped was still in the back of the kitchen cupboard, it was; he grabbed it along with a couple of spoons. This was the easy bit - so long as they weren't challenged and, if they were, he hoped the Invaders would swallow his gesticulations that they'd come for supplies. The tools went into his pockets and the honey into his backpack, he carried the tool box. He would soon have a use for the blankets tightly rolled up inside.

Chapter 7 - Clarity

Pilgrimage - 1980

'Are you sure Jen? I really don't like leaving you here on your own.' Rod, the Skipper, was in two minds.... he didn't want to leave his attractive young friend to venture back in time on her own... but he also had deadlines to meet.

'Honest Rod, I'm not a little girl anymore. I appreciate your concern but at the ripe old age of thirty it's time I faced my demons.' Jennifer's smile made light of her words.

'And it's not as though I'm here on my own ... it is now a tourist resort so I'm bound to bump into other people.'

In truth Jennifer would rather not bump into them – she felt tourists would be an intrusion into her pilgrimage.

The walk up the track had been made easier with proper steps and hand rails, and the adjacent foliage was trimmed back so it didn't impede travellers; there were even viewing platforms with seats so visitors could catch their breath and take in the view and their surroundings - endless miles of deep blue sea to the south and a faint distant smudge of a purple/grey island to the east. The hike to the village took 35 minutes; Jenny allowed herself regular stops to compose herself. Each step caused her heart to flutter and the knots in her stomach to tighten. By the time she reached the village and stood looking at the house she and her parents had inhabited she was struggling with her emotions and aware she needed to get a grip - easier said than done.

The old home which she had struggled to remember all these years came into view and, despite the fact she consciously denied having any recollection, when she bowed, took off her shoes and went into the main room from the genkan she instinctively knew where to go and where her old room was. And there were her childhood toys in a box and 'Big Ted' sat against the pillow on her futon, just as she'd left him. Her Grandma wouldn't let her take him with her, he was too big to fit under the tent of her skirt, so she had taken Sally instead, a tiny baby doll, wearing a dress and bonnet that her mother knitted to match the baby clothes she had lovingly produced for Jenny when she was first born. A smile broke through her tears, she could remember - she could remember her mother telling her she'd knitted the clothes. Such a small reminiscence but what joy and warmth it instilled in her. The Tour Guide, dressed in his uniform: a dark blue hip length Haori (jacket) worn over a matching striped Hakama (divided skirt) with white toe socks (Tabi) and woven straw Zori (flip-flops) arrived with the next tranche of sight-seers. He was stunned to see an adult Western woman reverencing the shrine and reciting, in soft muted tones, the names of the people who once lived in this house. Jennifer left the tourists to it, she was grateful she'd had some private time with her parents and couldn't face listening to the, albeit unwitting, asinine remarks of the onlookers. It was not their fault; they did not know who she was. And she had no wish to enlighten them. This was her own voyage of discovery; she was not prepared to share it.

The next stop for Jennifer was Ian Campbell's residence... she was sure she would have visited him with her parents because he was the only other fellow European on the island at the time. It always struck her as fortuitous that the aliens did not recognise the difference between Western and Eastern human beings in the same way that humans did; to them, all humans looked and smelt alike. This observation brought a wry smile to her features - somehow she didn't think you could ever convince people living in the world today they are all alike – especially when they are continually caught up in their differences.

Ian Campbell's home stood before her. A pergola covered in wisteria provided a shaded, feature walkway to his garden and there was his shed to one side, the door deliberately left ajar so tourists could see where he had tipped his tools. In the kitchen, the store cupboard and drawer were open too, in order that visitors could get a sense of how people lived then and the meagre tools at the disposal of the islanders. Jennifer loved the fact that the vegetable garden was once more being tended, this time by the Japanese Tourist Board, and, when she went to the tea shop that had sprung up to serve the tourists, she realised the produce from the garden was supplementing the fare served to visitors who ventured to the island. A light bulb moment shot across her face and she nodded to herself, of course it would be, even now it must pay to be as self-sufficient as possible when living on this Island.

Whilst the knots in her stomach were starting to loosen Jennifer couldn't bring herself to eat, not yet. She settled for a cup of green tea and, again, this small act brought back memories; the unique afternoon teas on the Hope & Charity when the refugees, forced to flee their homes and relatives, tried to come to terms and make the most of their situation. Those tea sessions had been a fusion of West meets East. Skip, his crew and Grandma took their tea, the western way, whilst the islanders, who usually drank green tea, of which there was none on board, affably made do with the compromise of sipping weak black tea served without milk. She remembered Skip commenting that it was just as well they drank it 'like gnats' it meant they could make the tea rations last the trip. Jennifer became aware her body was drenched in sweat, she felt exhausted. This was a full scale onslaught on her senses. She felt under attack yet excited at the same time. And there was still more to see, to hear, to inhale.

Her next stop was the meditation garden and pump room where the 3 Japanese islanders had hidden after they made their escape. Walking through the newly named Serenity Garden, Jennifer was amazed that it almost made her feel that way. She could feel her footsteps and heart beat slowing down to syncopate, rather than jar, with the rhythm of the landscaped woodland and water walks. The wooden bridge was there, arching across to the central island, still painted red. Yes, she knew it had been rebuilt and re-painted, but she also knew this was how it was - then. The Japanese were keen to retain this village and the whole area as a living museum and epitaph to their lost citizens.

The fragrance of jasmine weaved into her nostrils and recollections, she felt at peace, her stomach spasm released, soothing tears of relief flowed; whatever followed she could live through it. She suspected she glided, rather than walked, over the bridge, and it felt numbingly surreal to look down into the pump room where Ryuu, Kin and Sho had lived for three weeks. The rock now moved automatically as visitors stepped onto the viewing pad; there was no longer a noxious smell and the underground tin box was lit by electric light to enable visitors to see inside. The old clothing used for bedding had been painstakingly replicated to make sure everything looked as it would have done when the two men were found and scooped into the daylight. The pump and filter were back in working order and used on a daily basis; only grounds-men were allowed into the metal housing. The wall paintings made by Sho were lost in the shadows and obscured from direct view but hidden cameras now threw pictures of the murals onto a central screen in the floor; this way the artwork could be viewed but not fade in sunlight or be damaged by inquisitive hands. It was riveting to view and Jennifer peered intently as she leaned over the barrier surrounding the viewing pad. Each slide brought a fresh gasp from her speechless mouth. These were not fresh images to her, she'd seen them over and over again in books and magazines, but here, in this place, with the island's sounds and smells about her, they came alive. She had glimpsed these aliens through her grandma's skirt. She had watched her parents and friends being prodded away, like cattle, by masked creatures with bulging, flickering, almost twirling eyes. As a little girl she was scared and curious. She remembered she'd been told by Grandma to pretend she was playing hide and seek and not to make a sound; so she had kept Sally clasped over her mouth and nose all the while she hid within the folds of the skirt - just in case she forgot - luckily she didn't. She'd remained quiet and was not taken away with the other children. Tears of innate sadness trickled down the adult Jennifer's cheeks; she mouthed a silent prayer for all those lost, especially her parents and childhood friends. When the photos of Ryuu, Sho and Kin, gazed up at her from the floor she was spellbound. Somewhere in the back of her mind she had a picture of Ryuu leading the hunt for cicadas and their cast-offs as the children zigzagged this way and that on their way home from school; she was too young to go to school but watched this homeward procession each day as it passed their house. Sometimes they would stop at the garden gate and talk to her, a challenging but fun exchange of mime, words and actions. Jenny would try her best to mimic their language which resulted in immense amusement and shared laughter for all concerned. Jennifer had forgotten these initial forays into the Japanese language, although when she had gone to evening classes to learn it had not been as difficult as she'd expected; she had revealed a natural aptitude which, thinking about it now, was probably a reflection of those dormant peer group lessons.

As Jennifer walked around the second escarpment, to the copse of thorn guarded Locust trees she paused to listen to the cicadas clicking about their twilight business. The noise resonated around the track, it was impossible to pinpoint a specific position and to Jennifer it felt as though she was surrounded by speakers broadcasting a choreographed chorus of summer sounds. She'd grown up listening to their song at home in Brisbane and found it strangely calming as she approached the penultimate stop of her pilgrimage. She paused a while to collect herself for the next part of her trip.

The Locust trees were everywhere and at first it was hard to tell which were 'the ones' but then she saw the signs, against the trunks of four of the largest trees. These trees were now over 30 ft high, with thick trunks and piercing barbs - blades sharp enough to slice the legs off any misguided challenger. The branches reached out so far they looked as though they were clasping hands with their neighbours; each branch sporting beautiful fronds of double pinnate leaves dipping to display mounds of delicate snowflake flowers; the icing on the cake. These magnificent and powerful trees had once held the disintegrating bodies of islanders whose lives were deemed irrelevant by the Invaders. The investigating authorities had been at a loss to explain why the Invaders had chosen these trees, especially as it meant scaling their natural spiky defence barrier. In the end, they had determined it was probably because the branches were high enough to be seen over each others' heads, plus the alien creatures could fly to the branches rather than climb with the mutilated cadavers and that way the odour of decomposition was kept beneath them. They later discovered, from the aliens' faeces, that they ate the drupes (un-pitted fruit) of the trees. Modern day scientists were now putting forward the proposition that by using the corpses to attract insects they were encouraging cross pollination and thus ensuring lots of fruit for future harvests. It's hard to imagine this was the foremost reason in the Invaders' minds although it may well have been an inherent practice they automatically continued on the island.

The pun 'food for thought' crossed Jennifer's mind. She realised these seemingly irreverent thoughts and observations were keeping her sane. The adult Jennifer had to detach slightly from Jenny, the toddler, and the horror story of her childhood. A skill that had helped her through twenty-seven years and continued, at 30 years of age, to support her to look her demons in the face.

Beneath the trees was a man-made memorial to commemorate the last resting place of possibly 120 islanders and the bravery of another five. Jennifer perched on one of the basic wooden benches supplied for visitors to use. She sat in awe, understanding the significance of each part of the mosaic and the huge gratitude owed by society to the 5 individuals looking down on the whole scene from their pedestals. In the middle, wearing his kilt, stood Ian Campbell; around the base of his 5ft dais was an army of

giant Japanese hornets. Two Japanese men and women stood either side of him – they wore traditional costume and each figure had their name engraved on the plinth of their pedestal. Pedestals which, on closer inspection, transformed into 4ft garden sprayers with the hose and nozzle curled around the base, like a sleeping snake. Jennifer soaked up the memorial and what it stood for; she breathed in the scent of the trees and soil; she opened her heart to the pain and anguish of those that had been here before her; she heard the birds, the bees and the life existing there now. She was amazed how stable she felt, the past was now in the past, the not knowing was over ....
It was almost time to move on; once she had completed the final part of her pilgrimage.

An unexpected meeting

'May all beings be well, may all beings be happy, may all beings be peaceful and at ease, may all beings learn and grow. May all beings be well, may all beings...'

'Excuse me Ma'am. Do you mind if I sit here too? I will do my best not to disturb you.'

Jennifer opened her eyes and took in the aura of a blind Japanese man who stood before her.

'Is that okay? I'm truly sorry for interrupting your mantra.'

'It's no problem at all,' said Jennifer 'but I'm intrigued as to how you speak English so well ... and with an American accent.'

'Oh, I've lived most of my life in the States. I left this island just after my tenth birthday and hadn't been back until early last year. It was a trip I'd promised myself for my thirtieth year but I was a little late - it took a while to organise.' A wry smile twisted his face.

Jennifer adjusted her posture; she sat more upright and, turning herself slightly, moved over so she could better see the face of the man who had sat down next to her. He said no more, neither did she, for the next ten minutes they remained silent, lost in their own thoughts, and, for whatever reason, comfortable in one another's presence.

'May all beings be well, may all beings be happy, may all beings be peaceful and at ease, may all beings learn and grow.' Jennifer broke her silence and continued with the Metta Bhavana chant.

'Does that help?' asked the man. 'To accept what happened here and forgive those involved?'

Jennifer nodded her acquiescence encouraging the man to continue. He carried on as if he'd seen her.

'I was orphaned when the Invaders came to this island and haven't managed to let go of my anger and hurt. I think it's because I was taken to America and grew up with no sense of belonging and, even when I did start to fit in, I felt a sense of betrayal, mine mainly, as I let go of my parents' culture and beliefs.'

It was as if a plug had been pulled, he couldn't stop.

'Sho and Kin went with me which meant for a while I could still speak my mother tongue on a daily basis but gradually, I was Americanised. My foster parents were American and obviously I went to school there. My friends were mostly American children, or children of immigrants intent on becoming Americans. It was inevitable that I learnt to appreciate football matches and burgers and let my Japanese roots wither. I blame the Invaders ...and the Americans but, mostly, I blame myself.'

Jennifer recognised the feeling of guilt.

'Chanting Metta aloud helps me,' she responded - her eyes widening as she realised she might be speaking to Ryuu - or was he a Tourist Board impersonator, a part of the living museum experience? 'I too was orphaned at that time. I watched my parents taken away with the other islanders. I never saw them again.'

Her brain was ticking over quickly, how could she ascertain if this was the real Ryuu?

She needn't have worried.

'Are you little Jenny?' asked the stranger, 'You used to try and talk to us through your garden gate?'

'Oh Ryuu' cried Jennifer, it really is you?'

'Yep ... yes it is. What luck that our paths are crossing like this, at this moment in time. I was walking here today feeling very sorry for myself, thinking I was the only child from that time with no one of my generation to relate to. No one who had seen what I saw, smelt the same fear, and grieved the same losses.'

'I've read everything I could lay my hands on about that time,' said Jennifer, 'and listened to all the tales of the refugees when they met up in my grandparents' house. Unfortunately they have all gone now, including Grandma and Skip.' A tear prickled her eyelashes. 'I'm trying not to feel sorry for myself but I feel so alone at the moment. I'm all at sixes and sevens, not knowing what to do.

'Coming here last year helped me work out what to do. I needed to be back in my homeland, where I could feel close to my ancestors; so now I live and work here. Yes, I can work, despite my lack of sight.' He anticipated her thoughts. 'I hear people, things and shapes. I talk people through the film show that is played in the cavern, over there, twice a day, answer questions and explain how it felt, or at least, how it felt to me.'

Ryuu lifted his arm and pointed faultlessly to the entrance to the underground cavern where the crates remained intact, complete with their animal troughs. Visitors were permitted to sit on the frond bedding (changed each day) to watch the film show which had been inadvertently left by the aliens.

'Talk to me about it now, please Ryuu. I so need to know what really happened and how it felt, I was only three and my memories are mixed up with nightmares - I would really appreciate knowing the truth.'

And so Ryuu told her his and his parents' incredible story, and the reason why the aliens left and had not returned.

Ryuu could fill in the gaps in his story because of the film and the narrative of other survivors and refugees - but only he really understood his account, his anguish and struggle, and how he felt, nearly three decades later.

The tale of their time in the pump room was well documented so Ryuu didn't start there, other than to say that when he and his parents were kept in those crates, in the cavern, each day fighting to stay alive and watching their friends and relatives die in horrendous circumstances, he remembered crying and crying until he could cry no more and then just squatting in a numb stupor. His mother would reach from her crate to stroke his hand, he knew she was doing it, but he could not respond, he could not reach out through the shell he had created about himself. When he, his father and the other three men had taken off, running through the stream, they hadn't really thought through their plan, they just knew they had to get away. Thank goodness Kin had knowledge of the pump room. It wasn't until Ryuu was in the military hospital that he learnt the fate of his parents. His father and Takao had leapt into the sea to throw the aliens off the scent of the other three. Even now Ryuu's voice cracked when remembering the final parting from his father. Then his mother, believing that both her husband and son were dead, had not tried to swim again, giving herself up to the sea, to join her family.

'What about my parents?' asked Jennifer 'Do you remember them, were they in the crates with you?'

'Unfortunately yes,' responded Ryuu. 'They too did not return one day. One day neither your mother nor father returned. The listener in our midst, who understood the Invaders' language and was with them at the time, said your father was seen trying to save your mother in the waves and, in the end, neither of them made it back to shore. It was quite early on.'

Jennifer sobbed aloud, unable to keep her feelings in check. Ryuu waited for her to use the handkerchief she retrieved from her bag, saying nothing, allowing her the dignity of grieving the loss of her parents, again. He heard Jenny (as he thought of her) gulp, then, feeling her nod, continued.

'In some ways I was the lucky one. I could not see by then so it did not matter to me that the only light we had was from a small torch. It was Kin and Sho I felt sorry for. They were strong, determined men but gradually their will to exist was ebbing away. I did my best to feed us. It was truly wonderful being able to swim to the outside, to catch Koi and to breathe fresh air each day. Kin and Sho did not have that release. Sho started to record the invasion and what they'd seen on the walls of the pump room; this gave him a purpose, and Kin helped, catching the blood of the fish in cups he made from leaves. It was a double-edged task - as it only heightened our sense of loss and hopelessness - but we kept going with it.'

'You must have been ecstatic when you were found and rescued' commented Jennifer, 'how did you know it was safe to surface and call out?'

'I wasn't sure' said Ryuu, 'but by then I'd become accustomed to trusting my instinct and at that moment my instinct said shout for all your worth! So I did.'

Jennifer looked across to Ryuu; this reverie was painful for both of them but he could smile as he recounted the circumstance of their rescue.

'It was fortunate the Aussies had a Japanese speaker amongst them. He was able to put us at our ease and interpret for us. They couldn't believe how we'd been living, and we were a mess.' Ryuu screwed up his nose. 'We stunk and wore no clothes; they were so ragged and dirty we couldn't clean them but they were all we had for bedding, so we used them. At first I tried bringing in leaf fronds but they wouldn't dry, everything I brought in had to come through the filter trap, I had to swim with it, underwater, from the banks; luckily Kin could make cups out of the leaves which at least enabled me to bring water in for the men. It was then Sho started painting. He had the tools - cups of blood ink and fishbone pens.'

Jennifer nodded her silent encouragement.

'Once we were out of the ground and had been given some clothes, we took them to where the crates were; they had seen them in passing but hadn't understood what they were for. It was easier to recount our story with the actual props. The reality of it was shocking to them, I think the memories of the atrocities of the War were still in the forefront of everyone's mind and our incarceration and annihilation on top of that was almost too much to take in, especially as we were describing creatures, possibly not from our world, who could fly from tree to tree as well as swim like fish, deep under water. It still amazes me that they did not take over our planet.'

'I'm so grateful to Ian Campbell and your fellow islanders' said Jennifer. 'Because of them we all get to carry on with our lives; their selfless acts saved us all. That's in my opinion.'

'Mine too' agreed Ryuu, 'but I have this fear that they could return. The aliens I mean. They seemed virtually invincible at the time. Maybe that's because I was a boy of 10 and they appeared stronger than my parents and the other adults of our community.'

'No, I think you're right' Jennifer interrupted. 'I have nightmares that they will pop up in another thermal geyser one day and that we will not be ready or able to keep them at bay.

'I think I have more faith than you in that regard, Jenny. Science has moved on in leaps and bounds.'

They fell into silence again, each lost in their own thought processes for a few minutes, before Ryuu continued his story.

'We were taken from here to a military hospital in Tokyo, where we were medically examined and samples taken before being showered, fed and allowed to sleep. Then began a period of extensive interrogation, during which time we were kept apart. The questioning, despite being supposedly sympathetic towards a young boy, seemed endless. My mind was whirring and whirring, I hadn't realised there were so many things I should have seen and heard and just couldn't remember. As you can imagine, the scientists were particularly interested in my nose and breathing capabilities. They took x-rays, new fangled scans, and prodded and probed. They found it hard to believe I could not see them as I was always aware of their approach and form. Thankfully I could not feel colour so eventually they had to accept my blindness. It obviously helped that when Sho and Kin recounted their stories of the pellet guns they were the same as mine and, I think, as adults, their recollections held more substance. They explained that initially the children and adults given the language shot fell to the floor, screeching in pain, before fainting; but when they came too they had a strange buzzing in their heads that faded over an hour or so and then they could listen to what the aliens were saying to them and make sense of it but they could not see. We soon grasped we were to be interpreters, much good it did any of us. We still had to undergo the same trials and fail to fly or to swim for long underwater.'

'When did you realise you could breathe under water as well as understand and sense them, Ryuu?'

'It was after the second shot.' Ryuu's facial features distorted as he remembered the pellets, the pain and the shock of losing his sight. 'There were only 2 of us shot that time; one adult, my Aunt, Atsuko, and one child, myself. I don't think they'd expected us to develop a sixth sense and, after we escaped, I think they didn't want anyone else to develop our abilities - I think they thought that maybe I swam away, and my father and the others drowned, trying to. I suppose I could have tried to swim away but I just didn't think of it at the time and, in reality, I doubt I would have had the strength to get to the next island.'

'I remember reading a bit about your aunt; wasn't she the one who befriended an alien?' prompted Jennifer.

'Yes - she's the unsung heroine in all this. Her part in our survival has been overlooked - I don't think people want to entertain the idea that any alien could have been worth calling a friend. It's almost as though they see her as a traitor, even though it was her clarity of mind that helped Ian Campbell and the Elders with their venture.'

'Can you play the film and talk me through it' asked Jennifer.

'Of course, but first let me explain what we believe Ian Campbell was organising with the other four islanders left behind by the Hope & Charity. We have been able to piece together what they did in preparation from the actual film that the aliens recorded and left behind.'

'Mr Campbell had a hornet's nest he carried in his tool box. The others had garden spray guns filled with, what we now know, was water laced with the animal antibiotic left behind by Captain Maynard (traces of the spray were found in the crop spray guns discarded in the scrub. The islanders carried old cans full of cicadas; the insects' feet had been dipped in honey. I know, it sounds fantastic, the mind of the man that thought this up was astonishing, but thank goodness he did. If you look in his house you will see a selection of reference books about the insects, fauna and flora of Japan. He obviously had a keen interest and remembered what he read.'

The film was timed to start just as the other tourists came to the cavern. They all went inside, to sit in the crates. Jennifer was now feeling sick in the pit of her stomach; this was where her parents had spent their last days. If she was feeling this way, how must it be for Ryuu, he'd actually lived through this hell. She looked at Ryuu. His face was a mask - maybe not seeing was an advantage in this situation. She knew he could tell the size and shape of her, and the tourists, and he obviously knew they were in the crates. Hopefully their aroma was different from those kept here in 1953 - tortured and fed on bizarre fodder.

Ryuu had mastered his stoic approach and demeanour. He could manage being here but, what he didn't tell anyone and they didn't appear to realise, was that he couldn't bear to go back into the pump house, or swim in the sea. These days he used his underwater breathing and diving skills in man-made pools only. He once swam with dolphins in a tank in Florida, and that was amazing - he felt totally at one with them, and they with him. Maybe he'd do that again some-day but for now this was his place, making sure than no-one became complacent about what had happened or, as he believed, might happen again in the future. He knew Jenny understood because as an infant she'd grasped the menace of those creatures, their abilities and lack of respect for all sentient beings.

For the benefit of Jennifer and the other visitors, Ryuu spoke first in English and then in Japanese.

'Ladies and Gentlemen, please make yourselves comfortable and prepare to watch this most astounding film and listen to the account of what is believed to have happened on this island, three generations ago. If there are any of you who cannot sit on the fronds please let me know and I'll fetch you a stool.'

There was an older woman at the back who'd limped in with the aid of a stick, she asked for a stool. Ryuu, in the polite and solicitous Japanese way, gave his attention to ensuring she was comfortable and able to see the screen set up on the wall opposite.

He pressed the start button and there was silence as everyone stopped watched the story unfold on screen. Jennifer noted it was a silent movie and realised that she had been expecting a modern movie, like the one's she'd attended at the outdoor cinemas in Brisbane. Silly, of course it couldn't be like that. This was a black and white replay of actual events, characters didn't necessarily pose for the camera, the action was jumbled, and faces sometimes hard to differentiate - but, nevertheless, it was an authentic horror movie based not on science fiction but on fact; she shook her head to remind herself it was real and that all the characters in it were now lost, presumed dead.

'You will notice at this point', Ryuu paused the film, 'that all we can see is the back of the heads of the aliens. It would appear they were actually making a film of the insects devouring and dissecting the bodies of people impaled on the trees. It's what follows next that causes the camera man to change the direction of his lens.'

Chapter 8 – The Elders' attack

1953 - Pretend

Ess prodded Atsuko with the electric prong used to herd stock. He knew he had not activated the power button but those citiXens watching from the pOd did not. He did not want to hurt Atsuko but this had to look real. They must not realise he liked one of these Earthlings. He'd said he needed to get supplies from their homes to complete his observations of how they lived and managed to survive in these primitive conditions.

As he prodded he whispered ... 'Pretend, pretend, not hurt you'.

Atsuko automatically flinched as she was prodded ... she was pleasantly surprised it didn't shock her. She wasn't sure exactly what Ess was saying but she knew from the tone in his voice and the look in his eyes as he nudged her out the door and onto the trail that he was trying to be friendly. She kept walking at a regular pace, breathing in the fresh air, listening for the sound of any of her friends and family. There were no signs of life. The village was empty. She led him through the doorway of her home and automatically bent to remove her shoes. He watched; his attention captured by the simple process of changing from outdoor shoes to slippers. He looked at his bare feet. She gave him a little smile. He removed his mask and smiled back at her. Atsuko was amazed how approachable he looked when his whole face was exposed and he ventured a tentative smile. Ess was so glad he couldn't smell - he felt almost elated. She'd smiled at him. Inside the house they could not be watched. He reached out to touch her hand. She lowered her gaze and put both her hands in his. His touch was surprisingly smooth, not cold, firm yet gentle. Her hands were so small, her little fingers had virtually no grip - they tickled his senses. He was in awe. He put his fingers to his lips in the universal sign to keep quiet and went on to mime. It took a while, but Atsuko eventually understood that he was telling her there were wiggly creatures in the ground watching them outside all the time. It even looked as though he was miming these worms could get inside a person – but, seeing the look on her face, he hastily re-assured her she didn't have any inside her. Atsuko shuddered. It felt as though there was really no escape from these creatures. She led him to her kitchen and took the rest of the depleted stores from the cupboard, including tins and an opener. His eyebrows were quizzical; she allowed herself another gentle smile and showed him how it worked. He watched her put something in her mouth and eat it; bidding him to do the same… he decided to trust her and tried the fruit cocktail. The texture and flavour were totally new to him but not unpalatable - he sucked hard and started to relish the action and the sweetness. There was no more time to spare, they had to return. He pointed to the door. Atsuko hunched over to change her shoes, her shoulders going up and down in time with her sobs – it took a while for her to compose herself enough to complete the task. She turned to Ess and nodded when she was ready to leave her home – there was no going back. To an observer it looked as though her keePer must have given her a hard time. Ess prodded as gently as he could but did what was necessary to keep up the charade. Somehow he had to prevent Atsuko from being used as a breedinStock. She was too precious for that.

Back in the isoblution unit Atsuko washed her face and hands in an effort to compose herself. Ess had taken the tins and opener but she at least had combs, brushes, soap and towels to give to the men – there had been no blankets or tatamis. Their anxiety heightened as she explained about the worm-like creatures. They now knew they were constantly watched; every move, interaction, reaction analysed and each meal and toilet they produced dissected. They daren't refuse any of the food they were offered; they had tried that at the beginning and it had resulted in them being pinned down and force fed via tubes. They spent another day inactive, their minds working overtime surmising what was going on outside and what would happen to them.

Outside the Invaders had given up trying to find the escapees; they had come to the conclusion they must have drowned trying to swim away. They'd seen one of the bodies crashing with the waves against the rocks and expected the others to wash up some time soon. For now they wanted to relax and be entertained; to eat and make merry. The remaining eXpired manOids had been hung in the trees in readiness for the after dinner show but to begin with they would eat together - their daily rations of grubs, seeds, insects and grains, washed down with liberal amounts of water - followed by tiny pieces of fruit cocktail which Ess had brought back from his forage into the manOid's village. He'd reported he had eaten some with no ill effects and the scientists had subsequently analysed it as fruit, an edible food product long since exhausted from where they lived. They loved it. Slurping and feeling particularly sated and relaxed - buoyed up by the thought they would soon be leaving, they stood to watch the show. The knowAlls were not overly disappointed; they were taking four samplings with them, to experiment with at their leisure - in the comfort of their laboRatories back home.

The foreigners gave their full attention to encouraging and applauding the insects gnawing at the remains of the bodies hanging from the branches. This was the last of them so they were going to make the most of the sport while they could. The late afternoon was made even more pleasant because a gentle breeze was blowing the fetid stench of decaying corpses high above their heads and away into the tree tops. The merriment, squawking and noise levels were at peak resonance as Ian Campbell and the islanders sneaked up on them. Thanks to the message scratched by Atsuko on the floor of her genko they knew to avoid soil pathways as much as possible. They'd kept to the gravel drains and had only left them as they crept into the clearing.

It all happened so quickly. Sticky cicadas, thrown out of tin cans hit the aliens from both sides. They stood, stupefied in amazement. Unable to comprehend what was going on. They watched the insects attach to their skin and feathers. Black eyes bulging and swivelling in all directions. They caught sight of Ian Campbell knelt on the ground, opening a box. He banged on the sides with metal spoons. Tin cans clashed together.

Ian now knew the Gods had been with them when they'd had gone rummaging earlier; they'd unwittingly missed Ess & Atsuko by half an hour, enough time to avoid detection whilst Atsuko took advantage of the opportunity she created, crying over her shoes, to score her warning message. Ian also gave thanks to Lorna for keeping them safe by guiding them along a slower, worm-less route. Now he needed the breeze to help him. The hornets were angry, they'd been contained in the tool box since he'd used the mole grips and Stanley knife to cut their nest away from the tree and catch it in the blankets. Transferring the insects from the blankets into the box was a tricky operation but the team of Elders had the expertise and patience for such an exercise. What he wanted next was for the hornets to fly in the direction of the aliens. Ian had calculated the black masks would attract them. Hornets view the colour black as dangerous and generally attack it. He had made sure neither he nor any of his helpers were wearing black - so the hornets had no other distraction – their focus zoomed in on the black masks and fragrance of the honeyed cicadas. The elements were with him. The hornets, blown on the breeze, spied the black masks and flew at the Invaders. The Invaders, distracted by the cicadas didn't see them coming until it was too late. Squealing in shock and pain as they were stung they pulled the masks and hornets from their faces. The islanders now brought their spray guns into action. They sprayed the toxic antibiotic mix into the faces (and hopefully mouths) of the enemy. The attackers could see the exposed faces of their prey; they aimed at the slightly pointed chins and pursed lips of the strange beings; at the small nostrils in splat noses. The islanders kept on spraying. The aliens' feathers were covered with honey coated cicadas … unable to fly they were even starting to attract the attention of the insects from their human honey traps. Sweet honey was exceptionally alluring. The spray in the aliens' faces, whilst a nuisance and off-putting, was not disabling them. Fee ordered her fellow citiXens to chase the manOids but they did not listen … instead they ran away before circling towards the pOd.

The worMCamras kept recording the action from all angles.

Safe inside the pOd Ess watched the scene unfold on mothRWorm's screen. He turned as Wil reached the pOd and screamed at him to help prepare for departure. Ess was horrified. He knew that Atsuko would be condemned to a slow, agonising death in captivity as a labRat; never allowed a moment of privacy or a chance to interact with him. He disabled mothRWorm and took her recorder then triggered the cable link and connections to the central mind unit to ignite and melt. He did not want the knowAlls back home to see what was happening on this island - if the pOd ever returned. He did not want the eXpedition recording to be watched, or the worMCamras to continue to transmit their observations to mothRWorm. As far as Ess was concerned, the least known about this island and those left on it, the better. He had no wish to be tracked and taken back; there was nothing for him in his world. He hurried to the isoblution unit.... grasping a confused and scared Atsuko by the hand he pulled her out of the pOd and, prodding the men back inside, re-locking the door. He only wanted to take Atsuko with him. This was no altruistic liberation - it was Ess grasping at a small chance of happiness. He silently and briskly headed into the woodland, gripping Atusko's palm in one hand and the prodgun in the other, ready to fend off any attack.

Atsuko could hear and sense what was going on behind them. The hornets were swarming after the aliens; totally incensed at being confined and then let out to face the threat of black eyes over black masks looking down on them. They launched into action, going for the eyes and masks, not giving up when the owners of these black attributes started to run; the hornets followed them, holding on and stinging where they could. The aliens were letting out a deluge of howls and squeals, they didn't know what had hit them and, to their horror, found they couldn't fly - the combination of cicadas and honey impeding their flight feathers. They headed for the fissure, the safety of steamy water and their pOd. Atsuko could make out the shouts and hollering of Ian Campbell - vaulting into a battle cry as he chased after the creatures, her own people were joining in, making as much of a hullaballoo as possible to egg on the hornets and keep the Invaders on the run. All the time spraying them with their toxic solution, aiming for their heads, eyes and open mouths, oblivious to the fact that by now, they too were inhaling small droplets. These strange creatures might be equipped to swim and fly but their long floppy feet made them slow runners. Ian had strategically placed the infirm islanders so they could spray to best effect. They were so excited ... they each had found energy, hitherto lost to age, and, at this moment, felt reborn and regenerated, as they avenged their community and reclaimed their self-respect. A torrent of names, the names of loved-ones, tirade from very dry lips, and carry on the wind. When they run out of spray they hurl rocks and pebbles... anything they can lay their hands on, as they pursue the Invaders to the caverns.

Atsuko heard a few of the aliens regrouping in the third crater; most had retreated directly to the pOd... All were afflicted by stings and coughing, some almost choking. She wasn't so concerned about those in the pOd but she did not trust the murmurs and movement of the Invaders in the crater, they had ceased to run and there was purpose to their efforts. Ess held her hand tightly and was not interested in her gesticulations that they should return; that she didn't like what she was hearing. He knew what was likely to be happening and did not want to get involved or caught up in the nets. The citiXens were probably planning to throw trawliNnets over the island assailants as they ventured towards the caverns. He'd seen them catch fleeing samplings this way before and, although these manOids weren't fleeing believing they were the aggressor, the tables were being turned and they were about to be trawled and stopped in their tracks. He didn't attempt to share this information with Atsuko but concentrated on getting as much distance as possible between them and the activities in the third crater - activities which were obviously disturbing Atsuko's equilibrium. The sudden piercing screams followed by seconds of eerie silence echoed through the trees around them; her fingernails bit into his palms and she couldn't stop trembling. She knew something awful had happened; and she knew that Ess knew; she could sense the change in his body language, the tension and hesitancy.

'Ess, Ess. Please go back. Something awful is happening.'

Ess shook his head and kept walking.

He felt, rather than reasoned, her withdrawal from him. She no longer wanted to accompany him, no longer trusted his intentions or respected his decision making. He had no choice; his happiness depended upon her looking up to him. He started to veer off the track, taking them back through the trees towards the crater. It would be okay once she saw there was nothing they could do - she would go with him again, willingly, he was, after all, her saviour.

Ian watched in dismay as, almost simultaneously, his friends were caught in spiteful barbed nets and hoisted into the trees. He had been quick enough to evade capture himself; he'd turned, about to call to the Elders to follow him, when he caught a glimpse of the aliens in the branches. Instinctively he threw himself to the ground and rolled behind a rock, grateful for his military training and sustained fitness levels. He lay still, barely breathing. He didn't want to attract attention although he suspected the worm cameras would make his whereabouts known soon enough (he didn't know that Mother Worm had been sabotaged). The jubilant Invaders seemed to have more than enough to occupy them; they had 4 captives in their nets plus stings and coughs to worry about. The aliens hung the netted islanders from two poles which they jauntily carried on their shoulders. They played little heed to the bumps and moans as their freight hit the ground or swung against the trees. Ian was in torment; this was all his doing - he hadn't thought through what would happen if the Invaders retaliated. He assumed they would, of course, all die in this venture but hadn't considered in what manner. All were willing to give up their lives, including him, however watching this unwarranted cruelty was torturous. He should be there with them rather than observing from a distance their suffering and bravery. These old friends of his were battered and bleeding, yet, from the set of their mouths, intent on not crying out. He crawled through the scrub at a distance, his mind working overtime, trying to devise a way to help them.

Atsuko and Ess also watched the grisly parade. Ess was emotionless, Atsuko aghast; these were senior members of her community, revered and cherished for their knowledge and maturity. Every inhaled wince cut her to the quick. She sensed another onlooker. Not an islander, not an alien, but a foreigner nonetheless. It was Ian Campbell. She peered intensely around her and saw him in the undergrowth, their eyes locked. She realised the sight of her with Ess would perplex him. She held out her hand, beckoning him to join them. What now? He really had no option - he edged in their direction - never taking his eyes off Ess, watching for any sign of trickery.

Atsuko pulled her other hand free from Ess's grip. She grabbed Ian's hands and encouraged him to his feet. It was Ess who was perplexed. He did not understand the whispered discussion between the femanOid and manOid but he could see the looks Ian gave him when his name was mentioned. His eyes flickered. Had he made a grave mistake in walking away from the pOd? Sensing his agitation Atsuko turned to smile at him. Tilting her head and stroking his arm in an effort to reassure him. How could she tell him that Ian and the four older islanders had just done their best to maim and kill him and his fellow citiXens. Ian had explained to her what they'd done and how he hoped the mixture of hornet stings and toxic drug spray would prove fatal to the Invaders.

Due to his habit of staying in the background, Ess had escaped the initial cicada attack and not received a single sting, nor had he been in the line of fire of the spray guns. He and the young citiXen left on board to guard the pOd were the lucky ones. Ian knew from Atsuko of the coughing and spluttering as the aliens entered the pod; he was quietly confident that these alien creatures were developing an allergic reaction; their immune systems unable to cope with a synchronised attack of stings from the giant hornets and poison from the diluted antibiotic. The islanders would have been very satisfied to see the citiXens entering the pOd at that moment; all were struggling to breathe (hence the coughing) as they lapsed into anaphylactic shock. It seemed that the speed at which they collapsed depended upon the number of stings they received and the amount of spray they ingested, either from the direct spray to their faces or by the preening process they undertook in order to rid their feathers of honeyed cicadas and spray. Unfortunately for Ian, the sense of achievement was tainted, not only by the inhumane treatment of his old friends, but also because of the protracted, agonised death he had brought to bear on their assailants - causing other beings to suffer and squirm brought him no pleasure – but they had to go.

The four prisoners were broken and bleeding from the netting they'd endured and the violence of their journey back to the pOd. They were literally thrown into the isoblution unit to join the samplings held there. The men were appalled, they knew these Elders and could not believe their eyes. They had very little at their disposal to help splint broken bones and bind open wounds but did the best they could.

By now the aliens were in turmoil. Most too ill to function effectively and those that could were at a loss what to do. They had registered that Ess and Atsuko were missing, unaccounted for, and also another male manOid, the one that had led the attack. They were pulled in two directions, whether to focus on their ill comrades or to hunt for the missing manOid - who may have kidnapped Ess. Wil was one of those who could still function; Fee was one of those who could not. Wil wanted to close down the pOd and break away as soon as possible, whilst they still could. He was not a mediC knowAll and had no idea how to treat the presenting ailments, however there were other semi-functioning citiXens who wanted to catch the manOids, especially the main aggressor - he might be able to provide information about the toxin used which could help the knowAlls determine an effective cure. Observing the carnage Wil pointed out it was futile to collect more samplings and statistics if there was not a knowAll fit enough to draw conclusions and prescribe an antidote. As the most senior officer left standing he determined the sooner they left and got back to kaRRak the better. He just hoped Fee could last out until then. He might even be able to cold store her and others if they shut down before the pOd reached home territory. All this was tentative, he could feel a hot flush creeping over him, his skin and eyes were feeling unpleasantly tingly. If they didn't make a move soon it could be too late.

The Caverns, 1980

'At this juncture it is worth reflecting on the amazing coincidences and good fortune that had taken place within that 24 hour period ... without which the potential banishment of these super-beings from our shores would not have been possible ... super-beings with enhanced intelligence and physical abilities ...our shores being all those discreet kingdoms that exist on this, our planet, Earth.'

The audience was spellbound. Ryuu always paused the recording at this point.

'The successful exit of the forty refugees on the Hope & Charity was possible because the aliens were occupied hunting the five escapees on the other side of the island... The predators tracked their human prey towards the north west of the island, whereas the jetty was on the other side, off the South East corner ... and, whilst Ian had been preparing to put his plan into action, Atsuko had been wandering around their village with Ess ... where she scratched a message about the worm cameras.' Ryuu checked those listening were following the tale so far ....

'It was as if it had been a planned diversion - but it wasn't' a tourist shouted out everyone's thoughts.

'Yep ... if the escapees had broken away a day later... or if the body of Daiki - Ryuu's father- had not been seen by the flight scouts ... floating in the sea to the North ... the Invaders might have switched their concentrated endeavours to the opposite end of the island ... then the outcome might well have been different.'

Ryuu paused to allow the visitors' imaginations to do their work.

'Ian Campbell might not have managed to obtain the tools and materials he required to execute his plan ... the Invaders might have focused on the Hope & Charity and its cargo ... they might even have intercepted it and prevented Captain Maynard from landing or the people camping on the coastline from signalling to him ... it all could have ended so differently and - whilst we cannot guarantee this is the end - our World was given a reprieve ... a reprieve that was not made apparent to the general public for nearly thirty years - but more of that later.'

Ryuu pressed re-start and the visitors saw the empty caverns, with no sign of a pod or Elder. They also saw the films taken by ASIS as the refugees arrived in Brisbane; there was little Jenny, Grandma and Skip!

What none of them knew was that Ian Campbell stepped up to the plate one final time to save humankind.

Twenty-seven years earlier....

Neither Atsuko nor Ian could bear to leave the Elders to an unknown fate. They had no idea how to help them but at the very least they wanted to see if there was something they could do. It would mean going back, getting closer to the cavern, the pod and the aliens. They would need Ess to help with this. Would he help them? Could he be trusted?

Ess felt totally confused. Emotions he had not experienced since a child were coming in to play. A mixture of fear, love, terror and sheer excitement! His whole being was pumping. If he helped Atsuko she would be totally beholden to him and, if he saved this miSSion and helped the pOd limp home, he would be feted by his fellow citiXens. A win win situation. He did not care about the fate of Ian Campbell and the other manOids but he did care about his fate and his well-being. Better to be back home, feted, with Atsuko yielding and dependent upon him, than here, where he would have to live in hiding, permanently reliant upon Atsuko. He realised now that he hadn't thought this through properly before but, as if a bright spark had eXploded over his head, he registered how auspicious and favourable the situation was becoming for him - the citiXens would give Atsuko to him to express their undying gratitude.

Ian and Atsuko, oblivious to the machinations inside the head of the alien, saw only his weak smile and outstretched hand, indicative of an offer to help them, to lead them to the Invader's cavern and pod. All three walked in single file - Ess in the lead. They no longer needed to worry about worm cameras. Ess had indicated mothRWorm was rendered inoperative and proudly exhibited the recording chips he withdrew from his travel belt. Ordinarily the travel belt was worn to carry a currency card and the multifunctional communication device - coMMa - essential issue to all citiXens on exploratory miSSions. Ingeniously Ess had adapted his belt; it now had an extra secret compartment for his personal valuables; his father's golden comb feather, an ID picture of Atsuko and the verses he wrote; Ess had created a subversive dream realm to escape to, away from his loneliness and frustration, in the old-fashioned written word; and, of course, he now had a miraculous reality to look forward to - the warmth and friendship extended by Atsuko. Plus the recording chips were extremely valuable – tiTANium was in short supply.

Ess pondered his future with relish as he walked with a spring in his step towards the caverns. Before they came into direct view he stopped and turned. Ian grabbed his arm, yuk! Ian's hand was rough and unwelcome. The manOid was signalling to Ess that he had an idea; he wanted Ess to lead him into the pOd, as though he'd captured him; he did not want Atsuko to go with them, he wanted her to wait on the outside. Ess calculated that Ian was hoping to somehow perform the impossible and get the manOids out of the pOd. He knew that would not happen but now was not the time to tell him. He wanted the acclaim of capturing Ian; he could present Atsuko to the citiXens later, as his personal trophy. Oh yes, he could see it all, the welcome home, the public ceremony – he would no longer be ignored or treated as an odDBrew.

Ian stood in front of Ess; Ess prodded him, this time he flicked the switch so Ian's grimace of pain was genuine. Ess was enjoying the deceit, he enjoyed exercising control. It was a good job his masQ once again hid most of his face. He guided Ian through the labyrinth of caverns and passed the vacant crates. Ian found the smell revolting, he wasn't surprised the aliens wore masks; the sulphurous smell of the volcanic heat, the stale human sweat, faeces and food, all combined to generate nausea; he gritted his teeth and walked on.

Moisture clung to the cavern walls, algae already forming in the alien-made tunnels. Ian looked for markers to aid his exit. They were few and far between. The caverns had been created with symmetry in mind, not identifiable imperfections. He could not decide whether these beings were from outer space or inner earth – both options felt incredulous, but one had to be true. Actually, as he found out later, both were true. The creatures had come from deep underground, under the sea, where they nestled whilst the Earth was surveyed from their orbiting space-craft and a suitable emergence spot identified. The isolated Japanese island was pronounced perfect for an initial foray and trial tests. The evidence of the eruption of atom bombs was detected floating through space and the aliens followed this trail, convinced that a species willing to inflict so much damage on itself would not be overly concerned about the inhabitants of one tiny island. Some might view this as karma however all this information had yet to unfold to Ian; at this stage his eyes could only scour for the pod in front of him.

Almost impossible to differentiate against the cavern walls, he thought it was made from rock until a door slid open and he realised it was mirrored, its surface so highly polished that it reflected its surroundings. As they approached closer Ian could see his and Ess's reflections; he was un-nerved by the rapacious stare in Ess's eyes, so concentrated, so gleeful. Ian shook his head and looked again, the stare had been replaced by eyes flickering in all directions, watching and waiting for his comrades to appear. Maybe it was just his imagination, maybe it was purely a distortion caused by the mirrored surface of the pod. Ian's first step into the pod was surreal, the floor gave way, only a fraction, like the plate of a set of scales. Ess prodded him further along the corridor. Ian bit his lip, refusing to flinch although he did allow himself a threatening glare over his shoulder. Ess looked the other way. No, Ess could not be trusted. A door slid open to the left. Another, taller creature stood before him. This creature immediately pulled his mask over his face, his nose wrinkling in disgust, and glowered at Ess. From the rapid exchange in their piercing, squawking language Ian surmised this new character was furious. He seemed to be in the middle of a control room, a cross between an aeroplane's cockpit and a ship's bridge. The flashing screens and monitors were blinding. Ian couldn't focus, trying to look from one to another made him dizzy, he surmised that having eyes which could focus in separate directions would be a distinct advantage, especially if your brain could compute quickly enough to keep up. A very huffy Ess steered Ian from the control room to the

isoblution unit - there was another prodding. Ian gave a
sharp intake of breath, not from the prodding but from what
his eyes beheld. He temporarily forgot his concerns about
Ess and the Pod Commandant. His immediate objective
was to help his island friends. The three younger men had
done what they could for the Elders but they were in a bad
way, lying on the floor with bandage strips, torn from spare
clothing, used to dress their wounds. Totally stoic, each
managed a grim smile in Ian's direction. The interpreter
within the group of captives was able to update Ian as to the
state of the Invaders on board. Most aliens were
incapacitated due to breathing difficulties – their bodies
were shutting down. Unfortunately the four Elders were
also gasping; they seemed to have inhaled a significant
portion of the spray themselves - although they'd managed
to escape the wrath of the hornets. Ian was aware a sting
he'd received was starting to blister badly and had to
assume some of the spray had got into it. Fortunately, as
yet, his breathing was okay, mind you, he did have a bit of
a sore throat and his eyes felt itchy. Fingers crossed, his
immune system was strong enough to defend his body a
while longer; unlike their assailants, whose immune
systems seemed to be failing miserably. He spoke
soothingly, in turn, to his battle weary cohorts; they now
had a special bond and place in each others' hearts. It was
distressing to see them this way. The interpreter pointed
out the surveillance cameras and microphones. Ian got the
message and talked very quietly, his subdued voice
breaking with emotion as he asked if they knew of a way
out of this chamber. All three shook their heads. They
reported they had never been allowed out of the unit and
the only way they knew what was going on was by
listening through the walls and pipes to the creatures
comings and goings. The islanders were used to seeing Ess
every day when he brought their food and Atsuko had done
her best to glean titbits of information from him but, since

they had both gone out earlier that day, everything had changed. Ess had taken Atsuko out mid morning and deposited her back before lunch but then, without warning, a few hours later, had unlocked the door and grabbed her, whisking her away. That was just before the creatures started to return, wailing in agony. Obviously they now knew why there was so much commotion but were not sure if they'd been forgotten entirely or if the creatures realised Atsuko was no longer here. They had not seen Ess or any other Invader since the injured Elders were thrown into the room. That was until Ess thrust Ian in to join them.

Ian paced the room, diagonally from corner to corner, then backwards and forwards. He could see only one way out and that was through the entrance door but there was no lock or handle visible from the inside. There were inset lights to one wall and a shower head protruding from the wall and ceiling on the other side. There the floor sloped gently to allow the waste water to flow into a gutter and down a solitary drain. There was also a dispenser for toilet bags which the islanders were obliged to use - it was empty - sealed, used bags hooked limply on one wall. Ian frowned. There was no opening wider than a child's fist. He was starting to think the only way to break out was as they showed in the movies; create a commotion, attract a guard, pin him down from behind and then everyone pour out into the corridor - but what then? Ian concluded it was impossible to plan any further than that … 'what then' would depend on who opened the door, how many aliens were suffering, how many were functioning, whether Ess was on their side and whether the cool Pod Commandant was otherwise occupied.

Wil was certainly fully occupied. The mediCUnit was under siege; citiXens were leaning and squatting against the walls leading to it, desperate to get some relief, to be able to function, to breathe and stop smouldering without and within. The miSSion mediC was doing her best but she too was affected and her body was slowly but inevitably succumbing to a state of collapse. She didn't have an antidote, this was not something they had to contend with at home; insects were bred in strictly controlled bio-organic container farms and any stings or aggression had been removed by genetic modification centuries before. Unfortunately the problem had been exacerbated by citiXens attempts to preen themselves; now most were too ill to even consider preening, indeed, many were too sick to breathe unaided. There were insufficient oxygen cans and the few breTHren with any energy left were squabbling over access to them. Fee, wilted and bedraggled, directed the mediCAids to put those citiXens who had lost control of their bodily functions out of their misery; to stupORize them. This was a demoralizing activity. The mediC was used to repairing citiXens not putting them to sleep for an indefinite period of time. She surmised many would eXpire in that sleep – their breath too shallow to sustain them.

'Ess, go in, go in. See what nonsense about!' ordered Wil, totally pissed off with the banging and screaming coming from the isoblution unit. 'No time to pander, pander. No stop - stupOR the lot.'

'Might need, need eat and drink,' hissed a sullen Ess. He didn't appreciate having Wil order him about but Fee and the other senior officers were too incapacitated to deal with the pOd or its citiXens let alone their eXtraction from this hell hole. From what he could make out there was just Wil, himself and a relatively junior breTHreen, Gar, who was on his first mission, still standing; that was excluding the four manOids - currently making all the noise.

'Idea, idea - I go get, get provisions.' Ess was looking for an excuse to leave the pOd and bring Atsuko on board.

Wil was having none of it.

'Sod 'em ... Sod 'em. They hurt, hurt us. They starve, starve. The knowAlls utiliZe bodies.'

This was not going to plan.

'Go hose, hose hard. Shut them down!' Wil was in charge – and they would know it.

Ess stood at the isoblution doorway. He was preoccupied - his mind working overtime to devise a reason to go outside the pOd - one last time. He released the door but didn't step inside. He might not be able to smell but he could see, and it was a pretty gruesome sight; one of the older captives had died of their wounds - she'd been covered with a blanket in the far corner. There was blood stained clothing and puddles all over the floor. Ian Campbell stood before him with the interpreter at his side. Ian stared into the alien's eyes. No hint of friendship between them

Letting vent his frustration Ess snarled 'What's your problem, problem?'

'We need bandages and medication for our wounded and fresh water. One of our Elders has already died. Oh, and there are no sanitation bags left.'

Ess criss-crossed his eyes surveying the scene.

'See what do, do - but quiet, quiet or you all eXpire.' Ess nodded towards the dead femanOid.

He sealed the door and went back to the control room.

'One eXpired .... no water, no foDDer, no sandbags, need mediC. '

Wil shrugged his shoulders, he really couldn't care less.

'Maybe we use, use manOids to get away?'

'What you say Ess? ManOids help, help us?' Wil shrieked in disbelief.

'Why not? Four okay, okay. Us three, three not enough.' Ess waved his arms about him and towards the mediCUnit.. 'Put, put it to them. They help, help us. We leave, leave now. Else more havoc, havoc.'

'Hmmm.... Maybe .... Ask, ask .... But not leader - he stays, stays sealed, rotting, rotting.' Wil coughed and spluttered out his instructions.

Time was of the essence. The new coMMandant needed to set a course for home and let the satellite aPHid take them there. He doubted if any of them would be well enough to oversee the journey from start to finish, except maybe Ess, he was the only eXplorer not showing any sign of infection or allergy. Why was that? Gar didn't count - he was too juvenile and had been left on board all the time. It was all too much for Wil's brain at the moment, his body was screaming for rest but he had to keep going. Ess's suggestion to use the manOids' strength began to appeal to him.

This time Ess stepped into the unit, carrying a large bottle of water in one hand and his prodgun in the other. He handed the bottle to Ian and directed the interpreter, along with his 2 friends, to wait for him outside. They hadn't foreseen this. Ess indicated the water was to share between Ian and the older people and that he would return. What now? Split up and left in the room Ian couldn't communicate with Ess or understand him; neither could he attack Ess; he might actually be going to help them after all. Ian nodded his thanks to Ess for the water and turned his attention to his ailing friends. He surmised none of them would last more than another 24 hours - even his body was starting to tire - he was almost burnt out - a hornet's sting inflamed and seared his nerves. He shared out half a bottle of water between them, lay on a mat and fell into a troubled sleep; his mind active but his body exhausted.

In the corridor Ess gave instructions via the interpreter. The three manOids were to walk ahead of him and keep going until he told them otherwise. They heard the moaning and coughing of the afflicted aliens but saw no-one. Each man listened intently and, whilst anxious as to what was going to happen to them, they were also excited to realise how well the Elders' plan had worked and, the two of them with sight, were intrigued to finally see the inside of their prison.

'Stay, stay!'

They all jumped as Ess barked out the order. Ess went to a door to his left, knocked and opened it. The temporary pOd coMMandant came out; he looked the humanOids up and down quite disdainfully; his masQ securely fastened across his face; his intimidating black and yellow globes causing the men before him to look away.

'Propose, propose use them?' Wil asked Ess.

'Two as mediCAids. One with me batten, batten down. You have Junior,' he nodded in the younger citiXen's direction, 'work, work here. We return after check, check everything outside brought in. All secure, secure travel.'

'No, not agree. Use you here, here. Gar take talKer batten down. Leave, leave outside. Just get, get away. Two creatures to mediCUnit.'

The talKer had heard this conversation and nodded his head. As far as he was concerned they'd do anything to get these aliens and their pod to go back to where they came from and, maybe he would be able to get away. Wil, seeing the nod, called the junior citiXen, Gar, to him and eXplained what was involved in battening down. But first he was to go to the mediCUnit and use the talKer to explain to the other manOids what they were required to do. He was also to make sure that they knew the consequences if they played up. Gar left, giving all three humanOids a prod as they went. He was very angry at what these samplings had done to his fellow citiXens.

Ess and Wil worked in an uneasy silence. Neither liked the other, but each recognised they were the best chance their fellow miSSionaries and Fee had of making it home. Wil daren't take time out to go and see Fee, he needed to prepare their course; the initial part would demand his utmost attention, he would need to steer the pOd through the tuNNEls, down into the underground waterways and out into the ocean. From there they would follow the sea bed until they came to their launch platform. Once launched and away from this planet's gravity the pOd would be left to follow its pre-programmed route and link up with the satellite aPHid which, in turn, would transport them home. At that point he could go to the mediCUnit. He just needed to keep going for another mooNRing. He took a blast from his energy inhaler. He'd need more than one blast before this exit was completed.

Chapter 9 – Atsuko

Her Marathon

Two nights had passed since Ian and Ess left her there. She'd heard and felt nothing unusual since the rumbling deep underground yesterday evening, and she probably wouldn't have noticed that if she hadn't been sitting against the tree, listening and waiting.

Atsuko's stomach was also rumbling. She'd last eaten 48 hours ago and, other than drops of dew she licked from the leaves, she'd had no sustenance whilst sat, waiting... waiting. Fear and hunger were churning her insides over and over. She could not, would not sit there any longer. The aliens obviously hadn't located her with their worm cameras otherwise they would have come to get her by now. She needn't be foolhardy; she could walk along the cliff's edge, avoiding the soft soil that the worms might favour, but she would get back to the caverns, to see what was happening.

The journey took twice as long as it would normally - Atusko was extra cautious. She didn't want to attract any attention or mess up any rescue that Ian and Ess were undertaking. Each step brought fresh concerns and worries; her mind fervently creating stories in her head about what might have happened or be going on. What if she was the only human left on the island? What if the Invaders had move onto another island? What if... what if...? And there it was ... the entrance to the fissure that led into the caverns with the crates and the pod and who knows what else. There went her mind again!

She stood and focused; smelt the air, she couldn't smell them, couldn't smell anyone or anything unusual. There was the steam and sulphur coming from underground, in the distance the sound of the insects under the trees - working on the remains of old friends; she had to trust her instincts; she had to keep going. She inched towards the opening and entered – committed to following the footsteps that others had trod before her, even if they led her back into captivity. All seemed different somehow, she couldn't put her finger on it at first but then it dawned on her; she was entering the aliens' cavern but she felt no fear; why? Because she should. Yes, it felt odd, it felt very sad, but it was not scary. There were the crates - seeing them caused her to wobble – they were empty now but scraps of cloth and bed fronds remained; the water from the last hose-down stagnating in the troughs, more evidence that she was not dreaming. Where were they? She continued walking, slowly - her hands reaching out to stroke the sides of the tunnels; so smooth in one direction,

yet rough in the other, she could sense the machine that
drilled its way through the stone. The natural caverns
elsewhere on the island, made by the sea and underground
water, felt different, she could intuit they were made over
hundreds of thousands of years, worn away by nature, not
by mankind or machinery. She came to a halt, she must
have missed it in her reverie, she turned to backtrack her
route, she was sure the entrance to the pod was just after
this bend. When she saw the crates again she knew she
hadn't missed it, it just wasn't there anymore. But there
was a huge cavern, one she hadn't seen before, the one the
pod occupied? Her knees gave way; she crumpled to the
ground and started to sob. Now she truly felt scared; she
was alone – they had gone; not only the aliens but also Ian
and the last of the islanders. She had spent 2 days
expecting them to suddenly appear through the foliage,
rescued by Ian and Ess, but it hadn't happened and it didn't
look as though it ever would now. There was no sign of the
others; bizarrely, even bodies floating in the water would
have been reassuring. But there was nothing, no sign of
human or alien life. The only evidence of their existence
were the footprints in and out of the fissure leading into the
cavern.

Light-headedness was taking over. She needed to
eat and rest. She staggered back to the village. No sign of
life there either. She hadn't expected any. After a half
hour spent scavenging in hers' and her old neighbours'
homes she scraped together enough stores to keep her
going for a few days. Her solitary meal was tentatively
comforting. She lay down for the first time in days, on her
futon, in her home.

It was mid afternoon before Atsuko woke. She felt
refreshed. Then she remembered what she was doing there,
it was not just another day in her village. She was still all
alone and needed to venture back to the caverns, to explore

further; just in case she'd missed something. This process kept her occupied for the next 48 hours. She searched, ate and slept, then searched again. There was nothing – yet there was something. She could sense where the caverns changed from machine made to nature worn. She tried diving into the underwater sections, it was amazing how far she could go with her new found breathing techniques; but as far as she went, there was nothing to see, except fish, seaweed and crabs; funny how they all seemed brighter, louder, more vibrant.

Another time she explored the area around the jetty, where the older people had camped. There was no one there either; no one to welcome her, no one to talk to, to reassure her the aliens had definitely gone and were not, at this moment, attacking the next island. This thought had started to take hold in her mind, the more attention she gave it, the more it seemed a possibility. Despite her efforts, one thing Atsuko hadn't been able to find was the island radio. It had been kept in a room within the school house, along with the nurse's surgery and register of births, deaths and marriages. She could only assume the Invaders took it when they first went through the village and rounded up the islanders. She remembered that time acutely. She licked salt laden tears from her lips. Atsuko could recall exactly what happened to her, her family and those immediately about her when the onslaught started but she hadn't paid much attention to what was happening elsewhere. Where was the little radio Ian mentioned? The one left by Captain Maynard. What could she do? She needed to warn the other islands. Alone with her thoughts, pacing up and down, she felt impotent. Her family and neighbours were all gone, dead or kidnapped, she alone remained, she alone was the only one who could warn her nation they were under attack and let them know what happened here. It might happen again and again if they weren't ever vigilant.

After four days of eating, sleeping and scouting Atsuko felt a new lease of life, as though she could swim the oceans. She knew she couldn't but it would be good to try - with her enhanced swimming powers she might be able to make it to the next island. If the aliens were already there - so be it, if not, then she could alert her Countrymen to the dangers and explain what Ian Campbell and the Elders had done to combat the Invaders. Preparing herself for the journey was a leap of faith. She had no idea how her body would react to it, whether she would need to eat and drink, whether sharks would come after her. In the end she made the best decisions she could based on her limited knowledge of what lay ahead. She used whale fat to grease her body, found goggles and a hat to wear, even a pair of flippers for her feet. She found waterproof wrapping for some clothes and dried food. Water would be difficult. She had to take it in a glass bottle, not very practical, but then again, she chuckled to herself, this whole venture, in reality, was totally impractical. It was good to feel as though she was doing something constructive, trying to save the world. Another chuckle escaped her - a nervous chuckle this time.

The worms watched and listened .... but they have no one to report to.

It never occurred to Atsuko that she would not find her way to the next island – she trusted her newly developed sixth sense to guide her there. And so it did. Mostly she swam under water, coming up periodically for air. Her body felt weightless, completely at one with the sea and in tune with nature. If a storm brewed she dived deeper until it passed. The world below was a revelation. Smaller fish swam beneath her, taking refuge from larger predators. All were inquisitive – they rubbed her gently – she tuned into them - no she was not carrying any edible crustaceans but they could enjoy the little air bubbles that clung to her hair follicles. When she trod water to take a couple of mouthfuls of food and sip of water she almost resented the time her head was out of the water – afraid she might miss something. One time she felt something barge against her lower leg – it was a dolphin – being friendly and playful. There was actually a small pod of them, enticing her to swim and perform with them. For a few brief minutes she was caught up in the fun of it all but before long reality, or rather, land-based reality came back to her; there was no escape, it was spun in the cobweb of her mind. Oh joy, she could now call the sea her second home but her first allegiance must lay with mankind. She must continue. The dolphins escorted her for a couple of miles, leaping and somersaulting their ecstasy for life; for the first time since this whole soul-shattering business began Atsuko felt hopeful. Her fellow water creatures meant no harm; they accepted her presence as though she was one of them – why couldn't the Invaders be like that?

It was becoming shallower. The landscape beneath her was changing, more weed and coral; a sunken ship – no longer sad but an elaborate warren of shelter and anchorage for a host of sea brethren.

An island was in sight, so similar and yet so different from her own. It thrust, purple and golden, from the sea - she could smell humans, petrol, animals and no fear – all was as it should be here.

With some trepidation and mourning (she would miss her new friends of the ocean and her old friends and family from her island) she let herself be washed by the waves to the shore. She had to report to the authorities what had happened.

Her Reception

"The woman's mad."

"An absolute fruit-cake."

"She's lost her mind."

"I'll call the hospital" said the Harbour Master.

This was a larger island than her own; there was more infra-structure, more people, more workers, more everything – except the understanding to believe what she was saying. All these people knew was that it was impossible for any human being to swim over 300 miles across the turbulent sea, island to island. Yet this woman was so convinced and, in some ways, so convincing, with her story. She had to be a poor soul lost in her own dream world; to believe her would be to join her in her madness. The hospital would know what to do with her.

The hospital consultant was astonished. Atsuko was so consistent with her story, yet he could not believe her; his experience and knowledge told him such a swim was impossible. He ordered the nursing staff to clean and dress her. They fed her and tested her, watched her every move, fired questions at her every day. To Atsuko it was just a slightly more bearable version of 'crate-life'.

After two weeks of this they sent her to a mental unit. Atsuko became really agitated at this, her usually soft and gentle demeanour turned aggressive and she was loud in her protestations trying to convince them they must believe her. And so they drugged her, into a walking, compliant husk of a being. The story numbed within Atsuko's mind - which in turn was locked behind glazed eyes.

1953: The Authorities do what Authorities do

The intelligence services effectively 'shut down' the island. They controlled all communication media and put out that nearly all the inhabitants had perished in a medieval type plague, brought on by the island's rats breeding with some that had jumped ship.

The word was put round that the Hope & Charity and all of its occupants were being kept in quarantine for the same reason. Those that knew differently were sworn to secrecy, including the escapees, refugees, Skip and his crew. If they ever wanted to get on with their lives again no-one was to be told of their 'alien experience'; the whole episode was to be obliterated from the public eye. The three intelligence services worked tirelessly to trace the Invaders, any sign of their pod or the missing islanders but, whilst they found Ryuu, Sho and Kin, which meant they had confirmation of the refugees tales, they found no Invaders. They did however find piles of bones beneath Locust trees; the insects having completed their work had disappeared. The secret services felt impotent – not that they would admit it. They could not allow the refugees to go back to their island so they re-housed them all in Brisbane where they would monitor their movements and interactions meticulously over the years that followed.

Captain Maynard and his crew swore an oath to keep quiet about their experiences and were allowed to carry on doing deliveries – as usual – so long as they followed the publicised line that illness had broken out on the island; they must not arouse any undue suspicion. They all had regular assessment and debriefing checks to make sure they were complying. The refugees were housed within a 15 mile radius of each other and the watchful eye of ASIS. Their initial lack of English helped isolate them and keep them quiet. However, they were permitted to meet up for afternoon tea every couple of weeks. At first the authorities sent a psychologist and his assistant to supervise these reunions; then just the assistant; and by the time 5 years had passed they were on their own – with phone numbers to call in emergency and annual reviews to look forward to.

Meanwhile Atsuko languished in a mental institution on the outskirts of Tokyo. She soon learnt that to mention her previous life experiences or her swimming marathon and capabilities would lead to electric shock treatment followed by endless tranquilisers - a torturous therapy which in itself could send one insane. She had to keep quiet and the only place her story was held, outside of her head, was on the tapes collecting dust in a filing cabinet in the Senior Psychiatrist's office.

The days became weeks, the weeks months and the months grew into years. Atsuko's resilience was near breaking point – her mind was on the edge of reason – but she pulled it back from the brink. She hadn't been the sole survivor of the crates and pod to not live to tell the tale. She was sure life had some purpose for her; she just didn't know exactly what it was – yet. So she immersed herself in helping her fellow inmates, keeping her mind active and body fit, preparing for the next potential invasion or whatever might arise. At least she was in a Japanese institution where her meditation and shrine practices were viewed as normal. Little did she know that although Sho, Kin and Ryuu had survived, they were re-homed in the United States, where this spiritual activity was seen as evidence of intrinsic weirdness.

America in the early 1950s was not a particularly cosmopolitan society. Meditation was an Eastern custom that the American Establishment viewed with scepticism and mistrust. Their American hosts actively discouraged the two men and boy from any obvious displays of non-

Christian practices; Sho and Kin were resentful and, as many men before them, they found ways to practice their religion away from prying eyes. Poor Ryuu had no option; he was fostered to an all-American family where he was expected to muck in with his two foster brothers and become a fully fledged Yank under the long-armed guidance of the psychiatrist and scientists who'd worked with him when he was first rescued. Even his foster father was a scientist who worked for NACA (the National Advisory Committee for Aeronautics - absorbed into NASA in 1958). Ryuu was aged 11 by the time he was placed with the foster family; he was impressionable and eager to please, to appear normal (he certainly didn't feel it), to fit in with his peer group. His foster brothers protected him from the predictable teasing and ridicule he experienced at school on account of his heritage, looks and lack of biological parents and sight. He had extra lessons in American English and, fortunately, his agile brain was quick on the uptake. He was never going to be a tall man but judo lessons and his hidden sixth sense honed his defence skills so that he was able to floor any would-be adversaries in the school playground. He grew his hair to collar length so the scars above his ear and at the back of his neck were no longer visible. He wore dark glasses. Rock'n'roll was taking over the world. It was easier to camouflage he couldn't see. In his second term they nicknamed him Ninja, not disparagingly but out of respect for his athleticism and fighting skills. He played to this title and reputation, it kept him safe on the outside but inside he had a hollow, lonely spot - where his family and Japanese roots should have been.

1963

A decade later, as Ryuu left his teens, flower power took over. He was at Uni and now it was okay to be wacky, to explore eastern cultures and meditate. He craved his birth culture and language; avidly studied the Japanese language and history. The trade markets were keen to employ bi-lingual individuals so it looked as though his career was set – but he had a personal journey to undertake first.

His island was still shut down, 'being cleansed', but he could visit Tokyo and the island closest to his own. The native Japanese didn't know quite what to make of him: a Japanese youth, unable to see but knowing where things were, speaking with an American twang, wearing platform shoes, flared jeans and flowery tops, yet ever mindful of the respect and courtesy due to his Elders. Ryuu felt a strong pull to his mother culture but he also felt a sense of loyalty to his foster family and adoptive country. He held an American passport. Tokyo was busy and bright but in a different way to Washington. The sights, tastes and smells almost overwhelmed his senses, his mind a whirl with so many new and lost memories. He was used to vast spaces and American food; he needed to rekindle his Japanese taste buds. The smaller island was much calmer, not as quiet or welcoming as he remembered his parents' homeland but it brought unexpected solace to his soul.

He was back-packing, staying in different hostels or with associates of his American family who lived and worked in the East - and so it was on the smaller island. Post-war life was not easy for any oriental looking man or woman in America, many returned to their country of origin as soon as their work in the States was done. A Japanese professor who had worked with his US father in NASA for a while, offered to put him up. The professor knew nothing of Ryuu's true history and had assumed he'd been one of the lucky ones to survive the plague when it hit the neighbouring island; which sort of explained why he ended up an orphan and was eventually fostered in the U.S. One evening, during Ryuu's stay, the professor related an odd story he'd been reminded of by the young man's visit. A woman had been washed up on the shore about 10 years ago and had claimed she'd swum from his family's island; of course she was deemed mad and as far as he was aware, had been sent to a mental health institution.

'Do you know her name?'

'Mmmm ...Ai? Akumo? No ... I have it ... Atsuko ... Kind child.'

Ryuu sat in a daze. He knew that swim was feasible to a human like him, someone who'd received the implant from the Invaders. His swimming and diving had earned him wild acclaim in the school competitions but he'd never let on about his sixth sense and breathing capacity; not only was he sworn to secrecy but he knew, from past experience, that to appear too different and odd to his peers caused isolation and grief; no, he was not going there again. He now enjoyed the attention of his fellow students, even the girls looked at him admiringly, although none would go out with him for fear of what their parents and white friends would say. Some attitudes had softened slightly with the advance of flower power but the majority of middle class white Americans would only sanction their daughters seeing an able-bodied white boy from a similar background, or better. He was tainted, not by his education, prospects, manners or family, but by his blood origins and blindness – and he knew it – he never could forget he was being brought up in a foreign country. Unfortunately now he felt he didn't fit in Japan either. He was a nomad; back-packing was in keeping with his dis-enfranchised status.

141

Atsuko was not an unusual Japanese name. Ryuu recalled he had an aunt by that name but said nothing. He'd last seen her in the crates.

In the middle of the night he jerked bolt upright! The hairs stood up on the back of his neck. Somewhere deep in his subconscious had appeared the memory of his aunt being shot in the back of the neck; could she have survived? Was she alive and insane in a mental health unit? Heaven forbid! How could he find out?

Good Riddance - 1953

The pOd trundled into life and spun. In the isoblution unit Ian and his four comrades were strapped to the sides; the four bodies of the deceased Elders stacked, head to toe, one on top of the other, in the chiLLocker. Put there by the younger manOids under strict direction and with much prodding from Gar. He and Ess seemed to be the only citiXens little affected by the hornets and spray. The coMMandant was still giving orders but from a seated rather than standing position.

Ess was managing the controls; he had always known how to operate this machine but hadn't let on how adept and capable he was. Now was his time to shine. There was no going back for Atsuko but he would still be feted as a hero if he managed to steer them to the docking port of the aPHid. The race was on to get any of them back alive. He felt confident no one would ever know of his treasonous acts; he'd dropped his travel belt containing mothRWorm's recordings into a tree trunk by the entrance to the caves after he'd left Atsuko. No, no citiXen would ever know the truth about his near betrayal; a smirk of satisfaction oozed over him. He left Wil sitting in front of a screen in the control room to go through the final part of the start-up procedure. His task to check that Gar and the manOids had prepared everyone within the pOd ready for exit. They had. It was a pitiful sight that met his eyes: citiXens bloated, eyes sunken and tongues protruding as they gasped for breath; joints racked with pain; unable to quench a burning thirst through inflamed sore throats; two had already eXpired. The mediC was dragging herself around to give each, in turn, a stupORize shot as they were strapped down. Ess gave her a shot last of all, so she too had a slim chance of surviving the journey and being resuscitated when they reached their destination. And it was a slim chance. And they both knew it. The bodies of the eXpired citiXens were packed on top of those of the manOids – their fate would be the same – first as labRats, then as fodder and, finally, as manUre. Nothing and no-one was wasted in their world. Unhealthy burials and oZone damaging cremations were a thing of the distant past. One's name and memory lived on in one's off-spring. Each breedinPair was allowed two breWn, a male and a female, their gender engineered in the womb. The female took the mother's name and the male the father's; a single syllable name, handed down generation after generation. Ess never had a female siBling, he was the single produce of his breeDer's union, a lone, dysfunctional Ess. He refused to acknowledge the dysfunctional bit, disadvantaged for a while maybe, but a superior being; independent and insular, able to survive alone and live without his peers; he was stronger, more intelligent, more capable than anyone else. An unsafe delusional world beckoned him and he grasped it, willingly.

The spinning was horrendous. Cheeks and noses splattered inwards, hair parted and plastered back; lungs compressed; torso and limbs pinned to the wall, whichever way your head went when the pod first started its spiral path, so it stayed, for the duration. What felt like hours might well have been a few minutes but Ian was grateful he lost consciousness. He was amazed to find himself still breathing when the pod came to rest. There were no windows, he had no idea where they were but it felt cooler and there was the odd bang and rocking motion, as though they were in a boat, or rather submarine, beneath the waves.

Ian was basically right in his deductions; they were under the ocean, resting on the seabed, preparing for the next part of their journey.

Ess patrolled once more. Everyone was still strapped down. He reported to Wil then strapped himself tight in his seat. Wil whimpered his instructions for take-off. Theyl pulled muffle bands over their heads. The noise was eXcruciating, like a dozen jet planes taking off together but at a pitch so high humanoids could not distinguish it. The pOd turned 90 degrees and hovered above the seabed. The prisoners' nerves shattered by the vibration as the pOd went skyward, through the fathoms, through the waves and through the earth's gravity; leaving an almighty bang in its wake as it breached the sound barrier and entered limitless space.

The Japanese men were resigned to endure what they did not know and could not comprehend. They had seen and done things in the past fortnight that were totally beyond their comprehension, they were now on auto pilot, going with the flow waiting for an appropriate time to end it all - if salvation did not appear first. A possibility which seemed so remote as to be farcical. They were walking, breathing, living dead - dead to their kith and kin.

Ian was mesmerised by the experience; he'd come into this enterprise expecting to die but had no way of foreseeing what adventures would befall him before he did. He felt Lorna at his shoulder, brushing his arm and cheek as she turned and walked backwards in front of him, beckoning him to follow. He did with absolute pleasure; the men watched him beam with pure joy as he took his last breath.

They were docked into the aPHid before Ess undertook his next round. He released two of the manOids and ordered them to carry Ian's body to the chiLLocker and stack it with the others. The men were given a liquid feed from a tube in the wall, three gulps and no more before the next man took a turn. Ess, Gar and Wil each had their own feeding tube; the samplings had one between them. They tried to be as hygienically clean as possible and, when they were finally released from the restrictive safety webbing and the pOd was back on an even keel, they set about cleansing their unit of the sick and effluence that had escaped during the take off. This did not go unobserved. It was not long before Gar appeared and prodded them to the mediCUnit and anywhere else sick aliens were strapped. They were instructed to clean the nestBoxes and the citiXens. The aliens might be comatose but their sores and pustules were weeping and bleeding, red blood, yellow bile, green poison. Cleansing was a malodorous unpleasant business but the men had no choice and, being from the culture that they were, undertook each task with impeccable distain. They had to do the job well even if they felt it beneath them - knowing they would rather be killing than repairing the Invaders.

Chapter 10 - Magic

2010 - Reflections

The mosaic weaved its magic once more. Jennifer sat entranced at how this place and its memories helped her at critical moments. There was Ian Campbell leading the Elders to save mankind and there was Atsuko - swimming with the dolphins.

Ryuu had explained to Jennifer on her visit 30 years ago how he'd discovered his aunt held in a Japanese mental institution; they both had the same breathing pellet although only he had the language pellet. When he'd realised the professor's tale might refer to his aunt he was desperate to seek her out and to engineer a reason to pay a visit. At the time he nearly went full pelt into declaring their relationship and similar experiences and abilities but fortunately an inner survival button had stopped him. If the hospital and local authorities hadn't believed his aunt why would they believe him, popping up 10 years later with a similar story, they'd just put him down as a copy-cat nutcase. He needed to go higher. It had been so frustrating having to return back to the States but, as keen as he was, he registered he would need the help of the intelligence services to follow this through and rescue Aunt Atsuko.

Back in Washington he spoke with his foster father. It was the first time they'd discussed the true reason for his arrival and fostering in America - the topic an enforced taboo. They had both been primed before Ryuu moved in with the family that they needed to be discreet and keep what they knew to themselves, otherwise Ryuu would end up living in a military unit for his entire life – the authorities had no desire to fuel mass hysteria by being forced to explain what they could not understand themselves.

It was Gordon Wade who eventually contacted Ryuu. He looked a lot younger than the other intelligence officers and scientists Ryuu had met when he was ten, or maybe that was because he was so much younger then. Agent Wade must have been about 30; a shock of orange hair and swathes of freckles across his forehead, nose and cheekbones were the first things people noticed about him. He looked almost too chirpy to be taken seriously but he certainly knew his stuff. He was well versed in the incident that took place on Ryuu's island. He was extremely interested to hear about the possible existence of Aunt Atsuko and immediately started the wheels in motion to contact his Japanese counterparts... to find out more about her, her story, how she came to be in a mental institution and whether she had any family close by.

A week later he was back with Ryuu and his foster father. He had set up a meeting with Atsuko and his Japanese associates. The meeting was to take place in a fortnight's time, in the same military hospital near Tokyo that Ryuu and the other two escapees had been taken to in 1953. Gordon invited Ryuu to go with him; it was not an invite he was expected to decline and neither did he wish to. Atsuko was being transferred there, along with the tape recordings of her original interviews and any subsequent therapy sessions she'd undergone. The word was that the staff at the institution found her extremely helpful and placid these days. She no longer talked about her swim and how she came to be walking along the shoreline, wearing nothing more than a pair of flippers, goggles and swimsuit; with no form of identification and a bizarre tale of aliens flying between trees, maiming and killing indiscriminately, wiping out her whole island. The professionals involved with her care were perplexed as to why she should suddenly attract the attention of the military. They were told she was being transferred to Tokyo because her illness was beyond the scope of their small hospital on the island and, in an effort to locate her family, her condition and origins was going to be further investigated as part of a training exercise for military internees. They shrugged, there was no arguing with the military and perchance they would be able to reunite her with her family - although it seemed unlikely anyone was going to come forward after all this time.

The flight from Washington to Tokyo with Gordon, in a military jet, was very different to tourist class on a commercial airline. Ryuu was flummoxed by the noise; he attempted to strike up a conversation and talk about the move of the Washington Senators to re-form as the Texas Rangers, but it proved pointless trying to shout above the engine roar, it just gave him a sore throat; so he and Agent Wade sat with their own thoughts for most of the 15 hour trip - wearing ear muffs. He was glad to land; they were taken from the airport to their quarters on the military campus.

Snapshots of his rescue flashed before Ryuu - the first hot bath with soap and towels – wonderful. He still loved the smell of medicated soap and shampoo. A bed with a mattress had provided much needed comfort after a hard floor with rags, whereas now he was used to a sprung western mattress the futon mattress felt too firm,. Since his rescue he always wanted the curtains and windows open - to breathe fresh air. All three of the escapees never wanted to be in an enclosed space again. Memories bubbled through him. At first that trying to sleep by starlight was difficult; the moon and stars twinkled magically onto his face but he knew that out there, somewhere, were the aliens. The clean, simple furnishings had seemed luxurious; everything was awe-inspiring, as if he was experiencing it for the first time. But he wasn't, he was locked into a seesaw world of sorrow and inspiration, shedding tears for his lost family, for the pain and anguish his people had suffered and at the same time marvelling at his own survival and sixth sense. He was told this new safe place was all part of the same country as his island but it had felt so different; cooler, bigger, busier, noisier - more threatening somehow. Yet now, 10 years on, to Ryuu, the young American adult, it seemed sparse and utilitarian. He wondered how Atsuko was coping; he so hoped she was his aunt and that she knew him and remembered his parents. He would find out over the next few days but first he had to go through more question and answer sessions with the intelligence and medical officers – far more intense than his annual health checks back home. And this time he was not cushioned as he was when he was a naive young boy. The adult Ryuu felt mentally bruised and exhausted by the time they accepted his recollections of the invasion and his aunt.

They doped her up for the journey, in case she became disturbed and created a scene; they did not want to attract the public's attention. Atsuko's first flight was a dream; she dreamt she was being cocooned in a capsule of cloud, a trembling, grumbling, grey cloud. She tried to get out but was strapped in and couldn't break free. It was all very strange.

When she woke from the dream she discovered she was sleeping in a plain, small rectangular room. The walls were a blotchy cream, the window obscured by a shuttered blind, rattling in an unseen draft. A solitary bulb threw a muted cool wash around the void, creating indistinguishable shadows that merged with their background. There were two doors. Once they might have been painted a fresh white gloss but now they were yellow and stained. One slid open to reveal chipped white tiles, white toilet, white wash basin and the same grey lino floor as in the bedroom area. Even the towel was laundered grey, although it should have been white. Atsuko washed and changed into the day clothes left out for her; simple white cotton underwear (vest and pants) along with a dark grey tunic dress, white tabi (socks), straw waraji (thonged sandals) and a grey-beige cardigan. She cleaned her teeth and washed her face and hands; carrying out her toilet the same as she had done every morning for the past 10 years; a different place; the same routine. Her eyes never looked to the other door, the one with the glass observation panel that could only be closed from the outside. She never wanted to see if eyes were watching her; she blanked them out of her vision. Her steps were mechanical, her movements minimal; her gaze dropped downward, no expression or emotion shown. She padded back and forwards waiting for someone to tell her what to do; someone to tell her when she could go to breakfast, when she could walk the corridors, when she could pretend to be real.

Ryuu woke to a dreary, damp dawn. He found it impossible to get back to sleep and lay there watching the dull gloom of the day pervade his room. His alarm rung him into action; he swung his legs onto the cold floor, showered and prepared for the day to come. He felt no magic in this room now, but maybe the wand was yet to be waved. Gordon, after a perfunctorily tap on the door, escorted him to breakfast across a wet, drizzly quadrangle. The eggs and toast they were served were adequate, the coffee - abysmal. They sat in silence. Through the misted windows they could see across to the hospital, their view framed by globules of escaping raindrops running to the sill. Wide concrete steps and steel balustrade opposite guided visitors and inmates towards the solid, windowless double doors. Before too long they too stood at those doors, pulling the bell which clanged a single monotonous 'dang'. A grey uniformed warden pulled on the handles and ancient hinges creaked as the doors were swung inwards to allow entry into the endless, colourless corridor. Doors led off in regimented order, two by two; dark stained wooden chairs zigzagged alternately between them; each door had a number, a highly polished brass number, incongruous against the ageing paintwork. From deep within his memory Ryuu recalled his room had been number 7 and the bathroom was number 12. The hush felt heavy, unnatural, it was hard to believe that once he had been cared for in this building – as he started his road to acceptance and recovery. There was no sign of other staff or inmates. All Ryuu could see, beyond the warden's office, were doors, chairs and cameras; he gulped and re-set his shoulders. The cameras spied down from the ceiling, watching every move, recording every interaction. He and Gordon instinctively tempered their steps and cut short conversation before each took a seat and sat waiting for the Japanese intelligence officer and psychiatrist to appear.

Systematically pacing her room Atusko wondered what was happening; she knew not to get excited about anything and to be wary; to show little interest and only to respond appropriately when prompted. Usually she was allowed out in the morning and she was very hungry; she'd almost called out in case she'd been forgotten but then thought twice about doing anything out of the ordinary and attracting negative attention. Her steps became more frantic. She pulled at the buttons on her cardigan, wrapping it tightly round her. Her eyes watched her feet working independently beneath her.

The Japanese intelligence officer was suspicious of Ryuu – his American accent was off-putting; on the other hand, he'd felt he knew where he stood with Agent Wade; they both mistrusted each other! It was their job, their training.

The psychiatrist came towards the three of them congregating in the corridor. The preliminary bowing and handshaking over he led the three men along the corridor and upstairs to his office. He'd already looked in on Atsuko - observing her take breakfast; she appeared co-operative which was a good beginning.

His office was positioned directly above the entrance hall where he could observe all who came and went through the main doors. The brightness struck Ryuu as soon as he entered; his skin tingled, he could smell the newness of the decor. The room was well lit and stylishly furnished - in sharp contrast to the corridor. Gordon observed the green walls were a foil for some original Modernist paintings, apparently a passion of their host, but not to his taste. They sat in comfortable brown leather chairs and waited for the psychiatrist to finish talking and get on with playing the tapes.

What a revelation!

'That's Aunt Atsuko' gasped Ryuu 'I remember her voice. She sounds so desperate.'

'I expect she is' commented Gordon 'trying to convince them to take her seriously and believe her warnings. It's a shame this was not reported to our Intelligence Services at the time.'

'The hospital knew no different, they did the best they could' defended the Doctor.

'Any report such as this should have been brought to the Authority's attention' reprimanded Gordon's Japanese counterpart. He did not like his Service to be seen as failing. He knew the background to this claim by Ryuu; he'd read the file through and through; he wasn't about to be disadvantaged or found wanting.

'Let's see the woman and examine her; she might have changed her story after all these years.'

Or had it wiped out of her memory - Gordon kept this fear to himself.

Ryuu was grateful that Gordon was more approachable than the defensive Japanese officer. He was also thankful for his American passport.

A slight tap and the door opened. Atsuko stood there, her eyes wide open, dazzled by the light and opulence. Then she remembered herself and dropped her gaze, waiting for instructions. She walked into the room, as directed, with a limp - her left leg didn't seem to function correctly. Gordon raised his eyebrows at the medic.

'Yes, that was a shame' stated the Doctor 'it states here, in her notes, that the last shock treatment she had affected the nerves in her leg – that can sometimes happen, but this patient hasn't had any shocks for the last eight years, we tend to use drugs these days.'

'Aunt Atsuko?' murmured Ryuu, he couldn't just sit there and hear her treated as though she was some inanimate specimen. He stepped forward and put out his hands. Atsuko glanced beneath her brows in his direction, he reminded her of someone, her brother, Daiki, but Daiki was dead; he'd died escaping the aliens.

Involuntarily her lips whispered one word 'Ryuu?'

It was the only confirmation that Ryuu needed, he put both hands on her shoulders, drawing her close, his head bent to hers; he felt and heard her fears, she felt and heard his, not a word was spoken. He caught her as her knees gave way and she descended to the floor.

By now Gordon was also on his feet, calling for a glass of water, as he brought his chair into the frame for her to sit on. The Doctor had one of the nurses come in with a tray of refreshments – he looked stunned at first and then a little sheepish. They'd got it badly wrong. This woman had been telling the truth all along.

'Obviously this doesn't mean much at this stage' blustered the intelligence officer. 'We will need to re-check her story ...what she said on the tapes ... whether there are any camera recordings ...'

Ryuu knew it would tally perfectly.

Gordon understood the diplomatic need to save face. 'Of course, but let's work on the premise it does and afford this poor woman the dignity she deserves.'

Ryuu was horrified; the aunt he'd remembered was pretty, barely 20, with a light step and quick wit. This woman felt much older than 30; slight and fragile - she was frail and limping. He held her hand as tightly as he dare.

They moved Atsuko's meagre belongings to a guest room, not as swish as the Doctors quarters but no longer bleak and grey. The room had soft furnishings in lemon and pale green; there was a radio, jug of water and glass to drink from. It felt absolutely surreal to Atsuko. She couldn't bring herself to let go of Ryuu's hand whether they were in the Dr's office, walking to the dining hall for lunch, or going back to the hospital and into Atsuko's room to sit quietly and reminisce together.

Ryuu had remonstrated that his aunt no longer needed to be locked in, but that was a step too far at this stage for the intelligence officer; so he promised to be back first thing in the morning. Atusko had smiled through her anxiety as they turned the key - she just hoped she wasn't dreaming and that her brother's boy would return the next day.

He did, and the next, and the next. It was nearly a week before the Japanese I.S. were satisfied and Atsuko was given a room in the same block as Gordon and Ryuu, with a door she could bolt from the inside. There had been subtle changes in that time. Atsuko was addressed by her title and now spoke without being spoken to. Her wardrobe had expanded to a choice of 3 dresses and an outdoor pair of clogs. She had started to chuckle at some of their recollections of happier times on their island and when she spoke of her marathon swim, it was with blossoming pride. Ryuu said he was envious – he would have loved to swim with wild dolphins – maybe they could do that together sometime. Atsuko held his face in her hands, what joy, she was no longer alone and they shared the same sixth sense; words were totally superfluous at times. These intimate moments and exchanges concerned Gordon; he didn't want the other intelligence officer to become nervous and had a quiet word with Ryuu about exercising caution in his presence. Gordon instinctively felt this pair could be trusted and Atsuko certainly merited some support to deal with the big wide world waiting for her beyond the hospital grounds but he could not guarantee her release if the Japanese Authorities were minded to detain her for security reasons.

Gordon had been in contact with his boss who, in turn, had brought Sho and Kin in to his office to let them know about finding Atsuko. They were all keen to link up but the Japanese Intelligence Service did not wish to let Atsuko out of the country. Sho and Kin needed time and help to make arrangements with their families and employers in order to return to Japan for a visit. This would mean more people being in the know and create further risk of the real story coming out. Agent Wade, with utmost diplomacy, reminded their hosts of their mistake and prolonged imprisonment of Atsuko. In the end the Japanese relented, it made more sense to take Atsuko to Washington than put Sho, Kin, their new wives and children, through a 15 hour trip; the compromise was that Atsuko would be escorted to America by a female officer who would stay with her at all times.

Even before all these negotiations commenced the Australian Tri-Service Unit was back on the deserted island, re-combing every inch of scrub around the fissure for sign of the tree trunk housing the travel belt mentioned by Atsuko in her tapes. She said her alien admirer had left his belt there to pick up when he returned – which he didn't do in the 2 days she sat waiting. Atsuko narrated that Ess had indicated he'd taken the mission's recordings to ensure his future security. It was frustrating for the service men, if only they'd known about it before; they were now dealing with ten years of growth. Nature had been allowed to run riot in an attempt to deter sightseers and potential settlers. Fortunately the ploy had worked and the island had remained as it was when they left. Naturally the village was in disrepair, the tracks overgrown and the trees were taller but the soldiers knew the layout and set about clearing a route to the fissure and the caverns.

The tree trunk with its hidden cache was eventually located. A synthetic belt, bulging slightly with its owner's treasures, was buried beneath layers of leaves, insect and bird droppings. There were two dark metal discs, smaller than a dime, a tiny pencil and small notepad complete with scribble, a gadget pen, a stamp sized plastic card and a withered feather. The priority task was to find a way of viewing the aliens' recordings, if that's what the discs were. The scientists in Japan were up to this challenge and used the very latest computer technology along with new gen gleaned from the communication pen to construct a sophisticated deciphering and viewing box. Once the Japanese Authorities were convinced they had garnered all they could from the recordings they rigged up a screen and arranged a film show to which all three intelligence services sent representatives. The Japanese intelligence officer interviewing Atsuko was already primed as to what the recording revealed but he didn't share this advance information; he waited until the official viewing. The Australian SIS sent the feather off for analysis. American scientists had the job of trying to decipher the marks in the notebook. They were amazed to discover it was indeed made of traditional paper materials and the pencil made of wood and lead, manufactured at Dixons in Jersey – in the late 19th century!

Ryuu had a good idea what to expect on the recording, he'd seen the Invaders first hand, experienced their corral methods, their crates, their jabs and their inhumane treatment. He accompanied Atsuko to the premier. She sat - eyes bolted to the screen, handkerchief to hand as she dabbed the uncontainable well of salt water from her dark tear-rimmed eyes and sniffled a running commentary of what was happening and who was being filmed. Ryuu, prompted by his aunt's recollections, supplemented useful information from his own experiences.

It was amazing, everything was shown as Atsuko said it had happened. They could see her and Ess leave the caverns and return with tins of fruit cocktail. At all times

Ess looked as though he was in control although, very briefly, as they walked through the woodland his face softened and he smiled at Atsuko. Atsuko sat motionless at this point. She did not wish to be viewed as a traitor but remembered thinking at the time how lucky she was that this alien had taken to her; he might be their key to survival. She sensed he was lonely and isolated and felt drawn to befriend him; her heart was that open that she couldn't see anyone, even a torturer, in pain. She wondered what had happened to him... and Ian Campbell and the Elders ... and the three island men. She speculated the Elders must have died of their wounds but Ian and the others had still been very much alive when she'd last seen them; that was before Ess prodded Ian back on board and gave Atsuko strict instructions to wait for him in the copse. She remembered watching them go along the track that approached the fissure and seeing Ess pause as he threw a small package, which she recognised as his travel belt, into the trunk of a tree. And here they were, viewing the data Ess had stolen from Mother Worm. They had to believe her.

Over the next few months there were a lot of intense, clandestine discussions between the three intelligence services. The press was kept well out of the picture. Knowing that Atsuko had been telling the truth was one thing but how to deal with the fresh knowledge that the aliens had escaped with humans on board was another. They now had confirmation of what these creatures looked like but they still did not know where they came from, where they had disappeared to, and whether they would return. They felt there was a distinct possibility they had been to Earth before, otherwise how to account for the pencil and notepad in the travel belt? Yet again, they endeavoured to keep the information out of the public eye. The island remained 'shut down'. The worms left to their own devices.

No one anticipated the impact or change fermenting with the introduction of the Freedom of Information Act in the United States - signed by President Lyndon B Johnson in July 1966 and brought into force the following year. This act applied to the Federal Agencies and meant they could be held to account for their actions and the personal data they held on individuals. In Australia the Freedom of Information Act was not enacted until 1982 and the UK and Japan had to wait until 2001; however, from 1967 investigative journalists and astute individuals could claim access to information held by the Federal Agencies in the USA.

Chapter 11 - Uncovered

Late 1969

The Vietnam War spored a mini troop of investigative journalists through its Protest and Survive underground GI papers. Some of these same troopers were now back in Civvy Street looking for ways to make a living and many pursued their new found skills in journalism. They focused their research on stories fuelled by rumour and tittle-tattle overheard during their military career.

Two Veterans, Josh Hammond and Zac Wellington, teamed up and produced some great undercover stories that exposed the double dealing and inadequacies of both military and political advisors. They'd heard tell of a Japanese island that had been invaded by aliens in the 1950s and shut down by the authorities. There was no firm evidence to support these rumours but the stories had become more hardcore as they were passed down over the years; and, on the basis that there is no smoke without fire, the two budding journalists opted to dig deeper. They had started with their Viet buddies and gradually worked back to ex soldiers who were based at Washington at the time Ryuu, Sho and Kin arrived. They then looked for the 3 Japs who'd been taken to a remote military base and nursed back to health before being integrated into the U.S. They found Sho initially and he, inadvertently, led them to Kin. Ryuu dodged their radar, having been fostered with an American family in a different city. The two Japanese men had no intention of bringing him into the picture.

Whilst Sho and Kin were inscrutable and circumspect, not wanting to fall foul of the intelligence services, they could not tell a lie; and so it came about that by clever presentation of the facts, as they knew them, and by manipulative questions that prompted a facial or bodily reaction, if not a spoken one, Josh and Zac determined that something had definitely happened on the Japanese island from which these, now naturalised, citizens of the United States originated.

Fortunately for the authorities and the refugees other world events demanded the attention of every journalist: Nixon announced he was negotiating peace in Vietnam and started to withdraw troops but then the North Vietnamese president died and the following year the Yanks invaded Cambodia. There were a huge number of demonstrations, both against and pro the war, to be covered; ceasefires failed to hold, both sides breaking agreements ... in fact it was 1975 before the war was finally brought to an end. On top of all this there was the first walk on the moon followed almost yearly by other space expeditions until the space shuttle was launched in 1981. And then there was the Cold War - the USA and its NATO allies lived in a continual state of mistrust with the USSR and other countries from the Warsaw Pact - using any excuse to undermine each other and gather more weapons. Nixon tried, he initiated a period of detente in the 1970's that lasted until the Russians invaded Afghanistan in 1979; and then of course, there was Watergate extending from 1972-74, when Nixon narrowly escaped impeachment by resigning. All in all there were endless stories for Zac and Josh to investigate and report and it wasn't until 1975 that they were prompted to pick up the 'Island Story' again; their attention drawn to Japan because of its booming economy involving the use of robots in car manufacture and their domination of the electronics and computer industries. Was there a link? They requested document after document under the Freedom of Information Act; the authorities were tardy and it took nearly four years to get what they asked for.

1979

(Atsuko is aged 46; Ryuu - 36; Jennifer – 29;

Sho & Kin are in their late 50s)

In 1979, armed with their basic understanding of the event, the pair of journalists made more demands on the Federal Government under the Freedom of Information Act. What had happened sixteen years ago to make Sho and Kin homeless? What was the United States' involvement in shutting down the island? What bacterium had killed its occupants? And was there any risk to Americans who came in contact with the survivors now living in and around Washington?

Just asking these questions caused a huge stir and flurry. Suddenly every newspaper had journalists trying to get photos of the two Japanese men and their families. Aerial shots of the island were taken and reproduced in magazines. Sho and Kin were petrified. They had done nothing wrong and yet felt targeted, both by the press and the Government. They employed a solicitor to act on their behalf. The solicitor insisted the Government produce evidence to denounce the inference that their clients were potential plague carriers and that, in truth, they were keeping quiet about the reason for their migration to the US, for security reasons.

Ryuu was listening to all this from a distance; loathe to make his whereabouts known.

1966

The Japanese Government reluctantly allowed Ryuu & Atsuko to set up home in Tokyo. They were concerned the refugees would be recognised as islanders and attract attention from their neighbours. They needn't have worried. As much as Ryuu wanted to help his aunt re-establish her life and integrate into their new Japanese community he couldn't. It was difficult for them both; Ryuu because he was implicitly Americanised and felt like a duck out of water in his native country - and Atsuko because she was fearful of even her own shadow. She had been confined, mocked and disbelieved for so many years that now she couldn't even trust herself to make simple everyday decisions and choices; she had lost many of her life skills and felt utterly inadequate. They struggled for eighteen months ... neither settling - their anxiety and unhappiness causing them to withdraw into an almost hermit like existence with just each other for company.

Gordon Wade was horrified, they deserved better than this. He instigated negotiations with his Japanese counterpart and, eventually, pulled off an agreement to airlift Atsuko and Ryuu to the colourful obscurity of Chinatown San Francisco.

The first twelve months were the most difficult. Aunt Atsuko's English was restricted to the few nouns and verbs she'd laughingly tried when living with Ryuu in Japan. Now it was for real. She went to classes - with other Japanese and Asian immigrants. Here were people she felt she had something in common with – they were all struggling to understand a foreign language and a completely different culture to their own. Being with other people who were also trying to come to terms with a new life released her from her sense of isolation. For whatever reason, she was less afraid. Ryuu was absolutely ecstatic when his aunt made friends with a couple of Japanese women who lived close by. They would get together to practice their English and learn about the history of the States. When it was her turn to host one of these lively afternoon sessions Ryuu would come home to hear trills of excited speech and laughter from the kitchen. He beamed; he had been extremely worried how his aunt would cope when they were first deposited on the west coast of California. The hilliness was not a problem to them; the traffic a bit of a challenge: and there was an extensive choice of Asian food available in Chinatown so Aunt Atsuko could continue to re-hone her cooking skills. He helped too - he introduced her to pizzas and burgers and coca cola! In fact Atsuko learnt an awful lot about the American language, its people and culture, by watching TV - especially the adverts. Gordon Wade's housewarming gift to them was the very latest Porta-color TV set!

Money was not an issue; they were given a generous allowance by the American Government which met their everyday needs and Ryuu's university fees so he could complete his Masters in Business Management. Ryuu was assigned a 'buddy' to help him learn his way around the campus and he soon mastered the use of a portable tape recorder to record lectures. Ryuu could read Braille but generally his study and reference books were not available in that language so the other students took it in turns to read out loud to him, again, he'd record in Braille what they said for future reference, and then type up his assignments for submission. His foster mother had encouraged him to learn to touch type in his early teens and this skill proved invaluable with study and work. His key interest was history but his logic told him a degree in business studies would be far more useful and, fortunately, being bi-lingual and bi-cultural was quite an asset in the up and coming commercial money market. During vacation time Ryuu flexed his academia and skills by temping in the San Francisco Stock and Bond Exchange – he was a success. The future looked rosy. He and his aunt settled into their new lives and mixed culture; feeling financially secure and comparatively safe. On the surface they made friends and socialised but neither of them let anyone get too close; they dare not risk intrusive questions and intimacy. But they didn't complain, they had each other and, after all they'd been through, that felt an awful lot. Ryuu kept in touch with his foster family although never visited them in Washington in case he was recognised; he didn't want to have to explain the in-between years. It was just before his 36th birthday that the proverbial shit hit the fan.

The Shit

Josh and Zac were extremely tenacious when they got their teeth into a story. They had honed their investigative skills to a fine art and had a good nose for a cover up. They had always been suspicious of the plague excuse for the mass evacuation and closing down of that isolated Japanese island.

Over the years they might not have been able to find all the individuals mentioned in despatches but they had their military contacts and, as these service men retired and the years passed by, they were more inclined to talk about the stories they heard and the sights and action they'd seen. And so it was that eventually Josh and Zac asked the right questions at the right time and discovered a huge cover-up. What a scoop!

The official documents spoke of an invasion by aliens, not a pernicious infection. There was even purported to be a recording showing these alien creatures, their habits and treatment of the islanders, and the subsequent and immensely brave action by Elders of the island which led to the expulsion of the Invaders. The aliens had disappeared, not only from the island but also from Earth, or so it seemed, and had not been seen or heard of since.

The story ran for weeks – every day there was a fresh angle or insight into the actual event; much of it conjecture based on a glimmer of truth. In the end the three governments, in order to avoid any further speculation and subsequent mass hysteria, were forced to make a joint public statement. As it was they were having to blockade access to the island and one small boat had already sunk in its efforts to bypass the Navy in particularly adverse conditions. Aerial shots were harder to prevent but opportunely these just revealed an overgrown, verdant habitat with little sign of life except for wild boar and birds.

The Public Declaration acknowledged that the island had been invaded by creatures from an unknown world and that, through the valiant efforts of five older residents, they had been driven off the island in what appeared to be some sort of underwater vehicle, possibly a submarine – but there was no clear indication as to the type of machine they travelled in, nor where they come from or went to. No one had actually seen them arrive or leave and they were no longer to be seen. In the circumstances the authorities had no alternative but to assume the invaders came from outer space and had subsequently returned there. But despite repeated attempts through the years scientists had not been able to follow their tracks or make contact. Those fortunate enough to escape the island had been helped to recover, as much as humanly possible, from their ordeal and to resume their lives in different parts of the world. It was felt that their privacy and right to a peaceful life should be respected, therefore their identities would not be revealed.

Luckily this was in an era when there was an unspoken moral code that upheld the right of private individuals, not usually in the public eye, to go about their business unmolested by the press. In addition, the male survivors were afforded inadvertent protection because the recording only showed pictures of distorted bodies, alien creatures and the Elders. Atusko was prominent because of her walk outside with Ess but the naive 20 year old was not recognisable as the mature Americanised Asian woman in her mid 40's. Sho and Kin, unfortunately, had been located and, at their request, for the sake of their relationships and sanity, were allowed to give a planned and supervised interview to the press which was televised and transmitted around the world. This brought a little respite to their families and also presented a lucrative side-line in 'sold stories' – from fake refugees.

The few remaining survivors living in Queensland never came into the limelight, in their 90s they were deliberately ignored by the Australian Secret Intelligence Service. Their gentle afternoon teas continued even as their number diminished and friends and neighbours were none the wiser. In addition the Hope & Charity had a new

Skipper who couldn't help, he'd bought the vessel off an ageing Sea Captain who had passed away. Jennifer had kept her parents' surname, Dean, and so was left undetected and unmolested to care for her beloved Grandmother and Skip in the winter of their lives. She scattered their ashes just before their story appeared in the headlines.

Following the sinking of the small boat the Japanese Government considered their options and made a ground-breaking decision to open the island up to the public – as a living museum. It was proving costly and increasingly difficult and dangerous to keep sight-seers at bay; so they opted to allow controlled tourism – little realising how popular and lucrative it would be.

The village was restored, as were the crates and troughs. Walkways around the island were cleared and made passable again. The meditation garden and pump room reinstated to the way they were 30 years ago. The blood mural renovated and protected behind glass sheets. Information signs and leaflets were produced to guide visitors around the museum; the only actual inhabitants of the village were 4 tourist guides cum wardens, and they lived together on the edge of the village in a new, slightly incongruous, purpose-built house.

Ryuu and Atsuko were among the first to visit; they felt driven to pay their respects to their ancestors in an effort to release their ghosts. Visitors were put up on small cruisers that brought them, weather permitting, from the mainland. The jetty was rebuilt and lengthened to allow for easier disembarkation but there was still no guarantee that the capricious sea would allow one to get ashore or sleep comfortably. Neither Atsuko nor Ryuu could settle upon their return to San Francisco – their lives felt incomplete and shallow – Ryuu had an idea. He asked Agent Walker to set up a meeting with the authorities who helped manage the island; he knew it was predominantly a Japanese venture but did not doubt that the US and Australians were also involved in order to ensure their naturalised citizens and ageing troops remained un-harassed.

Ryuu produced a business proposition. He and his aunt wanted to build and manage a small spa hotel on the island; profits would go towards maintaining the fabric and integrity of the village, the caverns, pathways and garden - the living museum. They would provide a guided tour and film show for visitors and ensure that the memories and possessions of their ancestors were respected and endured. They would also commission a memorial to commemorate the heroism and key aspects of those few weeks. They had a good idea of what they wanted and the artist best suited to carry it out. They wanted it placed under the Locust trees which were bigger and even more imposing after all these years. The trees were to provide a fitting backdrop for a secluded memorial garden with a mosaic to celebrate the lives of the islanders who once lived there. There would also be statues to each of the five Elders, to pay tribute and immortalise their altruism and ultimate sacrifice for humanity. They acknowledged the island was too well known now for it to return to the way it was but as two of its original inhabitants they had every right to live there and manage such a project. They were prepared to invest their life-savings into it but would need additional financial support from the Japanese Government initially, and, obviously, the backing of all parties involved.

By the time Jennifer visited, 12 months later, the hotel was built. A simple single story building on the edge of the village; it blended into the environment; it offered a dozen double rooms, a restaurant cum tea room and simple, separate living quarters for Atsuko and Ryuu. The memorial was installed; the mosaic lay under the Locust trees where bones once piled up; the statues looked on from where aliens once stood to cheer on voracious insects. There were simple bench seats, made from Locust timber, where visitors could sit and contemplate all they could hear, see and sense on the island.

The ongoing development of the island as a living museum was reported in the world press and bookings came in fast and furious. The difficulty was access so Ryuu began the process of organising a helicopter service, complete with helipad, to bring out pre-booked guests. In the meantime visitors continued to come by boat. Jennifer was unusual; she arrived on her own, without a tour or cruise guide. He sensed her presence as soon as he entered the caverns and was amazed to hear the Buddhist chant from western lips. That was before they'd started to talk and when they did he felt effortlessly comfortable - introducing himself and talking about his history. He now knew why, she was little Jenny, the child that had escaped on the Hope & Charity. He remembered her parents; they had died during that horrific time; the same as his. They had a shared history; they were both survivors.

As he talked the visitors through the film show he could hear the gulped gasps emitted by Jenny, could smell the salt in her tears. When everyone else has gone on to the memorial he sat quietly with her; holding her hand.

'I have another piece of the story for you Jenny, one that very few know.'

Jennifer looked up, trying to read his face, it was then she noticed the older woman still sat on the stool Ryuu had brought to her earlier. His arm stretched out and his fingers curled to beckon his aunt.

'Jenny, meet Aunt Atsuko, a very brave, warm, woman and an exceptionally good swimmer.' He spoke with pride and humour.

Jennifer looked into the woman's eyes and saw another common spirit, they both smiled as they stood up to make their traditional Japanese greeting and bow in unison. Then they broke into chuckles as they realised how 'in tune' they were.

Fortunately Jennifer had planned ahead and booked into the hotel before she arrived on the island, so there was a room waiting for her and the whole evening to spend together. The Hope & Charity was not due back to pick her up for two days. She had deliberately kept this first visit short because she had not been sure what she would find and how she would feel.

They left the caverns and walked pass the memorial; the other visitors were still there and Jennifer wanted it to herself, she would come back later, to quietly honour her parents, Grandma and Skip.

'How on earth did you cope all that time in the hospital?'

'Oh, it wasn't so bad compared to the crates, or at least, it wasn't so bad once I realised to keep quiet and not prompt them to give me the shock treatment.'

Inadvertently Aunt Atsuko juddered with the memory, she tried to keep her voice and body on an even keel but there were some things embedded deep into her mind and muscle memory.

'I'm constantly amazed at how she coped and came out of it such a warm loving person' commented Ryuu, 'I feel so embittered at times.'

'You've been absolutely wonderful' said Aunt Atsuko, 'it was thanks to you that I am out of that place and able to live back on my own island. Without your help I'd still be over there,' her hand waved in the direction of the other island, 'a timid little mouse, frightened to be seen.'

'I was so excited to find you - but then devastated and angry to see how you were being treated .....'

They all paused in their steps, breathing in deeply, listening to the cicadas and thinking of Atsuko – locked away all those years and subjected to horrendous treatment and medication. Ryuu put his foot forward first to continue their walk back to the hotel.

'It has been a real privilege and pleasure to help you come out of your shell and re-discover the big wide world.'

'Wide indeed! I didn't know what had hit me when we were taken to San Francisco. I had of course heard of America but never imagined I would live there! Do you remember the first time you took me to a supermarket?'

Ryuu laughed .... and so it went on ... their memories were poignant, some extremely sad and others so sweet and full of hope.

Ryuu told Jennifer what had happened to Sho & Kin and how they now had new families and were settled in Washington DC. They had not seen them since their first reunion and he wasn't sure they ever would; they couldn't make a habit of it as they didn't want to attract the attention of the press.

'I was so young that my memories are blurred. Skip and Grandma were my surrogate parents and they did a fantastic job. I am so happy to have had them in my life and so sad to lose them.... but they had a truly wonderful marriage and I was blessed with a good education and stable home... that is .... a stable home after we reached Brisbane and were allowed out of the hostel.'

They walked in silence for the remainder of the journey to the hotel. Relaxed in each others' presence, and strangely at peace; they each reflected on their past grief and the joy they felt together.

'Oh, it's perfect' exclaimed Jennifer. 'I'd seen it from the village but hadn't stopped, as I'd wanted to see the caverns before nightfall.'

She was stood in the reception area, functional yet soothing; its timber walls and panelling sympathetically decorated to create a warm welcome. Soft lighting lit the corners where low chairs provided an opportunity to sit, take tea and recover from the sights and stories experienced on the tour of the island. Here one could feel cocooned, safe and at peace with the world. Her room was the same; a low bed with blossom print covers and toning blinds; a sliding door blended into the wall and opened to reveal an ensuite; a simple chair and round table took up the spot in front of the window through which she could see the lush green slopes leading to the cliffs' edge and, beyond them, the sea. But it was the sky that really grabbed her attention; it was sunset, the golden globe sent piercing shafts of light across the sea, streaks of gold and red melded around purple clouds; she could just make out sea from sky. Her heart lifted and opened .... she knew she was loved and being watched over. She dropped her rucksack to the floor and knelt in obeisance.

The Joy

The next morning Jennifer rose early, before the hubbub of the day ensued. She stretched and inhaled the morning air, noting the inescapable tang of sulphur on the breeze. She passed Atsuko, making her way to the kitchen to start preparing breakfast for the guests. A brief wave and smile was all that was necessary, Atsuko knew where she was going – to the final point of her pilgrimage.

During the walk there Jennifer focused on the beauty around her; the sweet fragrance of the jasmine, the bird call and chatter, the warmth of the ground beneath her feet, nature at its best. When she reached the memorial, the place where so many bodies had been used as sport and fodder, she realised she expected silence, but it wasn't like that. The birds and insects carried on as usual. Initially she walked around the mosaic, taking in the skill of the artist who had produced such beautiful colours and intricate shapes. The mosaic was framed with the names of those who had lived on the island at that time and died, or were never seen again. Her parents' names were there. She knelt on the ground next to them and cried; tears of sadness, tears of relief, tears of joy. She cried all the tears she'd been holding on to. Even though she had cried before, she had not been able to cry with her parents, now she felt she could. Her hand rested on top of their names, she traced the letters with her fingers; she imagined the family in the mosaic, on the beach with their little girl, was herself and her parents, watching the dolphins in the sea and the parrots in the sky. Two or three deep breaths and she felt her shoulders drop as she released all the tension she had been carrying. She hadn't realised how tightly she was holding on; holding on to what? Her fear? Her grief?

Her love? It was all their within her... it was part of her ... and it was okay.

Jennifer sat on the simple wooden seat provided, a single plank to perch on. The knotted wood and bark blending into the background, nothing was going to detract from the vibrancy of the mosaic and the quiet power of the Elders; their statues calm and dignified, supervised the last resting place of their families and friends. The remaining bones of those lost were buried beneath the mosaic.

What to do with her life? That was the burning question for Jennifer. Ryuu and Atsuko had this, their personal tribute and quest to ensure that their people and the sacrifices made were not forgotten. They lived with the knowledge that what happened could happen again. Those who had experienced the onslaught of the Invaders were ever alert; they had instinctive antennae that checked the sea, the sky, the springs and geysers, the rumblings beneath their feet. They hadn't heard them come before, they would not be caught out a second time. The question for Jennifer was what could she do with her knowledge, her experience and her money? The answer came to her as she gazed at the memorial, she would help other children like Ryuu and herself. Could she do it here? In Japan? It was a seed of an idea which she wanted to talk through with Ryuu and Atsuko.

'I think it's a brilliant idea, but could you live in Japan and cope with the different language and lifestyle?' Aunt Atsuko's question showed her inherent wisdom and compassion.

'Yes, I believe I could. I know it will not be easy at first but working with children who need a helping hand would spur me on; and I could learn Japanese as I helped them learn English – with an Aussie accent!'

Grinning, Jennifer looked directly at Ryuu whose American accent inevitably brought a smile to her face. She wasn't laughing at him but smiling with genuine fondness. In less than twenty-four hours the three of them had cemented a bond that would last a life-time.

'We could help find somewhere' offered Ryuu, 'I think you will need to be on the mainland, it would be safer and easier for people to access.'

The safer element in Ryuu's observation was linked to their inherent belief that the Aliens would return.

'We could come across to the mainland in the quiet season' volunteered Aunt Atsuko.

'Yes, once the winter sets in this place is virtually cut off and we get no visitors.'

'I could use my contacts in the field of child psychology to find out what resources are already available in Japan, if any, and whether they would accept an Aussie cum Brit helping them.'

'I'm sure they would if we were involved as well.'

'Oh it's so exciting, another project.... I never knew my training would be put to such good use.'

Ryuu's voice and words generated an unspoken commitment from the two women. It revealed how much he needed to be valued. Long ago, in his own mind, he felt he'd failed because, as a 10 year old boy, he could not save his parents. Jennifer was in awe of both him and Aunt Atsuko; she'd had it so easy in comparison. Being an orphan was not necessarily the worst thing in one's life, but it was life-changing and could leave deep scars and self-harming behaviour traits. Jennifer was determined to help other orphans or abandoned youngsters; to make up for those island children who had not been as fortunate as she or Ryuu.

Good as his word, the Skipper of the Hope & Charity was moored off the jetty by late afternoon the next day; it had seemed a good idea to limit the visit when she'd left Brisbane three weeks ago but now Jennifer wanted to stay longer. However, she had other commitments in Brisbane; the house, her job. So with a mixture of elation and disappointment, she boarded the dinghy that would take her to the waiting vessel and waved good bye to Ryuu and Aunt Atsuko. Jennifer was always happy to be on board the Hope & Charity but this journey back to Brisbane was different; she was no longer filled with the sense of trepidation and loss she'd felt on the way out; she had so much to look forward to and think about. Yes, she would always miss Grandma and Skip; she would also be forever grateful to them, their love and kindness; for instilling her with the wonder and joy of life. This new project was an opportunity for her to grow and give at the same time. And she would be doing it with the support of two lovely like-minded people, two fellow survivors who understood and shared her innate fear and nightmares but also knew how to live and love despite them. Her heart felt fit to burst!

As with most of these things, there was no instant fix. It took months of hunting and negotiation to find a suitable property and to get the necessary permissions and licences but, true to their word, Ryuu and Aunt Atsuko went into bat for the project, and the authorities, having seen how successful their efforts were proving on the island, were inclined to support this endeavour as well. Jennifer's credentials were impeccable and she was well-respected in her field; there was really no reason to exclude her, although there were obvious concerns about her ability to talk to Japanese children with her limited knowledge of the language. However, Jennifer had been practicing hard, and was coming along in leaps and bounds, planning her classes in English and Emotional Literacy; a fancy term for how to understand and manage one's own and other's emotions and thought processes.

The Japanese Government or, if they could afford it, a child's surviving relatives, would be required to make a small contribution to the schooling and house-keeping costs but Jennifer would pay for the building, and initial set-up costs. All three of the entrepreneurs would give their services for free. Finally Jennifer was relying on Ryuu to advise her how to invest sufficient funds to ensure she had a pension and modest income for the rest of her life. He had already done the same for himself and Aunt Atsuko.

'Hi Jenny. Can you hear me? We've found a place! Yes, I said, we've found a place!'

'That's terrific Ryuu. Where is it? When can I see it? Can you send me the details?'

'We can do better than that' said Ryuu. 'We can send you photos and meet you there in a fortnights time, if you can get away?'

'Oh... sorry... nearly forgot the main bit....it's just outside Tokyo, it's an old school with 5 stories; the top two would be ideal as dorms, one for boys and one for girls, each with a teacher's suite, then the 2nd and 3rd floors could be for classrooms, and the ground floor could provide a gym and recreation area; it already has a main hall, a Principal's office and staff room so you and the other staff could be on hand to keep your students safe and prevent any break outs!' Ryuu chortled at his own humour. 'It needs some work, the kitchen and bathroom facilities are not good enough for boarders but I'm sure you'll soon sort that out. The grounds are adequate and maybe you could start a gardening group to create garden and play areas the children would really enjoy.'

How Jennifer managed to keep quiet through this long statement of Ryuu's she didn't know, maybe it was because she hung on his every word whilst her mind was working overtime, painting pictures of beautiful classrooms, dormitories and gardens.

'I'll move heaven and earth to come over in 2 weeks; I'll start re-juggling my diary immediately. I'll aim to stay for a week, all being well, and then come back again as soon as I've worked out my notice and packed up my home here.'

A cold shiver ran through Jennifer's spine; it was the first time she'd actually thought about the reality of packing up her home - their home, Grandma and Skip's - and moving away. She shook her head and gulped, it would have to be done, she was a grown woman now and she would always have their love with her. She would put the house on the market when she came back from Tokyo and they had secured the purchase.

'I can't wait to see it; it's so exciting; I was beginning to think this moment would never come.'

'So were we. And it's just at the right time; our season is coming to an end, so we can come across to help you for a few months. Maybe we'll move into the school for the winter, camp out - kind of, and supervise the overhaul.'

'Listen to him' shouted Aunt Atsuko in the background, 'talk about jump the gun, you haven't even bought it yet.' She was giggling and the others joined in, they were all animated at the thought of this venture together.

Needless to say it wasn't a totally smooth experience; the property, when Jennifer saw it, looked a bit oppressive to her. Aunt Atsuko came up with some brilliant suggestions on how to soften the entrance and

179

facade with wisteria climbing up and trailing plants falling from window boxes. They could also have it repainted to compliment the colours of the plants. Jennifer liked this idea, and realised that Aunt Atsuko knew exactly what was needed to make a property inviting; after all, she'd had to live in some pretty uninspiring units. Ryuu was oblivious to this. His lack of sight meant he focused on practicality and whether a room or property was easy to access and move around. This one was. It had good vibes. He could imagine it providing a warm, buzzing sanctuary of learning, with quiet places, fun places and lots of loving kindness. He and Aunt Atsuko had talked things through - they would spend 6 months of the year on the island - over-seeing the living museum, the hotel and the tourists. They would also start to train a younger couple to help them. They realised they wouldn't always be able to show people over. For the rest of the year, late autumn through to early spring, they would live in Tokyo, hopefully at the school, helping Jenny and the children. Neither of them had children of their own, which, whilst they accepted as inevitable given their life experiences, did leave a void in their lives, and here was an opportunity to fill it. Maybe they would even be able to offer holidays on the island to some of the children.

The three of them had so many ideas and enthusiasm that it just had to work – and it did!

Aunt Atsuko and Ryuu enjoyed the winter camping in the premises and by the time Jennifer joined them they had quite a comfortable suite of rooms at their disposal.

It had been a painful time for Jennifer; going through all the stuff in the house; their home for nearly 25 years. Skip and Grandma weren't avid hoarders but there were toys, games, books, records, tools and linen in all sorts of odd places; tucked away - just in case. She could hear Grandma's voice - 'I can't bring myself to get rid of this, it might do someone a good turn someday', and quite often it did. What Jennifer couldn't take with her, and there was a lot she did thanks to the cargo hold of the Hope & Charity, she gave away to charity, to help refugees struggling to set up home. By the time she shut the front door for the last time she was exhausted. The voyage on the Hope & Charity was just what she needed, time to recoup and make the transition from an employed Aussie psychologist to a self-supporting philanthropic Matron. A Matron aged 31, what a scream! Thank goodness she would have her friends' wholehearted support.

Rod Christodoulou was a new-generation Aussie. His immigrant father had married a native 'Shelia' and he was the end result! He loved to see the look on peoples' faces when he introduced himself; his bronzed good looks and blonde hair belied his Greek ancestry - although his magnetic dark brown eyes were a bit of a giveaway. He had a soft spot for Jen and he had really taken to George Maynard. He had promised to look out for Jen on his last visit before Skip died. Jen hadn't known this, and didn't need to know, he'd have helped her anyway – she was such a lovely girl to have around – and she treated him like an older brother! Shame that, but maybe it was for the best, he had a habit of loving and leaving the women in his life, whereas a younger sister was forever. Jennifer gave Rod some of George's tools, and an old compass and sextant, no longer used on modern day ships, but a real treasure to a fellow seaman. He was glad she had these weeks to switch off, she'd looked washed out when she came aboard 5 days ago and was already picking up, losing herself in the routine of crewing, eating and sleeping; watching the waves, the dolphins and the whales go by. All too soon he was bringing his ship to berth at Osanbashi Pier, in Yokohama Port, within the huge bay that served as Tokyo Harbour. The task of unloading his cargo of wool and sugar in addition to Jennifer's container load of household goods took a while. Jennifer was waiting to say goodbye when he finally got ashore. Atsuko stood with her; the two of them keen to thank him profusely for his help and take him to tea. He accepted their thanks with some embarrassment and said he'd call in to see the school before he set sail again but declined their invite to tea; he wanted to wet his whistle and unwind with his crew. It was a traditional seafaring practice that he had no wish to break.

He watched the two women walk away, eyeing Jennifer's shapely rear and natural elegance, he was almost tempted, but reality brought him back to the present; she was about to open a boarding school for orphaned children and he was the skipper of a cargo ship, with a girl in every port – more or less! He adjusted his cap, turned and walked back up the gang plank to help his crew finish off before partaking of a little light refreshment.

Jennifer smiled to herself, she knew just what Rod was like, and enjoyed their banter during her time aboard the Hope & Charity, but she was never going to get serious with him. There had been other admirers over the years, and she was tempted once or twice, but then she had needed to concentrate on her career and now her school and children came first. The children were a constant source of wonderment. They came to the school bereft, angry and confused; full of fear, not knowing what the future held for them and angry at the world for taking their parents. Some had parents who were too ill to look after them - but the worst cases were those children who had been dumped in the streets, no-one willing to own them; these were usually the children of drug addicts - they had seen the worst of life and were the most defensive and aggressive, with the highest barriers; they needed her love and patience the most.

They never gave up on any child; some you instantly took to; you wanted to hold them close and soothe away their sorrow; others pushed you away with every physical and psychological tool at their disposal. Gradually, refusing to be put off, she and the teachers would dissolve their antipathy and help them discover healthy boundaries and coping skills. The youngest children they took in were age 6 and they were encouraged to stay until they were 18. During the holidays as many children as possible were placed in relatives' homes while others, who were too vulnerable, stayed with Jennifer in the school, or went to the island with Aunt Atsuko and Ryuu. One young man even went to sea with Rod! An amazing experience for both of them and one that resulted in the lad becoming part of Rod's crew at every opportunity possible; the skills he learnt on those trips helped him pass the entrance exam into the Japanese Maritime Self Defence Force. Both she and Rod were absolutely thrilled for him.

No day, week, month or year was ever the same for Jennifer. Grandma and Skip's constant love and support for not only her but the flow of transient people in their lives had prepared her well for this project; and she, in turn, was preparing others to take over from her. Jennifer was under no illusion; nothing stayed the same, and rightly so. Some of the young people who passed through their doors went on to teach and a few came back to their old school to educate and help other orphans with nowhere to go.

Ian Campbell's paintings hung in the entrance hall.

Chapter 12 – Nothing lasts forever

Retirement

There is never be a right time to retire, to let go of
the reins, but Jennifer had always maintained she would
step down at 60 and, now she was, and it felt too soon. She
was too young - had so much else to give - but so did the
other members of staff, and it was their time. These days
the school was self-funding; it was a well-respected
charitable institution that attracted generous donations from
ex-boarders and businesses, plus the Japanese Government
valued what it did and made a regular contribution to the
staffing and maintenance costs.

And so it was that Jennifer sat, on a warm summer's
evening, when it was quiet and the tourists were back at the
hotel or on their cruise ships, watching the moon and stars
twinkle the dolphins to life. How could something so
vibrant commemorate the death and destruction of this
island community? She thought she knew how and why.
Aunt Atsuko and Ryuu wanted to celebrate the lives of

their relatives and ancestors, not their deaths. They wanted to applaud the bravery of the Elders and Ian Campbell. They knew what a great service had been wrought here for all humanity and wanted visitors to feel awed and uplifted by the miracle of it, as they themselves were, as Jennifer was. Yet again, on this spot, it came to her: Ryuu and Atsuko had returned to their roots and so should she. She would go to England, to stay with Edward and Patricia Anderson; it was about time she understood her pedigree, where she came from and what life her parents had envisaged for her and her siblings. She was only 60; Ryuu was 67 and still going strong, organising everything on the island to his high standard; Aunt Atsuko (she would always think of her as Aunt) was in her late 70s and, whilst less active physically, mentally she was razor sharp, over-seeing the running of the hotel and training of the tourist guides. Jennifer knew their wishes; that their remains (once the scientists had checked out the bits that were of interest to them) would be cremated and their ashes buried in the ground, with their ancestors, under the mosaic. Jennifer had no idea what she wanted for herself. Thank goodness she still had time to explore her heritage and family ties. She would return to the UK and join Edward and Patricia Anderson in Binfield, Berkshire.

A journey of discovery

So, for the second time in her life, Jennifer packed up her belongings and moved - lock, stock and barrel; this time it was to England. Grandma had deliberately maintained UK passports for herself and Jennifer - as far as she was concerned they would always be British no matter where they lived. Jennifer had continued the tradition. The flight from Tokyo seemed endless; she understood why they called them long-haul flights. Not a trip she'd want to make too often. Jennifer arrived at Heathrow on a damp November morning, the light fog reminding her of Japan's morning mists, but it was different; it was cold and penetrating. She braced herself to inhale the chill – not the most welcoming of weather. The noise of the roaring aircraft and surge of people made her catch her breath. She thought she'd gotten used to crowds in Tokyo, a bustling Asian capital with an expanding community but here, in England it was different. The main language was English for a start and with it came a huge range of accents and dialects plus the foreign languages of visitors; and, of course, the baggage and fashion was as eclectic as the spoken word. Her senses were swamped, her body exhausted and jet-lagged. Happily the greeting she received from Edward and Patricia couldn't have been warmer. They were waiting at the arrival gate holding up a card with her name on ... along with flowers and a 'Welcome Home' balloon! Patricia had even thought to bring a knitted hat, gloves and scarf – perfect, Jennifer would definitely need them.

Hugs and greetings over she was grateful to lower her body into the soft leather interior of Edward's Jaguar. There was even a tartan throw for her to snuggle under. As Edward drove along the M4 towards the turn-off to Bracknell and Binfield Jennifer gazed out of the window. Everything seemed so small and dirty. She hadn't been prepared for this. She'd expected rolling green fields and quaint English villages. The wide open blue skies and endless space of Brisbane had not prepared her for 21st century England, neither had life in a boarding school in Japan. Jennifer crossed her fingers and hoped she'd made the right move; she reminded herself to go with the flow and not to follow her imagination. She must have dozed off, the smoothness of the car and gentle murmur of the radio crooning her to sleep; it had not been easy to close her eyes for long on the plane. When she awoke they were turning off the motorway towards Binfield. Properties were starting to look more quintessentially English; she couldn't help exclaiming when she saw the variety of thatched cottages with roses growing in their gardens. And the pubs, they were everywhere, with, what seemed to her, funny names. Edward said they'd take her to their local and introduce her to the neighbours - once she'd had a good night's sleep and they'd had her to themselves for 24 hours.

Patricia was in her element, giving Jennifer a guided tour from the front passenger seat; pointing out council houses, schools, Churches, supermarkets, hospitals and anything else they passed. It was all new to Jennifer; new and exciting ... and scary. This was where her family came from, this was her homeland, where she should have attended school and been brought up, with a brother or sister, or both, if her parents had lived. Her reverie was interrupted as Edward slowed down and Patricia announced

'Welcome to Honeysuckle Cottage.' The car turned into a shingle drive.

The front facade was a picture, there was an oak porch, stable door and latticed windows; the winter remains of honeysuckle clung to the walls. Jennifer commented on how well the garden was tended.

'That's Patricia's department' announced Edward, she's the green-fingered Anderson, I'm the one who earns the money - I leave all the house and garden decisions to Patricia, she's much better at it than me.'

'Quite right' chimed in Patricia, 'and I leave the car and gadget buying to Edward'. She smiled affectionately at her husband. They had a good division of labour and appreciated each other's strengths and quirks!

They took Jennifer inside where it was considerably warmer; the log burner alight - its flickering flame and red-gold glow an instant invite to make oneself at home.

Edward pointed Jennifer to a large sink-in sofa; it was a dusky pink and had enough room for 2 people to stretch out from either end.

'Sit yourself down while we make you a cuppa and bite of lunch.' I expect you're a little too pooped to take in much in at the moment but once you've had a chance to shower and nap we'll show you around the place.

'There are so many questions I want to ask, and things I want to see, but, as you say, I'm too exhausted for much at the moment..... I'm just extremely grateful for you taking me in like this.'

'Nonsense, you'd have done the same for us, if you could. To be honest we're so excited to have you here ... life's been a little dull since the girls left home, there's only so much WI Patricia can get involved with and golf that I can play.'

'Ah, I know about golf widows' said Jennifer. I had friends in Brisbane and Tokyo who complain about their husbands getting up at the crack of dawn to play 9 holes before going to work ... but what is WI?'

'I couldn't see Edward doing that,' chuckled Patricia as she entered the room with a tray of pretty sandwiches, scones, cream and jam. 'Thought we'd introduce you to an English Cream Tea ... it's the sort of thing we enjoy at the Women's Institute.'

Jennifer was none the wiser but she took the proffered napkin and tea plate and helped herself to sandwiches from the tiered stand. She was touched by their efforts. It was a shame she was feeling so bushed but, fortunately, they didn't seem to expect her to be any different.

'Travelling knocks me out' stated Patricia, I don't mind using the train but airports and planes seem to sap my energy. If we go abroad for a holiday I need another holiday when we return to recover!'

'Saved me a fortune' smiled Edward. 'We only book UK breaks these days.'

The scones and clotted cream with home-made strawberry jam (courtesy of the WI) were delicious.

'Mmmmm .. I daren't eat too many of these, I won't have a waistline left'

'You don't have anything to worry about, your Grandmother and Mother were naturally slim, the same as you.'

This simple statement sent an electric shock through Jennifer, she'd forgotten that here were family who knew her parents and grandparents ... a whole new world was about to unfold before her. She was glad she'd made the trip.

Life was a whirl for the next 3 months. Patricia took her shopping for winter clothes and showed her the sites of London. Edward introduced her to her heritage; showing her old family photos, their family tree and where her parents had been brought up. They both went to the same school and Edward had followed on, as had his daughters.

Christmas erupted with endless functions to attend. Dos for this charity and that, the village Christmas Fayre, the Carole Service in the Church, and a very fancy Ladies Night put on by the local Masonic Lodge, of which Edward was a member. The Freemasons seemed to have come on a long way since WWII. They were much more open about their charitable work and encouraged members from all walks of life and livelihoods to join. Women even had their own Grand Lodges! Choosing an outfit took up a couple of days. Patricia insisted on buying Jennifer her first ever ball gown, as though she was a debutante coming out, rather than a 60 year old woman being introduced to polite English Society. It was fun. They playfully looked in the posh London stores but no way would Jennifer entertain such extravagance. They ended up in TKMaxx, Guildford - a suitably upmarket area for Patricia and a reasonably priced store for Jennifer. They even managed to find a warm evening wrap (imitation fur) and glittery shoes with enough of a heel to look glam but not so high as to cripple the wearer! They steered clear of black and found a dress in just the right shade of midnight blue to flatter Jennifer's skin colouring and blonde locks.

Jennifer hesitated, 'this might be the only time I'll wear such a dress.'

'I doubt it; you're far too attractive to be left on the shelf.'

Jennifer burst out laughing. 'I'm on the shelf because I like it here! Come on, let's part with the cash and go for a coffee by the river.'

She had to admit the dress felt glorious against her skin and she was looking forward to her first 'Ladies Night'. It was as Edward and Patricia had promised; a lavish affair with lots of toasting, good food and wine, and some very glamorous outfits. What amazed her was how down to earth most of the participants were. They were all there to enjoy themselves and, at the same time, raise funds for chosen charities. They left at midnight whilst the younger members were still partying. Several men approached Edward for an introduction to Jennifer, and she was never short of a dancing partner. All in all a very successful outing for her ball dress. She could tick that one off her list of accomplishments.

After Christmas there was the New Year... this the Andersons celebrated with friends. They took it in turns to hold a New Year's Eve Party which involved silly party games, charades, a buffet, singing and dancing until past the bewitching hour - Jennifer and Patricia laughed all the way home - all of 2 streets away! They were slightly tipsy and the fresh air made them feel they had shed 30 years.... Edward smiled to himself, having Jennifer stay was a good tonic for Patricia. He felt proud to be escorting the two of them, they were fine Anderson women.

Winter turned to spring and before too long it was summer and there were yet more new experiences and adventures in store for Jennifer - polo at Windsor, the races at Ascot and regatta at Henley. All required new outfits. Jennifer emailed Aunt Atsuko about her outings, along with photos of her in her different regalia.... Aunt Atsuko was extremely complimentary and said she would have joined her if she'd been 20 years younger! But the excitement was starting to pale. Jennifer wasn't sure she really felt at ease with the excesses of the 'smart set'. She had seen too much hardship and struggle in her life. It was fun to escape to this life for a short while but it wasn't the real world. Pampered horses were magnificent beasts to look at but did they really warrant more money spent on their stabling than that to support an orphan in Zimbabwe or Rumania. Jennifer kept her inner conflict to herself, she did not wish to offend her cousin and his wife, who were wonderful hosts. However, she did start to withdraw slightly from the high life and took herself off to night school in the September intake. She opted to study British History, of which she knew very little, and also joined a volunteer befriending and counselling scheme to help adults with severe and enduring mental health problems. She felt her skills were useful and transferable to this group of people whilst their adultness would also present her with a fresh challenge. Finally, she joined a rambling club, something to make her get out of doors as the autumn and winter approached. It was there she met Viv, a 59 year old divorcee who enjoyed travelling around the UK and seeking out the lesser known landmarks and places of interest. For whatever reason, they immediately bonded, like kindred spirits. Maybe it was because they had both experienced loss and drastic change in their life. Or maybe it was just that they were both in the same place at the same time, walking through Wildmoor Heath with the Bracknell Forest Rambling Club; Viv wearing fluorescent pink hiking boots and Jennifer sporting a luminous bright green pair!

They instantly fell into step together and there was no turning back. They started off exchanging their knowledge of birds and butterflies; Jennifer was armed with a pocket reference book trying to identify the British flora and fauna she hadn't seen before and Viv provided a wealth of light-hearted commentary and deep insight. She understood the natural beauty of her environment but she wasn't a Green snob; she was not averse to dipping into man-made amusements. She introduced Jennifer to the fun of Victorian sea-side resorts such as Clacton on Sea and Margate; then there was Aldeburgh with its fantastic fish & chips, live-in converted 19th century mill and shingle beach with the amazing but controversial stainless steel scallop sculpture.

'Stunning is the only way I can describe it' explained Viv. 'It took my breath away when I first saw it, it was so unexpected – I stopped in my tracks and then couldn't stop laughing! I love it but as you can imagine, in this conservative area, it has caused quite a debate. Nothing quiet about retirement in England I tell you! You just have more time on your hands to pursue spiritual and cultural activities. I'm so looking forward to it!'

And there she was giggling again, an infectious, bubbly sound that Jennifer just had to echo.'

'I feel as though I'm in my teens again when I'm with you.'

'And why not, we're supposed to go backwards after a certain age. We no longer have to please anyone else and our life is our own .... no-one else is going to live it for us.'

They did coach trips to York and Bath... Jennifer's evening classes paid off – she was able to relate to the history of these old cities and, with a great deal of chivvying from Viv, managed to go round the Roman Baths. They were nothing like the thermal geysers and caverns on the island which was a huge relief. They had fun making up stories about the Roman ladies luxuriating at the baths, lying on couches, being served oysters and wine.

'What a life of Riley! Those Romans certainly knew how to live the good life.'

'I understand many of the inhabitants actually welcomed them and joined in their lifestyle – I'm not surprised.'

'Not so good for the slaves though – mind you, it seems slave labour was an accepted practice in those days – glad we don't have it now.'

'Ryuu and Aunt Atsuko had a flavour of it when they were captured by aliens on their island.' Jennifer's reference to her history just slipped out.

'What? Tell me more?' demanded Viv; she never missed a trick.

'It's a long story, I'll tell you after supper tonight.'

Can't wait.'

'Maybe I'll take you to Japan and our island someday.' Jennifer's voice was wistful; she wasn't sure she actually wanted to undergo another long haul flight but she couldn't imagine not seeing her island friends again.

That evening, after they'd eaten in the hotel, they sat down to enjoy a coffee and Viv, who'd thought she'd been on exceptionally good behaviour and wonderfully patient, blurted out:

'C'm'on then - spill the beans ... what's this alien business about?'

Jennifer took a deep breath and sip of black coffee.

'Do you remember all the who-ha in the newspapers about aliens some 30 years ago – don't look at me like that - you're not that much younger than me - you must have heard or read about it!'

Viv was genuinely gobsmacked for once.

'No, I don't believe it .... don't tell me you were involved in that. You would have been tiny, a mere toddler.'

The penny dropped.

'You were the little girl that escaped with her Gran and went to Brisbane with the other refugees?'

'Yes I am' whispered Jennifer, 'Keep your voice down pleeeaase.'

'Oops, sorry, yes, I can understand you not wanting to attract attention. It must have been awful for you, losing your parents like that.'

'It was horrendous and even now I have nightmares about it, as do the other survivors,' ... and Jennifer began to relate the whole of her life history and that of her friends, or as much as she could remember and cover in one evening. It took more than one cup of coffee to keep her going and a great deal of chocolate! Funnily enough, Jennifer had never gained a love for beer and spirits, but chocolate was a different matter. Fortunately the hotel served a chocolate with each cup of coffee they ordered. For once neither of the women worried about too much caffeine and not sleeping, Jennifer needed to keep awake to narrate her story and Viv needed to keep alert to listen to it – there was so much to take in.

At about 2am they went to bed, Viv in absolute awe of her friend's loss and survival. She would definitely love to meet Atsuko and Ryuu. It made the hairs stand up on the back of her neck just thinking something like that could actually happen in her life-time. She wondered what had happened to those who were taken away in the pod.

Talking so much about her past had a two-fold effect on Jennifer. It helped her exorcise her childhood demons, once again, and also enabled her to see things as a whole and how amazing it truly was that nothing worse happened to the human race. Living in England seemed a long way from Japan to her but would it be to the aliens?

The next day, not surprisingly, they were up late for breakfast. Their fellow coach travellers looked at them knowingly as they rushed into the restaurant to grab some toast and tea. Jennifer & Viv were the 'youngsters' on this trip, and their wayward ways were a source of entertainment and reminiscence to the pensioners on the coach. The 'youngsters' chuckled at their perceived youth and had no wish to enlighten the 'oldies'.

By the time they returned back to Binfield and Bracknell from this trip the women had an even stronger bond and were already planning their next little adventure.

'The West country next I think' said Viv, 'my father took me to Newquay when I was about thirteen, a very impressionable age, and I'd love to see it again.

'Suits me ... shall we do another coach trip or travel by rail?'

'I thought maybe we could invest in a camper van' volunteered Viv. 'Nothing too big 'cos the roads are narrow and windy, but it would give us more flexibility and, if we're gonna continue with our jaunts, which I hope we are, could save us money in the long term. What do you think?' There, she got the words out in a rush, she'd been thinking about this joint purchase over the past few days. 'And I wouldn't have to feel guilty about keep putting Dom into kennels, he could come with us.'

It was Jennifer's turn to be gob-smacked. 'Let me give it some thought' she said. Jennifer was a little less gung-ho than Viv and liked to think these sort of commitments through. She'd never owned property with anyone else before and, whilst it wouldn't be beyond her budget, she wondered how they would get on in such close proximity, the two of them plus Viv's Jack Russell, Dom. She also wondered if she would pass a British driving test.

'Take your time to mull it over' prompted Viv; she was getting to know her friend well and was quite prepared to give her thinking space. 'There's no urgency.'

'Just as well' laughed Jennifer,' you know me, ever Miss Cautious!

'And now I understand why,' a serious note came into her Viv's voice as she put her arm around Jennifer's shoulders and gave her a squeeze.

Another Venture

Edward had Patricia couldn't help being excellent and generous hosts. They were a lovely couple and put a lot of energy into helping Jennifer settle into her English life. Once they saw she was up and running, making her own friends and entertainment, they were happy with their part in the project and stepped back, making no attempt to interfere. As with their girls, they did their best to encourage Jennifer to spread her wings, knowing they would always be available to help, if called upon. Jennifer really appreciated the generosity of spirit extended by her cousin and his wife. They had finally accepted a small contribution from her towards her keep. They hadn't wanted to but Jennifer was insistent, pointing out she wouldn't be able to stay if they didn't let her pay her way; she wasn't without funds and told them to put the money towards their favourite charity if they didn't want to keep it for themselves. This appealed to both of them and they now gave Jennifer's rent to a different charity each month.

They were intrigued by Jennifer's practice of reflection and meditation, which led to some interesting discussions on Buddhism and other religions. Patricia went to weekly Yoga classes and said she always enjoyed the short relaxation period at the end, which seemed to include a type of meditation practice. So Jennifer went with her one week, and then another and another.... soon she was a regular and would have the odd chat with their teacher about his practice. And then she and Patricia would go for coffee and cake!

All in all, life was good and had settled into a routine which included the odd little adventure.

Jennifer gave the idea of a camper van considerable thought, researching the cost and likely maintenance requirements on line along with tax and insurance, petrol consumption; basically anything she could think of – and then she saw it, winking at her from across the road; sat on a neighbour's driveway - a beautifully maintained and totally eccentric pink and purple VW transit camper. She was completely smitten and went to take a closer look, peering inside and imagining herself and Viv sleeping and eating there. To her horror the owner came out of the house.

'She's a beaut in't she' it was more of a statement than question.

'Sure is Mate,' responded Jennifer, immediately going into the same Aussie strine that the owner spoke.

They both burst out laughing.

He was from Adelaide and had bought the 'van to move around the UK whilst visiting long lost relatives but he was due to return home and needed to put it up for sale in two weeks time. Jennifer asked how much, he mumbled an amount, not extortionate but a bit on the high side, he obviously knew he had a very interested party looking at it.

'Okay, I can't deny I'm interested but I would not be buying it alone so need to consult my partner in crime.'

'Well I've given you all the information about her that I have, and she's been good for me, can't be any more fairdinkum than that.'

Jennifer smiled; it was some years since she'd heard that turn of phrase.

'Can I come back with my friend at the weekend? Is Saturday morning about ten-thirty okay?'

'Make it 12ish can you? I'm out for a bit of a bevy with the lads on Friday night so it's doubtful I'll be up too early.'

'Great – see you then. Here's my mobile number if you need to change the time for any reason.'

They exchanged numbers and Jennifer walked back across the road with a smile on her face, having totally forgotten that she'd originally stepped out to get some groceries! That driving test was now a priority.

Viv fell in love with it too. It had an easy pull-out canopy so that the outside could be used as a lounge or storage area in the wet – a facet of British weather that could not be ignored. Jamie, its current owner, had put up with a lot of stick from his mates because of the colour but they soon changed their tune when they saw it's pulling power. At 33, bronzed and fit for the Australian outdoors, Jamie couldn't help being a success with the girls; he could even charm the more mature ladies. Viv and Jennifer laughed throughout their business transaction, knowing they were paying a little over the odds, but it was worth it, just to own such a fantastic camper and to listen to Jamie's stories and banter. They even went to his send-off party and he promised to keep in touch. Jennifer smiled, he was almost like a wayward son – and she doubted he'd be a good letter writer - but she would let him know how they got on ith Fuscia – the Vdub's name – by email and send the occasional photo. The whole episode of buying the camper left her with a warm glow... it had to be right.

Jennifer had a few lessons and took her driving test – yes! She nailed it!

They celebrated her success and christened their ownership with a visit to the New Forest for 4 nights, then Portsmouth and Falmouth, before going across the peninsular to Newquay. The weather hadn't always been kind and they made good use of their cagoules and wellies. But they had such fun: making friends where-ever they camped, trying local delicacies, and sitting outside at night just listening and watching.

By the time they reached Newquay they'd been on the road for a week and felt like seasoned campers, they could set up in under 40 minutes and throw together some fantastic one pot meals. Both of the women looked lightly tanned, slightly dishevelled and fully alive. They felt it. Jennifer text Patricia every couple of days, so she knew they were safe ... it felt good to have someone looking out for her; Viv didn't have anyone to do that for her. Or rather hadn't, until Edward and Patricia had very subtly taken her under their wing as well; she was always included in despatches and often directed Jennifer what to text!

Both women were now in their 60s but felt at least 20 years younger, and most of the time, acted as though they were. Jennifer felt a freedom and zest for life she couldn't really remember having experienced before. Viv Shoeman was elated to have Jennifer and her cousins in her life, the future looked rosy, she didn't think she would feel lonely ever again, and she certainly no longer felt the need to have a man in tow.

When they reached Newquay they first found somewhere to camp and then, having booked their pitch and set up shop, grabbed their rucksacks and started to walk down the hill to the harbour. Viv remembered kids diving off the harbour wall and wondered if that still happened. No it didn't, health and safety and all that. But it was very picturesque and busy with holiday makers and surfers. Newquay was renowned for its beaches, whether for surfing, swimming, sunbathing or canoeing in the Gannel Estuary. The young people there, in their surfing uniform of beaded necklaces and bracelets, shorts and sun-bleached hair reminded Jennifer of days spent at the Gold Coast or weekends at Noosa Heads. She had fond memories of going there with Luke and his family. The brothers were hooked on surfing and, when old enough, bought a panel van to go off at weekends with their mates. Unfortunately Jennifer was a little too young to go with them but in the early days, when they went as a family, she was often invited and would join in the fun - belly surfing and being tumbled by the larger waves. All Aussie kids living near the coast were brought up to give it a go. She was certainly too old now but loved to watch the youngsters enjoying themselves whilst she and Viv did some beachcombing. It was so hard not to pick up every piece of driftwood, pebble or shell that caught her eye. Viv laughed at her, they had such an array of mobiles made from Jennifer's findings that soon they would be able to set up shop!

'At least it keeps them off the shelves' commented Jennifer.

'We don't have any shelves' retorted Viv, 'and we don't do dusting!

More shared laughter and humour.

They were due to return to Berkshire in a couple of days. On the one hand they were looking forward to going home to their own beds yet on the other they would miss this carefree camping life. They would definitely do it again, hopefully next month and this time they'd allow for a longer trip. It would probably be their last chance before the cold weather set in.

With this in mind they were looking in the shops for little keepsakes to take back for Edward and Patricia. Viv said it would be fun if they all had a surfer's necklace and bracelet. So the hunt was on for 4 different sets of beads to suit each of them. Edward would probably wear a wooden set for a chill out BBQ or fancy dress do, Patricia favoured blue and white accessories, Viv was always drawn to bright pink or coral and Jennifer liked greens and blues. They wanted to ensure that each gift was chosen with care to suit its recipient. Jennifer was to choose Viv's and Viv to choose Jennifer's. Even this simple quest became a warm, joyous venture.

Walking down a surfers' street, looking at the array of equipment and accessories displayed outside, Jennifer was suddenly aware that the man ahead of them looked like someone she knew. She racked her brains... who could she

know here in Newquay? A friend of Edwards? Patricia's?
One of their fellow ramblers? No-one sprung to mind.
Then she heard the man speak, a deep voice with a faint
down under twang. Somewhere in the back of her memory
she knew that sound – it reminded her of Luke. No, she
shook her head; that was just because she'd been thinking
of the family outings they'd shared. Then he turned around
and spoke to the young man looking at surfboards. She
was almost sure it was him. This was just too much of a
coincidence – could she trust her instinct?

'Luke, Luke Osborne? Is that you?'

He looked up.

'Oh, sorry to disturb you, I thought you looked like
someone I lived next door to many years ago.'

'In Iris Street maybe?' A boyish smile spread across
the man's face.

'Yes', said Jennifer, beaming in return.

Viv stood a step behind watching the reunion play
out, her mind working overtime - what a good looking man
he was, dark hair with flecks of grey, just over 6ft tall,
tanned, and a very fit body, absolutely no paunch – she sure
hoped Jennifer did know him; not needing a man was one
thing, appreciating a good one was another!

'Fancy meeting you here'. He couldn't help
grinning at this old line.

'And after all these years!' She was astounded yet
felt remarkably happy.

'And I'm her friend, Viv. Viv Shoeman.' Viv
extended her hand; it was time to ensure her presence was
noticed.

'Oh, sorry Viv, this is an old neighbour of mine,
Luke. He was instrumental in helping me settle in Brisbane

and then led me astray on numerous occasions.' Jennifer couldn't stop herself – she was attempting to flirt with Luke!

'Totally my pleasure' Luke gallantly responded, 'You were a delight to have around and my Mum thought you were a real sweetie.'

'Those days seem so long ago yet seeing and speaking to you now is bringing them all back.'

'Oh, dear, I hope you're not remembering when I led you into that ants' nest – honest I just didn't see it.'

'I believe you – thousands wouldn't!' Jennifer grinned at Luke's over-acted contrite face.

Viv interrupted, 'So how come an Aussie lad is here in Newquay? Don't tell me you're a Surfie!'

'Not exactly' responded Luke. 'Although as Jen can tell you, we would often take trips to the Gold Coast and Noosa Heads. In fact, we taught Jen to belly surf. Oops, sorry, by 'we' I mean myself, my brother and my parents – Jen used to come away with us at times.'

'Yes, and you used to come on the Hope & Charity with me, Skip and Grandma.'

'Great trips as I recall.' He hesitated, 'how are your parents these days?'

A wistful sadness came into Jennifer's voice 'Unfortunately I lost them both ... nearly 35 years ago now.'

'Oh, of course, they were your grandparents weren't they, considerably older than mine. My parents are in their late 80s now but still on the ball. Playing bowls and watching the racing on the TV. Mind you, they won't do computers or mobile phones so I keep in touch by ringing them once a month... and I go over to see them when the season finishes here each year. My brother's just up the road to them now so he keeps me in the loop quite regularly. Where would we be without email and Skype!'

'Hey, do you two mind if we continue this conversation later? My tum is grumbling that it's lunchtime!'

'Sorry Viv, what kind of friend am I. Do you want to join us for lunch Luke or are you busy?'

'Can't at the moment – that's another story,' Luke nodded his apologies to Viv, with a cheeky grin. 'But I could make tonight – if you 2 girls are around?'

'We're staying in our camper just up the hill – you know Newquay better than us, where's the best place to meet up?'

'Well, if you trust me, you're both welcome to mine for pizza and salad about 8pm? I'm there on my own and, whilst I'm not the tidiest of men, I have no anti-social habits or predilection for wicked ways! We can eat on the terrace if this weather continues.'

'Jennifer, can we trust him?' How Viv managed to say it with a straight face was beyond her.

'Going on past performance .... mmm ... maybe we can,' winked Jennifer. 'Could we bring Dom?'

Luke raised his eyebrow.

'My Jack Russell' interjected Viv, 'he's house-trained and quite sociable.'

'No problem at all. The more the merrier, I'm sure Bella will cope.'

'Who's Bella?' it was Jennifer's turn to be curious. 'I thought you said you were there on your own.'

'A matriarchal white feline that owns me! There are loads of places she can retreat to if she doesn't like the company I keep.' Luke couldn't stop grinning. 'Great – that's a date – here's my address and phone numbers... in case you get lost.' He handed over a card. 'Women are not renowned for their navigational abilities!' It was Luke's turn to wink as he quickly turned on his heel.

They parted in great humour, looking forward to meeting up later that evening.

'I feel like a schoolgirl rather than a retired matron; I'm not sure we should be doing this' said Jennifer.

'Speak for yourself – I'm younger than you and still game for anything!' retorted Viv - the two women walked jauntily, arm in arm down the hill, totally forgetting about their shopping expedition. Fortunately, over lunch and a cuppa they remembered what they'd come out for and purchased their keepsakes before returning to Fuscia where Dom was waiting for them. He made it quite clear that he disapproved of being left behind to guard Fuscia whilst the women took themselves off to shop and lunch.

'Don't be so silly' cooed Viv as she stroked Dom's ears, 'you wouldn't have liked dodging in and out of peoples legs and anyway we would have had to have left you tied up outside shops; you can come out with us this evening – and I expect you to be on your best behaviour.'

Dom wagged his tail and turned over to allow Viv to tickle his belly. He approved.

'I'm sure he understands every word I say.'

'Well make sure he understands he's NOT to chase Bella' giggled Jennifer, 'we want a harmonious re-union.'

Dom pricked one of his ears in Jennifer's direction – both women erupted into laughter.

Supper in Newquay

By the time they approached Luke's home that evening Viv was totally in the picture as to how Luke fitted into Jennifer's life and how their families had lost touch once his parents moved to Noosa Heads. Both women were curious as to what happened to a twenty-something marine biologist that caused him to end up working in a surf store in Newquay. This evening's conversation should prove interesting.

As it was; Luke's house instantly aroused their inquisitiveness. It was a fusion of Australian colonial meets Victorian seaside residence; set back from the road and built into the hillside with a veranda out front extending onto a raised sundeck – 'the terrace'. And there sat Luke, waving to them to join him. He had a bottle of champagne on ice and 3 glasses at the ready.

'Thought we'd celebrate our happy reunion' he explained, 'it's not often I meet a friend as old as Jen.'

'What!!' both women exclaimed in unison.

'You know I don't mean it that way' apologised Luke – realising as the words came out of his mouth that they were in the wrong order.

'I mean a valued old friend from my childhood and growing up years.' He handed them a glass each, stood up and raising his said 'Here's to old friends' long may they remain in each others' lives.' The twinkle in his eyes did not erase the depth in his words.

Having taken a sip of bubbly Luke raised each woman's hand to his lips as he escorted them to their chairs.

'Please be seated whilst I finish slaving over a hot stove for the benefit of my illustrious guests.'

Jennifer and Viv sat and smiled, Luke was so cool. They took in the view. It was absolutely stunning. Across the descending rooftops they could see the cobalt expanse of the sea - the setting sun mirrored as it danced across the waves.

'There's nothing quite like British summer time, when the sun shines and the evenings are long and lingering,' observed Viv.

'I'm starting to appreciate them,' commented Jennifer 'thanks to your friendship and terrific ideas.' She raised her glass to Viv.

Viv blushed, 'oh, I couldn't be this daft without you around'. She raised her glass to Jennifer.

'Dinner is served,' interrupted Luke, returning with a tray laden with a tossed salad in a wooden bowl, a jug of dressing, a pot of coleslaw and 3 boxes of pizzas!

'We'll never get through that lot' cried Viv.

'Don't worry, I quite enjoy pizza for breakfast, lunch and tea' laughed Luke. 'No, seriously, I suddenly realised I hadn't asked what you liked or if you were veggie so I bought one veggie, one meat and one tuna – dig in, there's strawberries and cream for dessert.'

And so they did. The conversation was animated and serious, lively and reflective; and, over coffee, Bella made herself at home on Luke's lap. Dom gave her the eye from his position at Viv's feet but he'd got the message earlier and was not about to demean himself by chasing their host's cat. They were all extremely at ease with each other and by the end the evening had a good idea of their various life stories.

Both Luke and Viv had been married, but whereas Viv had gone through an acrimonious divorce, Luke was widowed. His English wife having died of ovarian cancer, discovered as they were trying to conceive a child. He'd met her when they were both in their gap year and acting as instructors on an Eco marine biology adventure holiday centre off the coast of Antigua. They spent many years travelling the world together, working on different scientific projects requiring marine biologists and eventually took the plunge, getting married in 1983 to start a family. Mandy's family lived in Cornwall and it was there they intended to settle and raise children (with regular trips to Noosa Heads). They had a son and daughter who were only 7 and 5 when Mandy was diagnosed with cancer; there followed a series of hospital visits and treatment spanning 3 years before she died. During that time the children were looked after primarily by their grandparents who, behind the scenes, also supported Luke as he tended to Mandy's needs. It had knocked the stuffing out of him and when it was all over he knew he had to be there for his kids; so he gave up travelling and took over the family business – her family's. It was the least he could do. He now ran the surf and diving shop owned by his in-laws which, in due course, would be passed on to his children. His son, Ben, 28 lived and worked in Exeter as an accountant - a bit of a black sheep that one – far too studious and mature for his age! Melissa, aged 25 had started a degree in Social Work at Exeter Uni following a very long 'gap year'; so was sharing digs with her brother. An affable arrangement; Ben was looking out for his younger sister in the way Luke had watched out for Jen. This left Luke living in Newquay, managing the business and supporting his ageing in laws and children to get on with their lives. There were times he felt lonely but generally life was good.

Viv's childless 25 year marriage had ended 13 years ago when her ex-husband decided he wanted a younger model. It had been a bit of a shock, especially as her ex was now married to a woman 20 years his junior and had a toddler aged two. He'd never wanted children when they were married. There was still a degree of pain and anger in Viv's voice when she recalled her break up, however she was intent on putting that to one side and doing the things she'd always wanted to do, no holds barred. She'd initially played the field and internet dating sites but, after a couple of defunct romantic interludes, decided she was happier doing her own thing, especially now she had such a great friend as Jen.

Jennifer had never married, never borne children, and yet had loads. Her work in the school in Tokyo brought her endless satisfaction and reward. Even now she had ex-pupils who kept in touch. And of course, there was Atsuko and Ryuu and, now, Viv; and her wonderful cousin and his wife who'd offered her the chance to live in England and get to know her country of origin. She rarely felt lonely but she certainly felt something on seeing Luke.... this last thought she didn't share with either of her friends.

The two women were on holiday but Luke was not; he had to be up early the next day; so reluctantly they made to leave at midnight and Luke insisted on walking them home! They exchanged contact details and promises to keep in touch.

Late Summer, 2012

Jennifer dropped Viv off at her starter home in Bracknell.

Viv joked when she'd first invited Jen round – she saw the irony of buying a starter home at age 52 – but she was not alone. There were so many like her out there; mature divorcees starting life again. Whilst Viv was eventually pleased to be shot of her ex she wasn't so sure that being out in the meat market was much better but, since teaming up with Jen, life had turned a corner. She thoroughly enjoyed their walks with the rambling club and jaunts to see the sights; Jen's friendship helped her see everything with fresh eyes. And now there was Fuscia - their camper – pure joy. This really was living the dream for Viv. As long as she could remember she had wanted to just take off and now she could, not quite abandoning her responsibilities, but free to take off on little adventures whenever she and Jen wanted. Their trip to the West country had been extremely successful and she was looking forward to getting away again before the autumn took hold.

As always, Patricia and Edward welcomed Jennifer back with a family supper but this time there were 5 of them. Their eldest daughter, Jessica, had come home unexpectedly with her 8 month old baby boy. The Anderson's were truly excited to see their daughter and first grandchild but, Patricia confided to Jennifer, they were also anxious about the reason for this visit. It would appear Jessie's long term relationship was going through a bad patch. The modern preference not to get married did not appear to give the enduring protection and security that a mother and her children need ... or that was how it seemed to Patricia - and Jennifer too - when she thought about it. It had never been a consideration for her beforehand; most of the children she'd dealt with in Japan had been orphans with no immediate family able to care for them.

Baby Eddie was just perfect; cute and cuddly; watching and responding to all he saw and heard with hands reaching out everywhere. He had a bum-shuffle approach to getting around and his doting grandparents had to be one step ahead of him when it came to moving ornaments and non-childfriendly obstacles out of reach.... but they overlooked the coal skuttle and recounted how they'd looked down to see him taste-testing lumps of coal, with blackened mouth, face, hands and clothes! Fortunately it was all washable, including the hearth rug which had survived a lot worse than that over the years.

Edward and Patricia tried not to interfere with their girls' lives, or Jennifer's. They were a generous and caring couple and loved their home being fully occupied. They only proffered advice if it was asked for and then with a great deal of empathy. Since Jennifer's arrival they'd helped her meet people and socialise, even trying the odd attempt at match-making – she'd met Mr Marks & Sparks, Mr Jovial Overweight Banker, Mr Ex Hippy with the proverbial bald plate and grey ponytail and Mr Pleasantly Normal ... all these introductions had been carried out as casually and informally as possible. Whilst enjoying the social whirl Jennifer was just not enthused to find a male partner. However, Luke had sparked something. Initially they'd exchanged emails, then a text every couple of days and now they would text at whim most days, they were getting to know about one aothers' preferences and habits – long distance. Luke would always email Jennifer to let her know if he was likely to be out of touch due to the rolling hills which created connection problems; one of the facts of life when living and travelling around rural areas - even in the 21st Century!

Jen had been home barely 2 weeks before Viv announced she had planned their next trip.

'I thought we'd try Wales. Drive through the Cotswolds, nip 'round Swindon and check out the Brecon Beacons.... there's a place called Seirian's Well that might interest you ... it's an old thermal spring.'

Jennifer felt herself take an internal step backwards at Viv's last words. She took a deep breath in and let the air out slowly, relaxing her shoulders. It was as though she'd been punched in the stomach – not that she ever had

– but it was how she imagined it would feel. With a shake of her head she reminded herself that she was a fully grown adult. Bath hadn't been a problem so why would Seirian's Well be any different. Recovering her equilibrium she responded.

'Oh, did you now. And when were you thinking of taking this trip?'

'Well, I thought we could go the last week in August and keep travelling throughout September... really as long as the weather holds.'

'Sounds a good plan.' Jennifer smiled. Viv grinned, her friend had worried her a bit there ... she hadn't seemed very keen initially.

'I think it might be a good time to leave Edward and Patricia's for a bit; they need time and space to devote to Jessie and baby Eddie ... I think recent attempts at reconciliation between their daughter and her partner have been unsuccessful. It doesn't look good. I've been wondering if I should move out and let Jessie have my quarters – I'd rather offer than wait to be asked.'

'Well, it would give her more room with the littl'un, especially if it's likely to be a permanent arrangement.'

'It's hard to tell what constitutes permanent these days. As the Buddha said, everything is impermanent, everything changes, nothing lasts forever.'

'Don't sound so morose.'

'Oh, sorry, I'm not, not really. Generally I try to welcome change but I was just thinking back to when I lost my parents and the anguish of all those children that came to the Hope & Charity School, they too had lost their parents. I think losing a parent through death or divorce or, in this case, separation, is to be avoided if at all possible. I hope Jessie and her partner sort things out so that baby Eddie knows he has a mother and father that love him.

Viv allowed her friend a few quiet moments before attempting to lift her out of the doldrums.

'And look at us! We're changing,' laughed Viv. 'Bits going South, brains losing track of why we come into a room, and we're no longer cheap to run – our maintenance costs are sky-rocketing!'

Jennifer upped her mood 'Definitely time to get out there and have fun – watch out Wales!'

'That's settled then ... And if there's time, I thought we could pop in to see your man friend on the way back.'

'He's not my man friend.'

'You can't fool me - even if you think you fool yourself!'

Viv was not blind, she saw her friends face light up when she received a text from Luke; and she saw the restlessness creep in when he hadn't been in touch for 24 hours. Oh yes, she knew the signs alright. She was happy for her friend but couldn't help feeling anxious about her own future. She'd so enjoyed these past months with Jen, she didn't want anything to change, and yet it would, it was, and so it should. The universe could not stand still for anyone or anything.

Wales beckons

It was all arranged.

Jennifer had moved her belongings into the largest spare bedroom in the main part of the cottage and Jessie and baby Eddie would consider the annexe their home, for the time being.

Patricia and Edward went to great lengths to persuade Jennifer from feeling she had to do this but she was adamant. She was travelling a lot these days and didn't need the same amount of space as a young mum and her baby. She wouldn't have it any other way. It was surprising how everything she really wanted could be housed in one large room. Really her whole life had prepared her for this ... yes, she'd had a home with Grandma and Skip but she'd never had a home of her own, she was used to sharing, her bedroom was her sanctuary and, so long as she still had that to return to, all was well in her world. Going around the country with Viv in Fuscia was hilarious and exhilarating and yet she could still look forward to having her few bits, neatly laid out, waiting for her when she got back. Not owning a property meant Jennifer had to deal with a sense of not knowing where she would end up but, on the other hand, it was a release, a release from the mundane and sameness of being tied to an inanimate fixture. Jen had mixed views – there was no right or wrong way ... just each had advantages and disadvantages – depending upon where you were in your life. And she was doubly fortunate, she had her health and sufficient income that she would not starve or freeze to death. For now, living out of a rucksack and on a day to day basis, gave a sense of freedom; long-term she couldn't imagine herself spending the rest of her days making her bed in a sleeping bag but she would concern herself with that when the day came.

There were no yoga or history classes during the summer holidays but a meditation group met in Reading each week and Jennifer made a point of going there when she wasn't on an adventure with Viv. It was run by western Buddhists who, along with meditation classes, provided an opportunity to study and explore the Buddha's teachings and how they could relate to everyday life in the 21st Century western world. Finding this group was the nudge Jennifer had needed to read and meditate a bit more – she was hoping that Viv might come with her one day. They had odd chats about the philosophy of Buddhism but Jen tried not to preach to Viv; it felt more appropriate if she just responded to any questions or comments as they arose. The Practice and Ethics were always with her, as were the emails and texts.

Texts whizzed back and forth, from Binfield to Newquay, and emails flowed from Japan to Binfield. Jennifer wanted her friends to know what she and Viv were planning. She hoped to arrange a visit to meet up with Ryuu and Atsuko in Tokyo; they were going to hibernate there during the winter season, and Jen wanted to take Viv to meet them – it was to be a surprise Christmas present. Luke would not be leaving for Queensland until the end of October, so there would be plenty of time to catch up with him as they left Wales – he said they could always sleep at his if the weather worsened and he had parking out back for Fuscia. Dom and Bella hadn't ripped each other apart on their first meeting so hopefully they would manage to remain cordial towards each other on a second visit. And so it was that, on a promising sunny morning in late August, Viv, Dom and Jennifer left for the Cotswolds. Poor Fuscia was fit to bursting, the women always joked about how much stuff they felt they couldn't be without when they packed to leave and how much they never touched when they were away..... pants and tops were washed out each evening, make-up totally forgotten; although hats, suntan lotion and moisture cream were absolute essentials!

The first part of the journey, along the M4, was old hat to them now, but when they took off through the Cotswolds the little stone villages were spell-binding. They had to keep stopping to have cream teas, buying pots of jam and cakes they really didn't need – or rather, their hips didn't need! It was just as well that a set of bathroom scales was not part of their luggage. Mind you, they also did a lot of walking and hill climbing so the extra calories were accounted for. Keeping in touch by mobile phone proved a bit difficult at times, reception was intermittent, but they became dab hands at tracking down free wifi, usually available in a cafe or library in the larger villages; and so they managed to send updates and photos of their journey to friends and family.

As planned, they crossed the River Severn, north-east of Gloucester, at the beginning of September; the weather was still mild and it was raining... they'd expected nothing less and had come prepared. Dom objected to his blue rain coat but Viv insisted – it saved a lot of wet dog smell inside Fuscia. They were a walking rainbow together; Dom in his bright blue coat, Viv in her pink boots and matching cagoule with red tendrils escaping and Jennifer in green boots and purple cagoule – just to look at them brought a smile to people's faces. And there was always a smile back.

Viv's red hair (she owned it was now the bottled version) and Jennifer's peppered blonde curls turned many an eye as they trundled through the small villages in Fuscia, decked in her pink and purple finery. The women had added pink, purple and white flowers to the dashboard along with an array of small toning cuddly toys they found in the various charity shops they checked out on their travels.

They could now set up camp in 30 minutes (under 20 minutes if they didn't bother with the canopy). Domino, to give him his full name, was also a seasoned traveller these days; he knew to stay close to his owner and her pitch, and his natural protective instinct made him a great pitch dog, he always let them know when their space was invaded; the two women felt quite safe under his supervision. He loved to sit up front, in between them, when they drove along; as far as he was concerned, he was top dog of all he surveyed, size was irrelevant. Jennifer loved him as much as Viv and Dom loved her in return.

They continued driving along the A40 until they reached Ross on Wye.

'Oh, I came here as a young teenager on a school trip' exclaimed Viv. 'At that time I was in love with Gareth, a boy in my year but in a different class. He kept looking at me at school discos but that was as far as it went; he looked at me, I dreamt of him. Wasn't love simple in those days?' It was a rhetorical question which was just as well, as Jennifer had no idea how to respond.

On the surface the Brecon Beacons reminded Jennifer of the Green Mountains, south of Brisbane, inland from the Gold Coast, where there was a wealth of rainforests and national parks, equally green to the eye. Obviously the Brecons were on a smaller scale but she was used to that now, everything in Britain was diminutive but beautiful nonetheless. They were heading for a lakeside campsite near Llangorse and hoped to use it as their base to explore the walks, woodland, medieval castles and caves. They were assured there were caves that even beginners could manage – another of life's little adventures that Viv fancied trying. Jennifer was all for staying above ground, especially after what she'd seen in the caverns and crates her parents had been forced to occupy, but she would do it – face her fears and all that. She had even agreed to visit Seirian's Well, about a half hour drive to the south – which was to be their last port of call before leaving Wales and heading through Bristol to Newquay - to meet up with Luke. They would probably stop a couple of nights en route to take in the scenery and local ambience. This trip they thought they would try to collect a selection of cheeses to take back to Patricia and Edward, each a reminder of where they'd visited –the extra pounds they were both carrying would be reminder enough to them of the fine fare they were currently enjoying.

The campsite was perfect, set in a glade between emerald hills decked with purple and pink heather, it offered a clean and well maintained toilet block; the two friends always checked the facilities out first; it was a good indication as to whether they should stay a second night or not. There was also a campsite store and small club house. That evening, after they'd set up, they sat under their canopy and ate quiche with a fresh salad accompanied by a glass of slim-line tonic and followed by fresh fruit and cheese. They'd discovered that drinking slim-line with a slice of lemon looked identical to a sophisticated G&T but kept them sober and, at the same, time lessened the amount of calories they consumed. Also they frequently planned to drive the next day so it paid to keep a clear head. Jennifer had never been a heavy drinker but she knew many who were. Viv had not quite taken the temperance vow but, having observed what scrapes drinking had led her into over the years, was determined to limit her intake quite significantly. She was all for growing old disgracefully but wanted to enjoy her entertainment - not be it for others.

All too quickly it was time to pack up and journey south. There was Seirian Well to visit ... it was on the outskirts of a town of the same name and approached via a brick built shaft and stairwell ... Viv assured Jennifer it was really quite innocuous and it might well be a disappointment. Inwardly Viv had dreams of being a writer and wondered if she could use Jennifer's story linked to the other thermal springs they'd visited to pull together a novel. It was just a thought at this stage but the more thermal geysers and springs she visited the more her imagination fired up. Jen didn't need to fire her imagination – she needed to subdue her memories and stop anticipating the worst – the return of the aliens, in her life time.

They opted for the scenic route, going off piste, as far as their satnav was concerned! There was little sign of civilisation and it felt disconcertingly more remote than it looked on the map. Some of the roads were extremely narrow; thank goodness they'd opted for a small VW Transporter and not a wider 'van. The hills rolled down and under them, then up and over them. Fuscia could have been mobile heather against the backdrop. By mid-day they were almost at their destination and decided to pull over for a cuppa and light lunch before they went exploring. They stopped off at a village about 2 miles from the Well. All seemed normal there. Jennifer was doing her best to keep a lid on her anxiety.

An hour later they were at Seirian Well.

'You know Seirian means sparkling in Welsh' said Viv. 'I looked it up.'

'No I didn't' responded Jen. The tension in her voice was not lost on Viv.

They got out of Fuscia and walked towards the entrance. Dom was agitated, staying close to heel and whimpering. Jennifer's senses were on high alert; she wished she had Atsuko and Ryuu here with her. Then she laughed to herself, it was just her imagination over-reacting - Dom was playing a silly game to get even more attention. By now Viv was cooing over him as she tickled behind his ears.

'I think I'll leave him in Fuscia. I've never asked him to go underground before and it might be a step too far for him.'

Viv left the windows open slightly and locked their camper; she didn't usually bother thought Jennifer, maybe Dom's unease was rubbing off on both of them. They put on their head torches. Viv had the tourist leaflet about the Well; Jennifer felt for the mace spray in her jacket pocket. It was the first time she'd thought about it on a trip, bought at Edward's insistence. Her phone showed no bars, there was no reception here. She wished she could be like Dom and avoid this subterranean tour. Viv headed towards the flint encased portal.

Seirian Well was derelict. There had once been a swimming pool there, built by locals for locals and filled from the naturally warm spring water. That was during the 60s, it was now a concrete slab dotted with weeds, puddles and moss. The actual opening to the Well was blocked with a chain and sign saying 'Danger – crumbling brickwork'. Alongside the entrance was another sign, promoting a regeneration project to revive Seirian Well as a spa resort. Wales was struggling economically and tourism was a growth industry, a natural spa pool and resort would appeal to tourists as well as provide employment and a leisure resource for surrounding villages. This seemed a great idea; it was on the river Taff which meandered through some spectacular woodland and green fields, before reaching buzzing Cardiff and melding into the now freshwater Cardiff Bay; salt water kept at bay by three locks.

'The Spring water is generally 21-22 degrees and past drainage problems have been sorted - all it needs now is the Council's motivation and money. Nothing new there then!' exclaimed Viv as she read out loud from the tourist leaflet and notes.

'The limestone strata blocks the water's decent to greater depths yet ensures it is deep enough to be warmed by the earth's core, before being sent back to the surface. A neat trick huh?'

Jennifer laughter was more relaxed this time – this was nothing like the caverns and sea entrance on the island – it would be of no interest to the Invaders.

Viv climbed over the chain blocking the entrance and started to descend the man-made steps beckoning to Jen to follow. Their head torches revealing the old brickwork; their hand torches highlighting the steps as they tentatively lowered each foot, ever downwards.

'What's that funny vibration I'm feeling?' asked Viv.

'I expect it's the trains at the railway station in the village' commented Jennifer, 'Noise seems to travel as vibration underground.' It sounded convincing.

They continued to edge into the depths, the daylight above receding into a faint blur.

'I think that's far enough' called Jennifer, bringing up the rear. 'Drop a coin and see how long it takes to plop.'

Viv hunted in her jacket pocket for a 2p – she wasn't going to throw a pound away! She let it slip from her fingers and made a wish.

'Plink.'

'It plinked' she observed – 'shouldn't it have plopped?'

'I don't like this,' murmured Jennifer, her voice low with fear.

'Let's go back to the top – I want to consider our options.'

'Hold on – let me try once more – I might have just hit an old piece of metal that kids have thrown down, or something like that, you know what I mean.'

'Hmmm ... go on then. Here, take this pebble, save your pennies.' Jennifer tried to make light of the situation but her heart was sinking to her stomach, the old fear and nausea rising.

A duller plonk this time - but definitely a plonk not a plop.

'Come on, let's get help.'

'There's probably a simple explanation.'

'We ... we shouldn't even be down here.'

'Don't be such a wuss and Miss Goody Two Shoes' laughed Viv. 'They rely on people like you and me to let them know what's going on – if anything's wrong.'

The two friends got back to the surface and drove into the village. Both lost in their own thoughts. Dom lay down between them keeping a low profile. Viv drove and Jennifer found herself stroking Dom, more for her own comfort than for his. They stopped at the Post Office and asked where the Council Offices were. It appeared the Community Council had no fixed abode in this village but was based in Cardiff. Meetings were held around the area at different venues each month so as many of the surrounding villagers as possible had the opportunity to attend. The Postmaster suggested they used the email link available free of charge from the computer in the library. So off they went to the library, parking first in the small car park next to the local store. By now they were starting to question their own senses and instincts and wondered if they'd imagined plonks rather than plops.

Once in the library Viv emailed the Community Council and Jennifer emailed Luke and Tokyo. They opted to stay in a B & B in the village that night – they wanted company and to be able to check for a response from the Council first think in the morning. Dom was content to sleep in the camper, he and Fuscia were good friends. After a look-see outing around the village and his customary evening meal Viv tucked him down with plenty of water and bedding. Both women enjoyed a hot shower and home-made chestnut pie provided by their hosts. They needed an early night - although their busy brains kept sleep at bay for some time.

The next morning the Council responded they intended to reply to emails within 3 working days!

'They've got to be joking!' squealed Viv. 'What if it's an emergency?'

The librarian on duty looked at them; she rose from her seat and walked over to their position at the computer.

'If you have an emergency I suggest you call the Police' she soberly advised.

She hadn't known what to make of these two women when they'd called in late yesterday afternoon but now sensed trouble was brewing.

'Oh no, sorry for my friend, she gets a little excited at times.' Jennifer was keen to make amends, not so Viv.

'We think there's strange goings on at Seirian Well' she spoke loudly. Viv wasn't shy in coming forward and she wasn't about to be intimidated by a woman of her own age and stature with a Welsh accent.

'Oh,' the librarian took a step back. 'Well, in that case you had better contact the Seirian Well Regeneration Society – their key man is Peter Lewis. Hold on I'll get his number for you.'

Viv grinned and poked her tongue out at Jen. Jennifer gave her the thumbs up and nodded 'well done'.

Then her phone rang. They both jumped - obviously there was an intermittent connection in this area. She whizzed outside to take the call. It was Luke, a really unexpected and welcome surprise. Her nausea abated for a few seconds - a different kind of nerves taking over.

'Hi Luke – this is a pleasant surprise! What can I do you for?'

'Hi Jen, I've been thinking about your last email and I'm intrigued – maybe I should pop over and help you girls out?'

Jennifer could hardly believe the girlish trill she heard coming from her own mouth 'You're asking for a wallop' she bantered, not wanting to own her fear.

'No, seriously, I am both intrigued and concerned. My marine background and muscle might be of some use to you.'

Jennifer couldn't resist – she felt oddly comforted.

'That would be great Luke – we're a bit out of our depth if the truth be known.'

And then, not knowing what possessed her, she blurted out, 'I'm shit scared and Viv's a bit tally-ho!' Then her good humour won out, 'She's building up a terrific relationship with the local librarian.' Jennifer was in teenage mode again.

By the time Viv came to join her, with the phone number and address of the guy leading the drive for regeneration of Seirian Well, she'd arranged to meet up with Luke on Monday. He was going to come up when the store was closed, just 2 days away. He would drive up early morning and be with them by 9.30.

Viv raised her eyebrows.

This was a new development – she'd picked up on a vibe between these two and anticipated a relationship at some point in the future but the heat had just jumped up a couple of notches, and all in the space of 5 minutes; interesting. Luke was blatantly concerned for Jen's safety and she very obviously wanted him there with her. The shop was always closed on Mondays but he was going to close through 'til Wednesday so he could join them. They needed to book him a room at the B&B.

Chapter 13 – The Welsh Adventure

New Friends & Lost Friends

Viv rang Peter Lewis and arranged to meet up the following day, Sunday, for tea and a chat. He turned out to be an ex hippy - without the pony tail - now living in his home town and passionate about good use of natural energy and resources. Peter believed that the government should work for the greater good and he just knew that regeneration of Seirian Well would have a positive impact on his community. Unemployment was high and there was little money to invest in social enterprise but he had a feeling, that, with an initial leg up from the council, a pool and spa at the Well could be self-funding and provide much needed local jobs. Unfortunately he was struggling to produce a business plan; not quite his forte. Jennifer made a note to put him in touch with Ryuu and Edward when this was over. Ryuu was a star with business plans and Edward had all the right connections to get funding for seemingly impossible projects.

They agreed to meet up the following day, Monday, at 10 o'clock, in the car park; they would all travel together to the Well. Peter didn't believe in taking two vehicles when one would do! The women smiled, he was quite a character, and they liked him. All being well they would have time to meet and greet Luke before whisking him off to Seirian Well with them. That would mean squeezing five into Fuscia, as Dom would not be want to be left out, so the women spent the rest of the day giving their camper a bit of a spring clean; taking as much out of her as possible, storing it in their bedroom in the B&B; making sure there was extra space for both men and their gear. They did manage to squeeze in a walk through the nature park for Dom's benefit. In reality their thoughts were elsewhere but Dom enjoyed it - although he complained about being on the lead. He couldn't see what was wrong with a bit of squirrel and rabbit hunting.

'If only he'd just walk at heel it wouldn't be a problem, but when he gets the scent of game he's off – he's male – he has a one track mind and cannot multi-task!'

'Don't let Peter or Luke here you say that' chuckled Jennifer, 'Definitely girls' only humour!'

They were eating in their camper this evening.... a last supper so to speak. They both sensed their holiday would change from tomorrow morning but didn't yet know in what way. They'd parked up at a well-known beauty spot to walk Dom, eat and watch the sun go down.

'Stir fry okay for dinner tonight?' checked Jennifer.

'Wonderful – chickpea and bean shoots?'

'Mais naturellement – the finest tins the supermarket had to offer.'

The women were in good spirits, they enjoyed their repast washed down with faux G&T.

'Fit for a King ... or Queen even' stated a replenished Viv raising her glass.

'Cooking on a boat is like camping on water – I've been apprenticed from a very young age to the finest chefs.' Jennifer smiled fondly at her memories of deliveries on the Hope & Charity.

Dom whined for his share, he didn't like to be left out, even if there was no meat involved.

They slept easier that night but woke early. It was a new morn and dawned a new episode in the lives.

Jennifer showered and tidied their room whilst Viv walked Dom. They both needed time to themselves each day and this morning routine worked for them. If they'd been in Fuscia Jen would have been washing up the breakfast things but as they were extremely well fed and catered for by their hosts that wasn't necessary, so tidying the bedroom and showering was a good alternative. Jennifer was grateful for the time to compose herself before meeting Luke. By 9.15 she'd receive a message, he was in the village, in the car park, where were they? Jennifer waved out their window, almost opposite the car park; Viv and Dom caught sight of him at the same time on their way back from their walk.

Hugs and kisses on cheeks were exchanged between Luke and both women. Dom was picked up and tickled. Viv noticed Luke stroked Jen's arms when he greeted her, she envied her friend.

Peter was there early as well; introductions made, the men shook hands and seemed to approve of each other. In the end they opted to take 2 vehicles. Luke had brought some underwater and climbing equipment that might be useful and Peter had his own climbing kit, torches and maps. Luke felt his 4x4 might prove useful and suggested Jennifer travel with him; she could make sure he didn't get lost and fill him in on the rest of the background info as they travelled. Viv smiled inwardly at this proposal and turned to Peter.

'Is your wife interested in the regeneration project?'

'Never had one .... who'd put up with me?'

Jennifer glanced at her friend, who looked wide-eyed and innocent back. Luke winked.

Viv made out to blank them; she was looking forward to the pleasure of Peter Lewis' company as she drove Fuscia to the Well. They led the way, Luke and Jennifer followed behind in his Range Rover. Dom was a little taken back at this stranger in Jen's seat but he soon succumbed to the mellow lilt of Peter's voice and even sat on his lap in order to see the landscape better! Viv almost envied her dog.... what fun!

'Ok, now for the descent – I have a pocket full of essential scientific equipment – pebbles – plus a plumb line and search light.'

'I've brought my diving gear and a blow torch, just in case we need it ...as well as a marine search light and additional climbing gear.'

'And we have our head torches and hand torches' volunteered Viv.

'So we're all prepared and ready to go, I'll lead the way, you girls bring up the rear – or rather ladies – no – women I mean', Peter's attempts to be politically correct were wavering.

Jennifer was happy to go last. As it was, Viv followed Peter and she followed Luke – his presence reassured her. She found herself mesmerised by the back of his head -...the soft curl of hair on his neck and the width of his shoulders ... then she almost tripped and was brought back to reality.

'Put your hands on my shoulders if it helps' offered Luke.

'I'm okay at the mo but will soon grab you if I feel I'm going to fall.' Jennifer knew the tremor in her knees was not because of fear of falling ... or of the unknown ... she knew only too well what could lie before them.

Their descent was a lot different this time – the searchlight lit up the walls as though it was daylight. Peter provided a running commentary as to the history of the place – he was very well informed. When they first entered the Well the brickwork was weathered and covered in algae but the further they moved away from the daylight so the algae lessened... eventually all they could see was brickwork, showing signs of wear and tear from water erosion where it wasn't always beneath the water level.

'Okay, we should be able to see the water from here. It's been quite dry of late but it never goes much lower than this.'

Peter shone the light to where he expected the water to be – it was and it wasn't. A little water was visible around the edges of a reflective shiny surface. Without the reflection of the light you would have mistaken it for brickwork and water, it mirrored its surroundings so efficiently.

'Hmmm, that's odd. The last time I came down here this cavern was a lot smaller; now it seems to extend in all directions and this object is nestling in its bowels.'

A perplexed Peter was shining his searchlight all around the area shaking his head and ducking down to look into the cavern above the object.

'It's a good job you're fit and slim' observed Viv. Her voice just above a whisper.

Luke turned to look at Jennifer. Her fingers were gripping hard into his shoulders. He had to prise them out of his flesh in order to take her hands in his as he faced her. She was motionless and grey.

'Are you two okay? I want to take Jen back up top – I'll be back down as soon as.... don't go anywhere without me ... I'll bring my diving gear when I return.' Luke's words were matter of fact, there was no emotion shown until he focused on Jennifer.

'Don't worry Jen, I'm here, I won't let anything happen to you ..... shhh ....' he kissed her forehead then rubbed her back and shoulders as he gently turned her round to steer her up the steps; all the time prompting her to lift her feet and keep going. It was a slow ascent. Jennifer was compliant in a robot-like way. By the time they reached the entrance she was shaking. Luke was really worried about her. She was in shock; he needed to get help.

'Yo!'

Luke had been totally absorbed in his task of helping Jen and hadn't noticed they were not alone.

There, by his car, stood a tall, lean American, totally incongruous in a suit and tie. Surrounding him were British soldiers, including a senior Officer going by the pips on the shoulder of his combat uniform. Two of the soldiers, guns at the ready, were checking over the camper, looking underneath with the aid of a mirror and taking photos.

'Can I help you?' It sounded pathetic, even to him, and he said it!

'I think you'll find we're here to help you. Captain James Elliott,' he extended his hand, 'and Agent Chris Savage, assigned to NASA USA.'

Luke held out his right hand while Jen still clung on to his left one; he noticed her grip was not quite so feverish.

'You must be Jennifer Dean.' Captain Elliott had taken in the situation. Almost imperceptibly he summoned a soldier. 'Sergeant Jones will you please take care of Miss Dean, I think she's had a bit of a shock.'

Sergeant Emma Jones wrapped Jennifer in a baco-foil blanket before presenting her with a hot sweet drink.

'How did you know we were here?'

'I told them' interrupted Agent Savage. 'We had an urgent call from Tokyo. Apparently Miss Dean emailed her friends, Ryuu and Atsuko, about her concerns as to what was at the bottom of this well. As soon as we got the word from our Japanese counterparts we contacted the British Military and hot-footed it over here.'

'Glad you did but can't stop to chat. I've left Viv & Peter down there, so need to get back.'

'Leave that to us, it's what we're here for.'

'I've got diving gear in my car – we might need it.'

'Why don't you go and help Sergeant Jones with Miss Dean and we'll go down below to your friends. Perhaps you and Miss Dean could fill in Agent Savage on the details of what you've seen so far.'

'Call me Chris – now let's go and see if your lady is recovering – something must have traumatised her down there.'

These men were good, they knew their stuff. Luke walked away from the entrance to the Well with Chris Savage as Captain Elliott directed his team.

The soldiers went in two by two, until eight of them were making their way down to the cavern. The rest were setting up field headquarters, listening on the radio to their colleagues' feedback. They had reached the last visible step, the cavern was full of water. There was no sign of anything metal, or Peter, or Viv but they did find a small hand torch, still on and shining towards the water.

This information was not shared immediately with Luke and Jennifer.

Jennifer had found her voice once more; garbled words were rushing out.

'It's them again. It's just like the film. It's the pod .... the Invader's pod..... we must stop them .... before they take the children.' She gasped for breath.

'Don't fret, everything is under control. Ryuu and Atsuko have helped from as far away as Japan. They called the American and Japanese authorities and, would you believe it, we now have the British Army here to help us.' Luke attempted a grin. 'Why didn't we think of that?'

'We weren't sure.' Jennifer cupped a mug of hot chocolate between her palms. She had stopped shaking and was now thinking aloud. 'Where's Viv ... and Peter?'

'The soldiers have gone to get them. They should be surfacing any time now.'

As Luke said these reassuring words to Jen he registered that actually they were a bit on the slow side to return. He tried not to let his imagination run away with him.

'Finish your chocolate and I'll go check where they are.'

He found Captain Elliott. There was a tension in his shoulders that hadn't been there earlier. Something was wrong.

'I thought our friends would be up by now,' commented Luke.

'So did I - but we can't find them, nor your metal object.'

'What? Oh my God! We need to suss out that cavern and where it goes. I'll get my gear.'

'Mr Osborne, Luke, please leave it to us, we're the professionals.'

'But you do believe us don't you? Here, I took a photo on my mobile.'

Luke pulled his cell phone from his pocket and scrolled to the photo. At first glance it looked as though he'd photographed brickwork but he knew otherwise and could see the tell-tale signs of the water marks around the edges and the reflection of the torchlight.

'That could be a big help. Private Adams – Mr Osborne has a picture for Reconnaissance to examine… Is Miss Dean ready to talk to us now?'

Captain Elliott directed Luke towards Private Adams as he walked towards Sergeant Jones and Jennifer. Luke was torn, he wanted to help the army find Viv and

Peter but he was extremely concerned about Jen's health; he wasn't totally convinced that the aliens had returned but he certainly felt a chill wind when he saw the pod in the cavern. He was already referring to it as 'the pod'. He'd seen the pictures on Wikipedia when he googled the Island Invasion after that special evening with Jen and Viv and what they'd seen down below was very similar. No wonder Jen was terrified - it was her childhood nightmare all over again. Luke quickly text his photo across to the number Sergeant Adams gave him and talked him through the water margins. Fortunately Viv and Peter had turned round as he took it so there was a portrait of them as well. As he recalled the moment he took the photo was a split second before Jen gouged his shoulders. He left the soldier and headed towards Jen.

Her eyes were searching for him, a weak smile greeted him.

'It's started again – we've lost Viv and Peter', a sob escaped her lips as she spoke these words.

'Don't worry, I'm sure we'll find them soon,' James Elliott had broken the news and tried to comfort Jennifer.

'You don't know them, the Invaders, they're ruthless; they see us as nothing more than animal fodder. We need Ryuu and Atsuko here. I know they're older but they're the only people able to tune in to the aliens ... they can swim, hear and sense things that other humans can't ... we need them here to help us – now!'

'Yes, we've already thought of that and your friends should be leaving Tokyo within the next 24 hours. In fact they were quite insistent they came to help us.'

Jennifer's smile was genuine this time; she could just imagine her two old friends asserting their views and capability to help. She tried not to think of what was happening to Viv and Peter .... she just hoped they would be in time to save them.

In the background Captain Elliott was communicating with his senior officers – this was serious. Analysis of the photo taken by Luke Osborne confirmed there had been an unusual object in the cavern, one that didn't conform to any form of submarine or drilling rig that he'd ever seen, and certainly nothing you'd expect to see in this part of the country. They needed to check with their computer records. Contrary to public perception the military had not forgotten about the Island Invasion 60 years ago, all available information and DNA had been extensively examined and re-examined as scientific research improved. However, whilst they could determine the possible weak spots of these alien creatures they could not determine what their pod was made of and how to disable it, or where these Invaders came from. Scientists, ever watchful for unknown space ships, had satellites scanning the Earth's skies, but nothing untoward had been reported in recent years, just a piece of meteorite from a falling comet which, luckily, fell into the sea, causing little damage to the environment and disappeared into the deep. Agent Savage was desperately trying to call his superiors, despite all the scientific progress made, his connection with the outside world was frustratingly intermittent in these hills.

As Jennifer recovered here senses she felt a bit of a fool; fancy reacting like that; and she, a grown woman. What would Skip and Grandma say? Actually, she knew exactly what they'd say. They'd tell her not to be so hard on herself; she had seen and heard things beyond most people's comprehension at such an early age that it was bound to have an impact on her. And it certainly was. First she'd lost her parents and now she'd lost her best friend, Viv, to the aliens. But this time she was big enough to fight back – and she would. Jennifer dug deep into her psyche and inherent resilience. Tomorrow she would get involved with the search - but not today, today her arms and legs refused to work.

Luke took Jen and Dom back to the B&B. He ensured their bookings were okay for another week and, after walking and feeding Dom, made to settle him down in his car for the night but Dom wasn't having any of it. He had slept in Fuscia because it smelt of Viv and her possessions but Luke's 4x4 didn't feel like home at all. Jennifer spoke with the landlady, who was somewhat curious as to where Viv had gone but, without giving too much away, Jennifer said that Viv was unexpectedly called away and that Dom was pining for her, so could he sleep in their bedroom until she returned. She promised he wouldn't cause any damage. The arrangement was cemented with the exchange of a £20 note.

Jennifer was as grateful for Dom's company as he was of hers. She made his bed up on the floor near to her but woke during the night to find him snoring in her ear – she hadn't the heart to tell him off. These were unprecedented circumstances. At least they weren't as alone as they had been on the island ... thanks to Atsuko and Ryuu they had the support of the army and the intelligence services. Captain Elliott seemed to know what he was doing and had an awful lot of resources at this command ... or so it seemed to Jennifer as she drifted into sleep. Utterly exhausted she slept solidly for three hours but then the old nightmares started to trouble her. That's when she discovered Dom sharing her bed ... she smiled ... he was not quite Big Ted but he was the perfect salve to her childhood fears. Six o'clock the next morning found the two of them up and out the door ready for a head-clearing walk and they were not alone, there was Luke, waiting at the garden gate.

With butterfly breath Jennifer smiled 'Good Morning' just as Dom launched himself at the back of Luke's legs.

'And a good morning to you Dom, and to you Jen,' Luke reach out to pull Jen to him and peck both cheeks. 'You're looking a better colour than you were last night, did you sleep okay?'

'Well enough. I was going to give Dom a walk before breakfast and aim to get back to the Well for 7am, how does that suit you?'

'Ideal. I wanted to get back there as soon as possible too but didn't want to wake you; I figured you needed your sleep after yesterday's emotional upheaval.'

'Yes, sorry about that, hopefully I'm back on track now.'

'Nothing to be sorry about, just take it easy and don't push yourself too hard; I doubt if we will be able to do much anyway, especially as the army are on the scene.'

'I wonder when Ryuu and Atsuko will get here? I'm so looking forward to seeing them... but wish it was in different circumstances. I'm assuming there's no news about Viv and Peter?'

'None that I know of ... we'll find out more when we get back to the Well. C'mon Dom – walkies!'

The three of them walked along the river's edge in silence. Jennifer watched her thoughts creating stories despite her trying to focus on the morning birdsong; Luke watched Jen's face for signs of strain or shock; Dom sniffed the verge as a matter of habit but at the same time kept one ear cocked for his owner.

Luke ate a Full English, Jen couldn't stomach much more than porridge and toast, Dom helped Luke with the bacon rind and a piece of sausage he said he couldn't manage. As planned, they were at Seirian Well for 7.

Chris Savage and James Elliott were already on site; they'd slept the night in the mobile field quarters and looked surprisingly fresh. They had men posted in the Well all night, along with the latest sound and vibration detectors able to pick up and record any movement underground. There was little news. No, Luke and Jennifer could not go back down the Well; they were directed to keep well clear of the entrance; frustrating, yet understandable for the anxious pair. After about an hour of hanging around they opted to go for a walk, to skirt the parameter of the site. They hadn't intended to do anything 'naughty' but Dom took off into some scrubland after a squirrel and they followed. By the time they found him they were about a mile from the incident headquarters, up a hill overlooking the verdant valley that led to Seirian Well and the village beyond.

As usual, Dom's attempt at squirrel chasing had proved futile but his attention was now drawn to a rabbit hole. He wouldn't leave it alone and was excitedly digging and yapping in turn. Jennifer grabbed him by the collar and whisked him up into her arms, shushing him and telling him that was enough. Luke looked at the enlarged hole Dom had created. His attention was caught by what appeared to be a flicker of light. No, it must have been his imagination. Dom was twisting and yapping in Jennifer's arms, desperate to get back to his digging.

'What's that?' exclaimed Jen, 'I thought I saw a light.'

'So did I.' Luke's voice was now a whisper and his hand signalled Jen to keep her voice down. Dom got the message as well.

Three pairs of eyes watched and three pairs of ears listened intently. For a brief second they heard it, a whirr, like a giant fan going around slowly – then it stopped.

'Did you hear that?' Luke asked Jen.

'Yes, and so did Dom, look at his ears ... and nose.'

Dom's head was tilted at an angle; one ear was stood up high and both it and his nose were pointing in the direction of a huge oak tree.

'I think we should get help' said Jen.

'You go and I'll stay here so we don't miss anything.'

'No way - I'm not risking losing you as well as Viv.' The words were out before she had time to think about them.

'That's nice to hear... but one of us has to go for help and I'm certainly not leaving you hear alone.'

'Then we'll stay together. It might well be nothing. Let's stay here for a while and see what happens ... if we hear anything else or see another light.'

'Are you sure? I don't want you to end up like you were yesterday.'

'I'm sure. I'm over that initial shock – it was the sight of the pod that did it – it was... it was just as if I was a little girl again ... but I'm not, and this is a totally different scenario. I can cope. Honest.'

Luke wasn't keen but there wasn't much else he could do, he didn't want to leave their location just yet ... he had a feeling there was more going on here than they could imagine.

Dom was becoming agitated again.

'Put him down – let's see where he goes,' said Luke.

Jennifer hesitated but after a particularly sharp jerk from Dom had no choice; he leapt from her arms and frisked off towards the oak tree, circling it and jumping up at the branches and trunk.

'It must be hundreds of years old' said Jen, 'its trunk is so wide .... and look at how gnarled the bark is – it's as though it's covered in warts and carbuncles.'

Suddenly Jen stopped in her tracks and pointed. Luke eyes narrowed and focused directly ahead. There definitely was light coming from within the trunk, a soft muted wash of the palest blue hue. It looked as if the sky on a hazy summer's day had been trapped inside and was trying to escape through the hollowed heart of this ancient oak.

'Do you know that fungi - virtually as old as the oak itself – will have eaten away at the dead wood over the years, leaving the living wood to support the life of the oak and its inhabitants?'

'Well it's definitely supporting some very odd inhabitants at the moment. Can you hear that buzzing?'

They walked around the trunk to the source of the sound and peered into an opening where once a branch had been – a split second later they pulled back.

'Hornets,' Luke stated the obvious.

'The Elders used hornets to chase away the aliens when they invaded the Island – this is creepy.'

By now Dom has turned his attention to the plaited roots beneath the canopy. The ground was soft and his snout was covered in soil, his eyes screwed up tight against the onslaught as his front paws tore at the spot he determined had to be exposed.

And there it was again, the same defused blue glimmer. Jennifer and Luke watched, spellbound, as Dom exposed more and more of the void beneath the oak. This was not a natural cavity; he was uncovering a machine made grotto illuminated by thousands upon thousands of glow-worms.

'They're using insects and worms again,' whispered Jennifer in a tremulous voice.

'We don't know that for sure,' Luke reasoned. 'We really must get help now. Come on, put Dom on the lead, we'll go back together – I can't imagine this not being here when we get back.'

And so they left. Walking as briskly as possible back to Seirian Well and Captain Elliott. Luke held Jen's left hand, her right hand held Dom's lead; the blood pumped fast through their veins. Both bodies in flight or fight mode.

Hunters & Hunted

Ryuu and Atusuko were met at Heathrow Airport by Agent Savage. They were disappointed, somehow they had expected to see Agent Gordon Wade; they forgot he would be retired by now. When Ryuu had rung the emergency number he had for the US Intelligence Service he'd asked for Gordon ... but was directed to a female agent who managed incoming calls from dormant entities. He gave his name and immediately his details were on the computer screen in front of Agent Malinowski. He explained his concerns over an email he'd received from a friend in Wales, Great Britain and when he elaborated that his friend was the only surviving toddler from the Island Invasion Jennifer's details were pulled up on screen as well

- as were Atsuko's. Whilst listening to Ryuu Agent Malinowski was multi-tasking ... she alerted her superior to the call and put it on broadcast. Naturally it was automatically recorded. By the time the call with Ryuu ended at least another half dozen agents were examining the files and recordings of the call and past interviews. This was categorised as a phase 4 priority; phase 10 being the lowest.

USIS rang its Australian and Japanese counterparts. After a brief on-line conference it was decided the UK Intelligence Service would need to be brought up to speed and that USIS should get a representative over there immediately. The Japanese would arrange to transport Ryuu and Atsuko to the UK within 3 days and the Australians would research the background of Luke Osborne. They would leave MI5 and MI6 to investigate the background of the British citizens involved and also to check out the site in Wales. The Yanks would be there but would remain in the background at this stage.

'Hiya. Hope your flight was okay?' drawled Agent Savage as he held out his hand, 'call me Chris.'

'Hi' a simultaneous response from Ryuu and his Aunt. Ryuu bowed over the agent's hand as he clasped it, next to him Aunt Atsuko gave the traditional Japanese greeting.

Chris smiled, a broad inviting smile, he was well-practiced at putting people at their ease.

'Have they found anything yet?' Ryuu's voice was clipped and to the point, he was accustomed to the direct American approach so didn't bother with the polite formalities of his culture.

'Nothing yet, as far as I know, but let's get to the site and we'll find out for ourselves.' Agent Savage's arm was outstretched directing them towards a waiting limo.

'I was hoping to see Jennifer's English home in happier times' mumbled Atsuko who hadn't slept well since Ryuu replayed the voicemail he'd received from Jennifer. Memories of the sounds and smells of those times were coming back to haunt her. She wondered if Ess was still alive ... they had no idea of the aliens' ages or life-spans; only of their eating and sporting habits.

'We're going across London to the City Airport and then on to Cardiff by helicopter.'

'How long will that take?' Ryuu was anxious to find out for himself if the Invaders were back; he also wanted to ensure Jenny was safe and sound. He had grown quite attached to their friendship; bonded through a shared history.

'I can never get used to this driving on the wrong side' commented Chris Savage as he instinctively ducked away from the oncoming traffic – and he wasn't even behind the wheel!

'It's certainly not what we're used to' Ryuu kept his response neutral. He was still coming to terms with the speed with which they'd arrived in England and the reason for their visit. What would the Invaders find of interest here? A self-perpetuating food and worker chain?

'I googled Wales and Seirian's Well before leaving Tokyo. Doesn't seem to have a lot to offer except spa water; rolling hills with sheep and dis-used coal mines. Oh, and wet weather.'

Ryuu felt Atsuko shudder next to him – he reached out to hold her hand – it felt cold and fragile beneath his. He knew reassurance was impossible ... they felt the same fear.

'My aunt could do with a rest and warm drink.'

'Hopefully we can grab one at the airport before our chopper leaves.' Chris Savage couldn't afford to be too sentimental over these seventy year olds; he had a job to do and so did they.

Fortunately the septuagenarians were still on the ball and quite alert. They climbed into the back of the Eurocopter and put on their ear muffs. Atsuko was grateful for the short comfort break they'd been allowed in the waiting area. For her and Ryuu, with their expanded hearing capabilities the flight could prove excruciating, even with ear protectors. They both had ear plugs and muffs. They sat back to endure the 3 hour flight.

'I can't believe you can't bloody find it – what about heat detection? Vibration? There's got to be some way of tracking it down.' Chris concluded the British Army was ill-equipped for a task such as this. Sending men in two by two was like something from Noah's Ark rather than modern day search and find methods.

'Okay, I hear you. The fabric of the hillside is difficult to negotiate. Yea, I've heard of the Aberfan Disaster – loads of kids died in a colliery slip didn't they? Nope, never heard of the Neath Disturbance but I'll look it up. Okay, okay, didn't I say I heard ya'll ... you know what you're doing, it's your goddam country ... I was just sayin' that we would have got in there by now with some tunnelling equipment.' Chris Savage was both exasperated and frustrated when he snapped shut his cell phone ....but managed to present a smiling demeanour as he rounded the corner to escort Ryuu and Atsuko onto the helicopter. They half grimaced back and followed with their hand luggage.

Chris Savage had not realised his discreet mobile phone conversation could be heard through solid walls by this pair. They now knew of Viv and Peter's disappearance and that the metal object at the bottom of the well had also vanished.

The hour drive from Cardiff to the Well site was a lot quieter and slower ... there was no option in the winding Welsh hillsides. Agent Savage drummed his fingers on his knees, Atsuko glanced at Ryuu and then to the scene beyond the Range Rover's windows.... green, hilly and isolated .... with ample tree and shrub cover ... not quite their Japanese island, but ...., his body language told her he was thinking along the same lines. He squeezed her hand and took in a deep breath, as did she. Chris Savage looked at them in the rear view mirror, 'damn the inscrutable Japanese – he wished he knew what they were thinking'. Patience was not a virtue of his, action and getting things done were his forte. It was his turn to breathe deeply and remember his training.

'Alright in the back their folks? We'll be on site in 20 minutes and I've booked you into a quaint Welsh pub for the next few nights, B&B they call it here. It's near where your friend is staying.' He noted the flicker in their eyes at this last sentence.

'That's excellent news,' responded Ryuu. 'It will be good to spend time together, once we have been to the Well and seen if we can be of any help.'

'I kinda' expect everything to be under control when we get there' were the words he said out loud. He tried to sound relaxed and confident in this new partnership with the British Officer and his troops. 'Ya never know, the Brits might have found the missing couple and the metal object turns out to be an old tin bath - and we could all be on a wild goose chase' were the words he said to himself.

'We've got to see him.'

'Please let us through.'

Their loud pleas reached the ears of their prey. Captain James Elliott walked across to the sentry and nodded him to admit the couple into the inner sanctum of the military incident unit.

'Hello again, what can I do for you?' He extended his hand to the doorway of the mobile unit.

'We think we've found them,' blurted Jennifer 'up the hill and in a tree'; she was quite breathless but determined to get her words out.

'Whoa, take your time. Sergeant, please bring us 3 teas; do either of you take sugar? No, I seem to recall you didn't from yesterday.'

Luke sat next to Jennifer with his arm touching hers; Dom drank water from the bowl the Sergeant produced for him.

'We were going for a walk across the hill, aiming to take a back route round to overlook the Well as we weren't allowed on site today,' explained Luke.

'Incident units are generally not the best place for civilians,' James Elliott observed, almost apologetically.

'Anyway, we let Dom off the lead and he was busy snuffling around when he started digging and yapping at the base of this really wide, old Oak.'

'Yes ... and when we approached it we could see a soft blue light coming out of knots and gapping roots.' Jennifer had recovered her breath; she was not as fit as Luke and Dom and had struggled to keep up as they half run and half trotted back, but she had not given in and here they were now, trying to convince Captain Elliott that they had seen what they'd seen and were not pranksters.

'Here, I took another photo on my mobile phone,' Luke offered his phone across to the Captain. 'I know it's a bit fuzzy but you can just make out the faint blue glow against the bark of the tree, it was coming from inside and when we looked between the roots there were thousands of glow-worms.' He swiped his finger across the screen to reveal the second shot.

'You're a pretty smart scout, wasn't it your last photo that got us here?' James Elliott smiled with his lips but his eyes were elsewhere. These were sobering pictures.

'Can we borrow your phone while we download these for interrogation?' It was hardly a polite request. His hand was already passing the phone to Sergeant Jones to deal with.

'Could you take us back there? Can you remember the way?'

'I'm sure we can – especially with Dom to help us.' Jennifer gently stroked the hound on his head. He was now sitting by her feet looking inquisitively from face to face... it was as if he sensed something was about to happen.

'Okay, take a couple of minutes to finish your drinks and I'll get some men together.'

'I suggest you bring climbing equipment' prompted Luke, 'and diving gear.' He so wanted to get his from the car but knew he wouldn't be allowed to join them.

In less than 2 minutes Captain Elliott was back with half a dozen soldiers plus climbing, diving, photography and GPS equipment. And a whole lot of other bits and pieces that neither Luke nor Jennifer had ever heard of.

'Here's your phone, we've downloaded the pictures and the co-ordinates of where they were taken, so let's go.'

Jennifer's eyes were wide open, how could they do that? She looked at Luke, he shrugged his shoulders and reached out for her hand for the return trek. Dom obediently fell into step next to them.

It was an uphill climb back and their legs were starting to feel the pace as they tramped through woodland.

'There it is!' Jennifer pointed and tried not to yell with delight, her voice reduced to a stagecraft whisper.

A soldier's arm came out across her and signalled them to keep quiet and stand still. Luke and Jennifer obliged but Dom was pulling at his lead in a very excited and determined way. His head yanked through his collar and he was off!

The soldier gave chase and caught up with him as he dug, yet again, at the base of the Oak. Flat on the ground, peering over dog's head the soldier signalled to his colleagues. Yes, there was something, they would need climbing gear to get down.

'Oh, I so hope they're down there and okay.' Jennifer gripped Luke's hand tighter.

They watched the soldiers lower themselves down into the abyss beneath the ancient oak. One of them had Dom under his arm, on a makeshift lead.

'It looks as though Dom's in the Army now.' Luke tried to lighten the moment. 'He should be able to find his mistress ... if anyone can.'

They watched the soldiers' progress on the field camera screen set up in front of Captain Elliott. The view below was amazing... the glow-worms throbbed out light as soon as the soldiers' torches moved on.

'It reminds me of a film I once saw, where the aliens tried to communicate by sound and light.'

'These aliens use insects as tools to carry out their gruesome exploits'. Jennifer's voice was harder; the little girl gone, the mature woman taking hold again. 'I hope they know what they're doing down there.'

'Down there' they were following Dom's nose. The abyss seemed to be the pivotal point for at least a half dozen caverns leading off. A single soldier stayed within the base of the tree sending pictures and readings back to the Captain, the others tracked Dom.

The route he chose was dark and damp. They needed their head torches. At times they had to get on their bellies to go deep into the earth's bowels. Not a word was spoken. The men gave their full attention to the task in hand - on high alert for an attack or any sound in the sightless black around them. Above ground Jennifer and Luke held their breath, the screen taking them every step of the treacherous journey. They could hear the men below breathing, the silence around them surreal. They couldn't understand why the troop were in single file until a soldier's foot dislodged a pebble and there, lit by torchlight, was a mesmerising ripple of water, six inches from the next man's shoulders.

'Surely they can't be there.' What Jennifer didn't add was 'alive' but that's what she thought.

Luke watched in controlled immobility, as if any movement from him could trigger a catastrophe.

Captain Elliott quietly and confidently gave orders, for more men and equipment to be sent to the site and for the men below to continue to follow Dom. He peered intently at every picture, questioning if there were any untoward odours or vibrations - nothing - just the expected dampness and smell of minerals in the soil and rock, spiders' webs along the walls and flat worms every now and then. The underground water was surprisingly warm, similar to that at Seirian's Well. And there was still sufficient air to breathe.

Then they smelt it, bat guano; the inhaled ammonia fumes brought tears to the soldiers' eyes and they gripped their lips together to prevent themselves from coughing or retching. Multi-purpose balaclavas were quickly pulled up over their noses.

'Surely not ....' Jennifer didn't finish her sentence; she felt Luke grip her arm. Captain James Elliott shifted his weight, all eyes were on the screen.

'They're entering a large cavern.'

'Look at the floor. .. Look at the ceiling... Look at the walls... What's on that ledge?' James directed the soldier with the camera. The soldier zoomed in.

'I think it's them. Don't look,' Luke turned Jennifer's head into his shoulder, fearing the worst. She was gently sobbing but turned her head back, intent on witnessing the scene.

'uh huh, u huh....' it was a pitiful sound, but it came from the ledge.

Two soldiers, the best climbers, were edging their way up the ragged wall, with pitons and rope and other equipment that seemed to miraculously appear from their rucksacks. What seemed an age was probably less than five minutes.

'They're alive.'

'In poor condition but alive.'

The onlookers heard gagging as a trickle of water was put into their friends' mouths. They had been lying with their faces to the wall trying to keep away from the edge. Their bodies were cocooned and held fast in what looked like neoprene straight-jackets. Their rescuers left them like this for the decent, lowering them as gently as possible the thirty or so feet to the ground.

It was Peter and Viv. Weak legs refusing to support them when they were released from their bonds, their enlarged irises sensitive to even defused light.

'I feel I should say, what took you so long, or some such crass phrase ... but all I can think of is thank God you found us. Thank you ....Thank you...'

'That's Viv, I can hear her,' Jennifer was beaming.

'How long have we been here? They jumped us from nowhere ... we just didn't see them coming.' Peter was trying to explain their capture.

'Hold that thought until we get you out of here .... we'll want to know the ins and outs of everything when we get you up top,' the Sergeant in charge didn't want to be hanging around longer than necessary, especially as he now had two civilians to protect and get back for interrogation.

He gave the signal for the two climbers to go further up.

'There must be a way out further up, the bats would not come in the way we have.'

'Here Sarge!'

'There's a light at the end of this tunnel – looks like daylight,' as he said it the soldier ducked his head, a bat flew over him to settle on the ceiling with its brethren.

'We have your co-ordinates and will meet you from above. Can you get the couple up there?' James question brought a smile to the soldiers' faces and a thumbs up. They went about their business silently and efficiently.... completing the installation of ropes and pulleys to winch their human cargo to safety.

The civilian onlookers above watched the screen in awe. Despite the stench and dark working conditions these soldiers performed a miracle and Viv and Peter were brought back up the wall to a tunnel above and then led into daylight, with sunglasses over their eyes.

'It was like that for Ryuu and his fellow survivors' commented Jennifer. 'They had to have sunglasses to cope with daylight when they were rescued. And it's not exactly sunny weather.'

'No, I don't remember it starting, but I can feel the drizzle now you mention the weather. Here...' Luke wrapped his jacket around Jen as he looked for hers; dropped earlier in their haste to get back to the incident unit with news of their find.

'Oh, poor Dom,' Jen chuckled lightly 'his pride is hurt.'

Dom was being winched up the wall stuffed into a soldier's rucksack. He had greeted his owner so enthusiastically that she had yelped in pain as he jumped up catching her with flailing claws. Nonetheless, she had given him a cuddle and reassured him he was a good boy. His tail expressed his excitement and approval of the required response. Now his ears were compressed against his head which he was trying to hide in the soldier's backpack.

'I think he's probably scared and confused. But he'll be fine once he's back up top with Viv.' Luke's observation was pretty accurate.

'Can we go and meet them?' asked Jen.

'Not at this stage ... but you can meet them back at the Incident Unit. I don't want any of you near where we need to be working ... and we need to get DNA samples from them first.'

From this Luke and Jen correctly assumed that Captain Elliott expected to continue the search for the aliens.

'We have them.' Viv and Peter were back on the surface with medics on hand to assist and get them back to the Incident Unit.

'You go back, Jen; I'll stay here and see what evolves.'

'Sorry Sir, we can't have you remaining here, you will need to go back with the lady.' Captain Elliott had slipped away and his second in command was politely aiming them both in the direction of the prescribed Unit. They undertook the walk down the hill with renewed optimism.

'About time, that's great news.' Chris Savage was as complimentary as his disposition and training determined.

'Our ETA is 16:30 at the Unit but I think our guests will need to sleep before they can help us, if indeed, they can help us at all.' Ever the sceptic, Chris was a professional Loner; experience had taught him to trust no-one, least of all those who promised the most. The Japanese pair were difficult to read but he could see their tiredness and understood it. They had been travelling for nearly 24 hours and that would knock him out let alone someone 40 years older.

'Fine, but we're moving their accommodation - in fact we now have 6 civilians to house, oh, and a dog.'

'So what's occurring? What's the solution?'

'We've found a holiday home, away from the village and nosey landladies and neighbours.'

'Sensible ... how many men will there be on watch?'

'Two on the outside and one on the inside ... you.' A small smile of pleasure broke the intensity of James Elliott's face. 'I thought you'd be the best man to keep an eye on them, you might pick up information that has been overlooked to date. They might tell you something they thought was of no importance but, with your training, you'll recognise if it is.'

He could sense the stiffness and resistance in Agent Savage ... but ever the professional his response was affirmative.

James was pleased with himself; that would keep Chris Savage out of their hair whilst his troop got on with the task of hunting down whatever it was that had taken and cocooned the civilians. He understood the agent's angst but didn't appreciate his underlying criticism.

'They looked like birdmen, like the ones Jennifer talked about.' Viv was shaking now. Her initial elation at being found had given way to the shock and horror of what they'd been through; replaced by thoughts of what could have happened, or, indeed, might yet happen.

'One of them kept shouting Succo, Succo at us. Sounded a bit French to me so I told him we didn't have any sugar ... but not sure he understood.' Peter was slightly less shaky but still very pale.

They were both wrapped in survival foil blankets and fed recovery rations; sweet and nutritious, but hard to get down when your gut is in turmoil.

'We were stood on the steps, Peter was in front and I was looking over his shoulder.'

'Yes, we were peering into the darkness, trying to make out if the Well led anywhere.'

'Then I dropped my torch and, when you turned around to help me look for it, they sprung from nowhere!'

'Not quite nowhere – I think they came from the water – I seem to remember hearing a splash - as though something was breaking the surface.'

'And there was wet, I vaguely remember wet hands on me ... then I was out for the count.'

'It was as if they prodded us with something and then - nothing.'

'I can't believe my brain has no recall ... I've always prided myself on my memory.'

'Maybe a truth serum?' Viv was now letting her imagination run riot.

'Well, thanks for all this.' James Elliott nodded to the Sergeant. 'I think we'll carry on this conversation in the morning, when you've had time to rest. The Sergeant ..... here will take you to your accommodation – we've organised clean clothes, toiletries and food to tide you over.

'Oh, aren't I going back to my room with Jen?' Viv was disappointed, she was looking forward to seeing her friend again, 'and what about Dom?'

'They'll be going with you. You two, Luke, Jennifer, Ryuu, Atsuko and Agent Savage. Sergeant Jones and another soldier will be outside all night so you have no need to worry. We will get your belongings from your B&B tomorrow. Peter, do you have a key hidden outside your house or will we need to break in to get whatever you need?'

'Oh no, no need for that, Jill at no 34 has a spare key.' He looked at Viv. 'She often takes in parcels for me and does some cleaning when I need help.'

Viv nodded her understanding and acceptance of the arrangement. Not that it was anything to do with her really but she welcomed his explanation.

'Ruu and Asko are funny names, not sure I'll be able to get my head or tongue around them.' Viv was back in good humour. 'I remember Jennifer talking about them, they're very close friends of hers from Japan; they both survived the invasion of their island, like she did.'

'I think the names are Ryuu and Atsuko, not wishing to be pedantic, but it's only polite to get someone's name right.'

'Ree you, Ree you, Ree you; At sooco, At sooco, At sooco; howzat?'

'What did you say?' asked James Elliott.

'Oh nothing, just practicing the Japanese names, not used to them and don't want to get it wrong.' Viv was embarrassed.

'No, I realise that, say it again, just as you did.'

Viv repeated her exaggerated version of the names.

'Oh, I get it, Succo, was not sugar, it was Sooco, Atsuko.' Peter was pleased with himself.

Captain Elliott inclined his head, 'it might well be.

'An Enforced Holiday

The cottage was delightful; it was a perfect holiday retreat set at the end of a long drive hidden behind lush woodland yet with its own secluded lawned garden. Dom was in his element. Jennifer half heartedly acknowledged the beauty of the place but her mind was elsewhere ... how was Viv? And what about Ryuu and Aunt Atsuko?   It was such a long way for them to travel – how would they cope? She was struggling with her fears and memories, her mind taking her ahead to untold unfolding stories ... it must be the same for them.

'Why don't you choose a bed and have a lie down? I'll bring you a hot drink up – what would you like?' Luke could feel her distress and apprehension, even he was anxious about what else could happen and he hadn't been there ... the first time ... he was trying to imagine what it must be like for those who were.

'Go on, I'll be up in 5 minutes to tuck you in,' he smiled. 'Look there's hot chocolate sachets here, fancy one of these?'

Jennifer appreciated his efforts and was sorry she couldn't be more affable. 'That would be lovely .... it's surprising how exhausting - emotionally and physically - all this is. I didn't realise I was so weak.'

'Not weak at all, you've done amazingly well but best to rest when the body demands it.... off you go,' his hands stroked her arms as he bent to kiss the tip of her nose before turning her around and pointing her in the direction of the stairs.

It was amazing how efficient the security services could be ... all their stuff was there, hers and Viv's, in a twin-bedded room with Dom's bed to one side. It felt wonderful to come out of a hot shower, sink deep under the duvet and make out it was all a dream and that Viv was in the bathroom and would be curled up in the bed next to her when she woke.

A cup of cold chocolate stood on the bedside table, the curtains were drawn, she was sure it was dark outside.

'Quiet Dom, you'll wake the other guests.'

Then realisation dawned ... this was not their B&B; there were no other guests. What was Dom barking at? Her stomach turned as her memory kicked in.

Tap tap; 'are you awake?' A head peered round the door.

'Dom!' cooing and giggling filled the air. It was Viv giving Dom as good as she got.

Jennifer sat up in bed, amazed, grinning from ear to ear; tears trickling down her cheeks; her hand came up to cuff her nose .... Luke's hand appeared with a tissue.

'Oh, just look at me ... utterly undone... Viv. I'm so glad to see you ... I thought... well you know what I thought ... '

'Give us a hug you big soppy ... it will take more than a couple of birdmen to put me down.'

Which wasn't quite true but Viv wanted to reassure herself, as much as her friend ,that she had survived the experience of being trussed up and suspended on a ledge in a lightless cavern for hours on end.

'They've given Peter and I the once over and we're both A1, or at least, as A1 as we ever were.' Gentle laughter broke the tension. 'How are you? Luke said he'd sent you to bed and you were asleep before he even brought you a hot chocolate – that's not like you ... to miss hot chocolate.'

'All the better for seeing ... and hearing you. Looks as though Dom is ecstatic as well. I know when I'm second best ...' Jennifer chuckled as she looked at Dom's eyes doting on his mistress. 'You know he led us to you - don't you?'

'Clever dog – when this is all over I'll treat you to a steak! Told you he was a great companion didn't I? A bit noisy at times but infinitely less troublesome than a man.' Viv winked as she let out this quip. 'Present company excepted.'

This made Jennifer realise she was propped up in bed, sporting tousled hair and a black camisole, with Luke, Peter, Viv and Dom's eyes on her.

'Well, if you would all leave me for a few minutes I'll make myself presentable and join you downstairs. What time is it?'

'Just after midnight, I wouldn't bother too much, I expect we'll all be needing our beauty sleep soon – but let's catch up over a cuppa in the kitchen first – after Peter and I have had a chance to take a shower and change into our own clothes. The Army took our rags and gave us these beautiful khaki tracksuits.' Viv gave a twirl. 'Not sure if they have a best side or will catch on but at least they're clean.'

he men left the women to it, chuckling with relief as they went.

'Seriously, how are you?' Luke asked Peter.

'Physically, remarkably well, considering; mentally, a bit shook up. It's not every day one is captured by aliens; rescued by the Army and debriefed by the Intelligence Services. It will be good to talk with normal people.' Peter smiled and shook his head. 'That Viv sure is a bit more than normal; amazing woman, don't know how she's managing to bounce back so quickly.'

'They're both special ladies. Unfortunately this is not over yet so we may all need to dig a little deeper. It's good to have friends you can rely on.' Luke put his arm around Peter's shoulder just as the front door opened again. They looked at each other and headed for the stairs.

Private Adams and Agent Chris Savage were escorting two elderly people through the porch into the lounge; each carried a small overnight bag. Their body language spelt out their weariness.

'Hello, you must be Aunt Atsuko and Ryuu,' Peter extended his hand; Luke's followed.

'You look all in; can I get you a drink and something to eat?' Luke felt for these older guests.

Peter took their coats and bags and beckoned them to sit down. 'The girls will be down in a minute.'

'Jennifer will be so happy to see you' chimed in Luke.

Then they both stopped as Agent Savage held up his hand. 'They had a light snack about 8ish and probably need rest and sleep above anything ... no doubt you will all have lots to talk about. We don't want to stop you chatting but do need to know of anything you remember that might help us ... so I'm going to stay with you.'

'We understand ... do you want a drink or anything? Is yours the locked room over there?' Luke pointed to a door leading off to one side. He'd checked out all the other rooms whilst Jen was sleeping ... there were 4 bedrooms upstairs, 2 twin-bedded rooms with en-suites and 2 single rooms sharing another bathroom. His and Peter's gear had been placed in the other twin room so he assumed the single rooms were for Ryuu and his Aunt. The ground floor accommodation provided a spacious, beamed lounge straight off the porch with access to a large family kitchen/breakfast room, utility room, loo and conservatory. He'd wondered what was behind the locked door and thought it must have been a dining room cum study.

'Yeah, I'll be down here all night, in case you need me. Don't worry about me, I'll keep a pot of coffee on the go and sort myself out. If you need anything in particular that we've overlooked, just let me or Private Adams know and we'll do our best to get it for you. Any medication? Specific dietary requirements?'

'Thanks, we'll let you know.'

Throughout this exchange Atusko and Ryuu remained quiet, taking in their surroundings and the men. Atsuko used her eyes, Ryuu his entire body and sonar. They got the measure of Agent Savage on their journey but Luke and Peter were new to them - although it appeared their own names and history preceded them.

All eyes focused on the latest arrivals.

'A cup of coffee would be most welcome, thank you for asking.' Ryuu's voice was clear and precise, with an American burr.

Luke kicked himself for forgetting they'd both lived in the States for some time.

'Coffee coming up' he sung out as he headed for the kitchen.

'A weak tea for me,' Atsuko's voice followed him, 'black, please'.

His mind actively considered whether to let Jenny know her Japanese friends had arrived. Too late, he could hear footsteps on the corridor approaching the stairs. He was going to need lots of mugs.

He returned to the lounge a few minutes later to find Jenny sitting on the sofa between Aunt Atsuko and Ryuu chatting in a mixture of English and Japanese. Agent Savage hovered in the background listening intently. Viv curled in an armchair with Dom on her lap and Peter sat on the arm next to them... listening to the chatter with his hand resting lightly on her shoulder.

As soon as he saw Luke he cleared a space on the coffee table for the tray.

'Don't know how you all take it so I've brought in milk, sugar, hot water and chocolate digestives.' Luke was pleased with his tray of goodies and 8 mugs of coffee; he'd even remembered the soldiers outside. He delicately handed Atsuko a floral tea cup and saucer he'd located in the kitchen.

'It's so lovely to see you again ... just so awful about the circumstances.'

'We feel the same way. Ryuu and I have been meaning to come to your homeland for many years and never quite made it ... how are your friends, we understand you were captured by the Invaders?' Atsuko looked at Viv & Peter.

'Fortunately we're both in one piece, thanks to Dom.' Viv tickled the ear Dom pricked up at the mention of his name. 'He looks very smug with himself – and rightly so.'

'It was really odd. One minute we were talking on the steps in the Well, deciding whether to stay there or go back up.'

'Yes, I remember shining the torch along the cavern and seeing black water. You said it would probably take Luke a while to get his diving gear and, when I turned round to speak to you ...'

'Yes, I dropped my torch and needed help to find it; then there was a little splash and I looked up into bulging eyes – then everything went blank.'

'Before we could do anything they prodded us with something and then – nothing; until we came to in that blue underground room.'

'I was shit scared I can tell you.' Viv nodded her apologies to the Elders present. 'The lights kept moving ... and then I realised they were worms.' Viv shuddered. 'We were tied up with our hands behind our backs and feet in front of us.'

'Yes, they sat us up against a wall, which felt muddy and damp, and the scruffy looking one, with dull feathers and only one eye, kept coming up and poking us and saying 'Succo'. I thought he was asking for sugar, in French, and kept telling him we didn't have any.'

Aunt Atsuko gave a sharp intake of breath but didn't interrupt. Chris Savage barely moved but his eyes focused on her.

'Then we heard a dog bark and I called out for help.'

'And that was it again. Another prod and we woke up cocooned in some kind of wetsuit type webbing on that ledge.' Peter grimaced. 'The smell was disgusting.'

'You can say that again.'

'Disgusting…. it took a while for my eyes to adjust to the darkness and they kept watering … but when I realised our predicament I whispered to Viv to keep very still and not jiggle about.'

'I'm glad you did. I was about to crawl, caterpillar style, to find a way out. I didn't know you were behind me.' Another shudder swept through Viv. 'I don't want to think what might have happened.'

'Instead you lay there, in front of me, trying to wiggle your fingers free.'

'Without success – my next thought was I might be able to turn over – without knocking you off the ledge,' Viv patted Peter's hand which was now on his knee.

'I'm glad to hear it – and then what?'

'Not sure, I wondered if I could bite you free – not bite YOU but bite and tear the webbing.'

'Your mind amazes me.' Peter turned to face their audience. 'Then we heard Dom barking below and soldiers telling him to be quiet.

'We tried to call out and realised our mouths were so dry we could hardly make a sound; it was more of a groan, quite ghoulish in fact.'

'I licked some moisture off the rock in front and tried again.'

'But it was enough, and here we are.' Peter squeezed Viv's hand.

'It was awful having to leave the army to it' said Jennifer. 'I forgot how resourceful they are - on the island we had no help - except ourselves - until Skip arrived.'

'What was really interesting is that when we were being de-briefed we realised Succo might have been Atsuko.' Peter's eyes turned to the Japanese woman.

'I can't believe it ... but from your description it could be Ess, the Invader who befriended me; although he had two eyes.'

'He only befriended you because he wanted you for himself.' Ryuu's comment was clipped. 'Did they wear masks?'

'Do you really think it could be him Aunt Atsuko? Would he come back to find you?', Jennifer asked.

'I'm sure I'm not the reason the aliens have returned but Ess might ask for me, especially if he doesn't realise that humans do not automatically know all other humans.'

'Yes, they wore black masks.'

'I wonder what happened to his eye?'

'I wonder if the army has tracked them down yet?' Ryuu was not inclined to consider the lives and well-being of the Invaders.

'I expect we'll hear soon enough, in the meantime I think our visitors need to rest. Let's get to bed and resume this discussion over breakfast.'

'Good idea, Luke - I'll cook us eggs and bacon in the morning and we'll be able to think more clearly then.' Jennifer was concerned for her old friends and could see Agent Savage itching to hear more. She had a feeling their input would be required early the next day.

Jennifer helped Aunt Atsuko upstairs to her room. The others followed behind. Luke carried the tray of dirty mugs to the kitchen. He didn't rush clearing up and slowly loaded the dishwasher ... he needed thinking time. What did the aliens want this visit? Could Aunt Atsuko and Ryuu be the key? Were they really too old to be involved? He removed his shoes and trod silently up the stairs, turning off lights as he went, leaving just the landing light on in case anyone needed to come down before daylight.... this was an unknown property to all of them. Then he saw Jennifer's head pop round her door.

'Couldn't go to bed without saying Goodnight - and thank you for all your help today.' She lent up to kiss his cheek. Luke turned his head slightly and caught her lips. The kiss was fleeting but the embrace was longer. No words were necessary ... they both slept better that night.

The smell of bacon wafted through the cottage. Pots of tea and coffee were in the middle of the table, along with a jug of fruit juice.

Jennifer and Viv had enjoyed preparing breakfast together. There was brown and white toast, butter, marmalade, jam and even vegemite! Where the intelligence services had found that she didn't know but Jennifer knew it would be a treat for Luke, as well as her. She had a quiet chat with Ryuu when he came down and was re-assured. He and Aunt Atsuko were bearing up to the travelling although they were both very concerned about the future of the human race. Ryuu thought that maybe their super senses might help locate the Invaders' base but it would depend on how many of them there were what could be done to stop them. He'd seen the film of Ian Campbell's attack over and over again and doubted the same thing would work a second time - however he did think that the aliens' seeming co-dependency on insects might be used against them somehow – he just couldn't think of a way, yet.

'Eggs, bacon, tomatoes, mushrooms and toast, a veritable feast' Peter announced. 'I might use this hotel another time.' He glanced behind him to Agent Savage, 'When life is less stressful.'

'That's putting it lightly,' stated Viv, munching through toast and marmalade.

'This is a very good breakfast Jennifer,' pronounced Aunt Atsuko, 'not what we're used to but very nice nonetheless. Have we heard anything?' She too glanced at Agent Savage.

'Nothing yet and we weren't allowed to walk Dom far this morning, just around the perimeter of the garden.' Jennifer looked in Chris Savage's direction.

He could no longer ignore they're eyes. He'd taken up the offer of a bacon butty and was eating it stood by the door.

'There's no news,' he stated. 'So far the UK authorities have been unable to find any further trace of the aliens. There are divers exploring all the underground caverns but, as you probably know, there are miles of them in this area, some explored and some unexplored, and many quite perilous to navigate.'

'I think you may need our help.' Ryuu's words were softly yet firmly spoken. 'Atsuko and I might be a little slower these days but we are fit and healthy and have the benefit of experience on our side. Not only do we know what these creatures look and sound like but we also have a sixth sense that helps us tune in to their movements and, in case you've forgotten, our underwater swimming abilities are not impeded by diving equipment.'

'I'll let me superiors know of your kind offer,' was all that Agent Savage said as he disappeared into his room.

'Are you sure, Ryuu? It could be dangerous.' Jennifer was anxious for her old friends.

'I'm sure it will be dangerous,' came Ryuu's response, 'but we didn't come all this way to watch from the sidelines as the Earth is about to be ransacked ... again.'

Aunt Atsuko nodded her agreement. 'If Ess is asking for me we might be able to tempt him out of cover. He might sense me calling his name - if we were underground and within his hearing distance. Plus we know what to expect and we would know they were approaching long before they were close enough to prod us ... or the soldiers.'

'Yes, we could be a great asset to the armed forces.'

'But what could the army do against birdmen with superior powers and knowledge and equipment?' asked Viv.

'Use insects.' Ryuu stopped there as Chris Savage returned.

'Carry on, please' he beckoned Ryuu. 'In what way could we use insects?'

'We're not sure yet but wonder if butterflies might be a way to distract their attention and perhaps caterpillars could be used to poison them? We know they eat, as well as use, grubs and bugs. It's only an idea at this stage ... it needs exploring and re-fining.'

'It sure does', chortled Chris Savage. Convinced these elderly Japanese pair were bonkers and wondering how he could explain their suggestion to his superiors without being considered doolally himself.

'When I lived in America I remember being warned that the Puss Caterpillar AND the Saddleback Caterpillar are extremely noxious; kids were told to leave them alone as their bristles could sting and cause not only a rash but nausea, shock and breathing problems. The birdmen,' Ryuu nodded in Viv's direction as he used this term, 'may not have come across them yet and not realise the risk. If they were debilitated by caterpillar stings then maybe the Armed Forces could capture them.'

'And what would the butterflies do?' Agent Savage was still sceptical.

'I recall they are drawn to bright colours and are fascinated by flying creatures. They left the birds alone on the island although inadvertently decimated them by taking the insects and grains they lived on.' Atsuko came into the conversation. 'It might be we can't get butterflies to fly underground, if that's where they are, but if they were in another root cavern, like the one you described,' she looked at Peter and Viv, 'then maybe we could distract them. Maybe we couldn't do both things at the same time, or wouldn't need to, these are just ideas. A modern day version of Ian Campbell's successful defence, he came at them from more than one angle, not knowing which might work.'

'Yes, and he drove them away and kept them away for over 50 years.' Everyone around the table nodded at Ryuu's statement.

'Okay, okay, I'll talk to them at Incident HQ and see what their response is.' Agent Savage was googling poisonous caterpillars as he spoke ... there may be an inkling of savvy in this idea.

Chapter 14 - kaRRak

1953 -The Home-coming

The pOd travelled on; oblivious to the disaster unfolding within. Wil succumbed to his infection, deteriorating by the hour. Ess and Gar kept the craft on track to the satellite Aphid. Docking was relatively simple but explaining the condition of their fellow citiXens was a little more difficult. CoMMunication with kaRRak had to bounce through space off a vast aPHidLink ... it was slow and disjointed. When they did get through they had to repeat themselves. It seemed incredulous to the home-based knowAlls that a stinging insect had brought such devastation to the miSSion. Ess and Gar took travelPips and retired to padded nestBoxes for the remainder of the journey home but first Ess had to stupORize Wil - if he was to have a chance to survive the journey. The toXin was shutting down his airways, muscles and memory. Ess was sorely tempted to lessen the dose but Gar was watching him. There would be no hero's welcome awaiting them on their return.

When they arrived on kaRRak, before they were allowed to disembark and enter the citiCApsule the sanitation sKWad pulsed the entire pOd to kill any germs or bacteria. The mediCs were then allowed to go on board and had to apply around the clock administrations to save the uneXpired crew. In the end there were only four of them: Will, Fee, Gar and Ess. They were supposed to have brought back fresh blood for breeding stock and alternative foDDer sources, instead they reminded the dwindling population of its vulnerability; perceived superior brains and skills were not invincible.

The three manOids in the isoblution unit miraculously survived. They'd escaped contamination from the insects and spray but not starvation. They were emaciated and very weak, lying unconscious on their mats amidst sewage and bile.

The medic knowAlls managed to identify the venom that caused the damage to their citiXens' respiratory systems and produced an antidote; too late for Fee's miSSion but it would be on board all other eXploratory units. There was even a pre-miSSion inoculationPip made available that, whilst causing feather loss as a short term side effect, gave 90% immunisation to the user.

Ess was at a loss; Fee and Will had been given permission to breed as soon as possible - it was felt their off-spring might have a degree of immunity to pass on to future generations. He was alone and missed the richness in life he had felt around Atsuko; his daily interactions with her, their time away from the pOd; simple things that filled a void in his life. He tried all sorts of distractions and even became more outgoing for a while. He joined an eXtremeKlub and, not caring whether he lived or died, he took part in some waCKy esKapades; catapulting gorges;

tight-rope walking across moving glaciers and bouncing on a giant band from a space platform. That last activity cost him an eye; a blood vessel burst – a messy and painful business.

Whatever he did there was no female citiXen prepared to consider him a breedinPartner. In fact the more eXtreme his activities the further away they backed. Why couldn't they understand he was trying to show he was as good as any other citiXen - despite his odDBrew qualities. He even paid for a weekly preening session to compensate for his inadequacy in that department.

CitiXens were kept alive for 130 suNRings and he had 91 to go. He needed a mate, a fRend, a purpose to life.

The sKWark went out there was to be another blueWorldeXploration. It was almost 60 suNRings since the last trip. The knowAlls boasted they could equip future miSSions with eXcellent resources to deal with blueWorldeOids and any toxic indigenous species. Ess volunteered his services. Fee and Will did not ... but their sonSson, Wil Jnr, was desperate to follow their example and volunteered to be the junior crew member in the communications unit. Because of his experience and maturity, Ess was allowed to make the trip as adVisor to the pOd's coMMondant - Mol, a fully fledged space eXplorer and transport teCHno. Each citiXen enlisting for the trip was given a Pop that enabled them to understand basic Japanese; kaRRak knowAlls had yet to realise that the blueWorld, was full of people who spoke different languages. The crew chose whether to take the inoculationPip - or not. Ess chose to; Wil was young and vain, the thought of feather loss put him off - despite his breeDers' pleading. Approximately 40% of the crew felt they were as invincible as Wil Jnr and declined the Pip.

The three manOids brought back from the first expedition were aghast to find they survived the eXperience. They had been left to fend for themselves in the isoblution unit without food or fresh water whilst the alien crew battled with their own debilitating health issues. After two weeks in the unit the prisoners shredded the skin on their fingers trying to break down the wall where the feeding tube protruded – congealed blood darkened the area and bore witness to their desperation. They were reduced to drinking their own urine and chewed on a leather belt. When the pOd reached kaRRak they were unceremoniously rolled into transportation nets, without barbs, and winched to the knowAlls' labs. There they received sufficient mediCare to enable them to live but, oh, it was a miserable existence. They were kept in a sterile labCell under constant watch with camRas recording their every move. They were regularly milked in order that their sperm could be extracted for breedinPurposes. When their sperm count dropped and they could no longer be used for breedin their brains and bodies were utilised to eXplore what it took to cause pain and pleasure in 'Oids. The knowAlls saw nothing untoward with eXploiting manOids in such a way; as far as they were concerned they had a duty to find out how lesser beings worked and how they could be programmed and improved to kaRRak dWellers advantage.

The condemned men's lives as labRats were torturous with no privacy and no control; it was a living hell and they yearned for death; they became consumed with the idea of committing Seppuku and were determined to outwit their captors. They were never given cutlery or access to sharp instruments. They lived in a labCell without windows or door handles; in all their time with the aliens they never saw the outside world or knew anything about their captors' environment. They practiced meditation to remain sane, a daily event that became a quirky curiosity to the knowAlls who monitored the manOids' physiology before, after and during their sits.

'See, see this,' the knowAll chuckled as he called his colleagues to the screen. 'ManOids odd, odd. Get odder, odder. Surprise, surprise.'

'Yo. New to me, me too. What do? What do?' The questioner was twisting his neck trying to see what was happening on the screen.

'nYa, nYa sure. Norm sit, sit on floor. Sing, sing Omm. Feels warm. nYa, nYa this. Faces down, down. Long, long time. Hold, hold, hands.'

The two observation knowAlls looked at the screen for about fifty wingBeats, waiting for something to happen.

'Fingers loose, loose!'

'Asleep? Asleep?

'nYa, nYa! nYa right, nYa right .... nYa life, nYa life.'

Swivelling eyes finally remembered to focus on the auto-stats graph. There were no respiratory emissions.

'FlyinLocusts! Bad, bad. Still have eGGlings. Need check, check bio connections.

'Bring eGGlings in, in. See if react, react.'

'Yo, yo, later. First see, see. What stop breathing, breathing.

And so the three men put an end to their misery. They suffocated; heads down in their sanBags, side by side, holding hands, each determined not to panic and give up. They never got to see their eGGlings, the confused bi-products of cross insemination between a variety of eggs and their sperm. Germination and gestation taking place under the clinical eye of the breedin knowAlls. EGGlings were viewed as the flotsam from essential experiments in the process of finding the ultimate workAid; a worKaid that would follow the aliens' directions and undertake menial tasks, a worKaid that was mindless yet knew everything, a biddable, living, breathing computer on legs.

Mankind and all sentient beings were to be the tools of kaRRak citiXens; as far as citiXens were concerned other beings were less gifted than them and therefore of less value, with minimal feelings and needs. Whether equipped to provide labour, foDDer or amusement, all creatures were only useful if they served a purpose. The dWellers had no conscience, no remorse, for them there was nothing wrong in their actions. They were tampering with nature in order to better production and outcome; to ensure their continued eXistence. They had the intelligence and thought processes to accomplish such things so therefore they were doing no more than expected of their ilk.

The goal of the next eXpedition to the blueWorld was to obtain more specimens, not only of manOids but also of other land, air and water creatures. The pOd was equipped with vast storageCells, stacked one above the other. The specimens were to be cocooned in a life-sustaining weB that held them in suspended animation until they were required for eXperimentation.

The information gained from earlier miSSions had been put to good use and this latest venture was prograMMed to succeed.

Chapter 15 - 2012

Another Re-union

Ess's hearing had not improved with age and he refused to get help for it; neither had his temperament but he was now far more astute and knew how to manipulate his fellow citiXens whilst not showing his distain; to use their greed to his advantage. He'd persuaded them to let him come on this trip because of his eXperience and knowledge of where the best specimens could be found. In actual fact he longed to find Succo. Over the years his memory had played tricks on him and he was now convinced that she truly cared for him and would be eagerly awaiting his return. No female citiXen had ever responded to him as she did - she was in tune with him - and he with her.

The pOd had landed in the blueWater, as before, where it nestled at the cusp of the Eurasian Tectonic Plate for some time whilst knowAlls took readings and aquatic samples. It then followed the sea bed until it could break through into caverns and infiltrate the manOids' land. This time the break through point was South Wales, not an island of Japan.

As far as the miSSion coMMondant was concerned all manOids looked the same and she was very happy when they came across the manOid and femanOid just above the water line. They had stored them temporarily in a worMRoom but the femanOid kept crying out and trying to escape so they had weBBed them both and transported them to an underground cavern, high on a ledge. To Ess they looked noticeably different to Succo and the other islanders, all except Ian Campbell that is. They certainly spoke differently. They did not understand the words he said in his pre-programmed monotone Japanese. He scooped up a crude communication instrument they dropped on the steps. The femanOid had dropped it as she turned to face them, just before she was prodded.

Despite the cold and his dislike of swimming he had joined the citiXenScouts in the water, so he could look for signs of Succo. They couldn't believe their luck when they found the 'Oid specimens perched at the water's edge, looking the other way ... too slow to understand what was happening. They had to buBBle them to get them through the water back to their land base - the worMRoom within the tree roots where they had established a safe haven that could also provided them with a multitude of insect and small mammal samplings.

The instrument was some sort of primitive coMMunication mechanism. Unfortunately the linguist knowAlls could not yet decipher the written and spoken messages contained within it but the pictures showed a far different world to that on the island. MiSSion coMMondant, Mol, took Ess's advice to proceed with caution and keep on the move. It was more important they collected viable specimens rather than encounter a large mass of beings. In truth Ess wanted to keep moving to look for Succo.

When they came back and found the manOid samplings gone and footsteps and scrapings of many other specimens they were both angry and perplexed. As far as they were aware, from the last expedition, these manOids could not climb or swim very well and they certainly could not fly ... yet they had managed to reach the 'Oids on the ledge. The aliens called a foRUm back in the pOd to consider their options.

'BreeDers said manOids resourceful. BreeDers said eXpect odD actions. Use, use prodgun. Vote, vote continue miSSion. Net more, more 'Oids.'

'Beware hotHead, hotHead, Wil. Prodguns, prodguns – valid point.' Mol was a good leader and allowed everyone a voice.

'Import complete, complete miSSion. tAg, tAg many 'Oid creatures here. Ideas, ideas, Ess?'

Ess counted off his fingers.

'Larger land mass. BreeD quickly. Essential have femanOid, femanOid sampling.'

The aliens had not got their heads around the gestation period of humans as they failed to obtain a female specimen on the other miSSion.

'Could go blueWater. Find island, island,' suggested Ess.

'Or go where minions of 'Oids. Jump, jump up, tAg, tAg some. Minions, nYa miss, miss a few. So, so many.' Mol was thinking aloud.

Ess was not happy at this alternative option. He was convinced he would find Succo where there were fewer people.

Mol determined they would move a little further along the caverns, near an 'Oid habitation, and endeavour to grab 10 samplings, 5 manOid and 5 femanOid, before finishing their miSSion. But they would only do this after they had completed their trawl of fish, insects, mammals and birds. They seemed to be doing this efficiently without causing any unwanted attention. They would only take up Ess's suggestion if they didn't succeed with the tAg and go tactic.

And so they continued. Within the pOd the knowAlls attempted to decipher the language on the coMMunication device whilst the miSSionScouts brought in squirrels, foxes, badgers, moles, voles, rats, mice, dogs and cats. Horses, sheep, pigs & cows followed. The Scouts always wore masQs, complaining of the smell and distastefulness of their task. Each specimen was cleansed and put into a holding buBBle cocoon immediately it entered the pOd; the Scouts went into isoblution units to remove any traces of contamination. They were under strict orders not to take back any germs or noxious smells.

Then he heard it, her name, on the device.

'I'm so excited, Ryuu and Atsuko are coming over. Just wish it was in happier circumstances.' Jennifer had rung Viv's phone and left the message, just in case she could hear it, not realising at the time it was in alien hands.

Ess didn't alter his eXpression but his body involuntarily straightened and he stopped breathing. Both Mol and Wil Jnr registered the change but said nothing.

The miSSion headed south - towards Cardiff. They were following 'OidBeats. Eventually they had to come nearer the surface to check out the inhabitants. They took the coMMunication device with them in case any more messages came through. They couldn't understand the words but the voice seemed to have an effect on Ess. Mol was hopeful the knowAlls would get a breakthrough and let them know what the words meant very soon.

This was their second mistake.

The Plan

'If I can get within earshot of Ess he will recognise my voice, I'm sure.' Atsuko was trying to convince Captain Elliott and Agent Savage that she, as well as Ryuu, should be allowed to swim in the caverns and help look for the Invaders. She and her nephew had faith in their enhanced capabilities; the younger men just saw two aging Japanese people, who, whilst wiry, seemed to have little muscle and substance on them. They'd heard of Atsuko's epic swim and of Ryuu's survival techniques but they were hesitant.

'Don't look like that, just because we're in our seventies we're not useless. Where we come from people our age are respected and revered for their experience and maturity.'

Captain Elliott was taken aback, he thought Ryuu was blind - how could he see his expression?

'I can feel your expression.' Ryuu commented without being asked.

'And read minds,' thought James Elliott.

'A useful tool, wouldn't you say.' Ryuu grinned - but was deadly serious.

'You can't afford not to let us help you otherwise what was the purpose of bringing us half-way across the world.'

'It just goes against the grain to let you go into a danger zone.'

'We volunteered for it, which is why we came. We know these Invaders. We can help, if you'll let us.' Ryuu was not pleading, he was being factual.

Atsuko nodded her agreement. 'If Ess is with them he's arrogant enough not to conceive that we could capture him. I'm sure he'll be tempted by my voice and not be put off by my smell.'

'Smell?'

'These creatures hate our smell and always wear masks, except Ess, he has no sense of smell.'

Agent Savage piped in 'Where would you enter the river ... if we let you?'

'At the base of the tree; or the big cavern where you found Viv and Peter. I doubt they'll return to the Well.' Ryuu was confident in his response.

'The longer we leave it the more headway they will have. We need to move quickly.'

'Yes, please let us get going, now.' Atsuko was pleading.

'Ok, but you'll wear wetsuits and tracker sensors.' Captain Elliott knew he really had no option.

'Talking of trackers, we've just had notification that the missing cell phone has come to the surface, just north of Cardiff. We're checking it out.' Chris Savage turned to go back to the mobile incident unit. His stride lengthening purposefully as he covered his ear to hear more clearly the report on his headset.

Three pairs of eyes turned in his direction. 'What!'

'It could mean nothing, we cannot say any more than that at the moment.' The agent's face was emotionless as he turned away for a second time, Captain Elliot beside him.

Ryuu shared the news when he and Atsuko were brought back to collect swimwear and spare clothing.

'If the birdmen have it they must be moving south, towards the Bristol Channel.' Luke spoke his and the others' thoughts aloud.

'Oh no...' Jennifer's voice crumbled.

'What is it?' Viv was concerned at her friend's reaction.

'I rang you ... on your mobile ... just in case you could hear me ... I wanted to let you know help was on the way ... I told you Ryuu and Atsuko were coming ... I might have let the aliens know too much.'

'Even so, I'm sorry, definitely not. You cannot come with your friends. This is a military operation and we cannot take bystanders.' Captain Elliot's voice was apologetic but firm, he was not to be swayed. Nor was he convinced that Miss Dean's phone message would give much information to the Invaders.

'But what are we expected to do whilst you're all searching for the aliens, just sit here?!' Viv was exasperated. 'Pretend we're on holiday?'

She wanted to be in the thick of it. Jennifer's hand on her arm stopped her saying more. And the squeeze of her fingers promised an idea.

'Well, okay, if we must - we must. We'll be waiting up for you for when you get back, Ryuu, Atusko.' Viv hugged them both. 'I supposed we'll have to make do with the travel scrabble.'

Peter almost choked, trying not to laugh at Viv's amateur dramatics and doleful look. He could see right through it. Funny how easy it was to know some people; or at least, how easy it was for him to know Viv. She gave him a wink just as she covered her face in her hands pretending to have a coughing fit.

'Please take care. I'll be with you in spirit if not in body. You're both very special to me.' Jennifer's words to her friends as she saw them out the door were heartfelt and touched all who heard.

'So what do you have in mind?' Viv barely allowed the door to click shut before she rounded on Jen.

'Sshh. Let's walk Dom, look he's eager to go out.' Jennifer put a finger over her lips and let her eyes do the talking as she beckoned her friends to follow her outside.

'Great idea, I think some fresh air would do us all good. Just let me grab my jacket and walking boots.' Luke indicated to the others to do the same.

'How about a picnic? I'll make up a flask and some sandwiches – we're bound to get peckish if we're out for a couple of hours.' Jen busied herself in the kitchen with lots of cluttering. Peter and Luke rammed as much of their climbing equipment as possible into their rucksacks.

Dom sat patiently at the door, waiting for the promised walk.

'We're taking Dom for a long walk and we're gonna have a picnic as well, so don't expect to see us back for a couple of hours.' Viv told the solider at the gate.

'It might rain Ma'am.'

'Oh, it's bound to – but we're all prepared – we're in Wales after all.' Viv twinkled her eyes mischievously. 'We're fully equipped.' She pointed to the waterproofs bulging from her backpack. 'We have to find something to do - none of us are soap addicts.'

'We might even stop for a drink at the While Lion in the next village if we get a chance.' Peter was entering into the mood of the adventure.

'Yea, see you when we see you.' Viv gave a nonchalant wave as they all took off up the lane pretending they were going for a holiday ramble.

'Do you think we fooled him?' Viv asked.

'Well you were pretty convincing,' Peter put his arm around her waist in a playful hug.

'Whether he believes us or not he can't do much until we don't come back.'

'Sounds mysterious. What do you have in mind Jen? We're all here because you gave us the nod.'

'I thought we could follow the water down stream and see where it leads us. If your cell phone has gone south I figure it didn't travel there on its own and that the Invaders might be following the river to surface on the outskirts of Cardiff.' Jennifer looked to Luke and was pleased to note he nodded his agreement.

'Brilliant idea – but a lot of the water is underground where we can't follow it.' Peter had a point.

'But we know where it surfaces, or rather you know as you're local. You can guide us to where there are rivulets, streams and ponds?'

'Yea and maybe we can cut a few corners by leaving out the obvious spots around here. There's a train route isn't there? Why don't we travel half way on the train?'

'That's a good idea Viv but I think you'd attract attention, you with your red hair and pink boots!' Peter smiled warmly. 'Cardiff is not that far, we could probably walk it in two and a half hours, if we don't stop to admire the scenery. There's a cycle trail we can follow most of the way.'

'Suits me,' Luke was totally prepared with a rucksack on his back and walking stick in his hand. 'I was looking forward to using this old friend; it's done many a trek with me.' The stick was gnarled and none too straight, about five foot in length with a crook at the top to rest his arm in when he felt the need. The protective varnish brought the wood to life and Jennifer just wanted to reach out and stroke it.

'Did you make this?' she asked.

'Yep, many years ago. If I haven't lost the knack I'll make you one - if you want?'

'I'd love one, yes please.' Her eyes held his.

'Come on you two!' Viv shouted from ten metres in front. 'We can't afford to lose any more time.'

Luke held out his hand and Jennifer took it. They ran the short distance to catch up with Pete and Viv. Dom was scouting further ahead. The sun broke through but there was a grey cloud looming over the Brecons.

Up ahead

'Those old'uns are amazing. I don't know how they do it. You wouldn't believe the guy is blind, it's like he's got radar or something.'

'I know what you mean. They just keep going, gliding through the water effortlessly. Even when they have to crawl like a worm through the narrow channels they do so without a word.'

'Yea, and the blind guy is in the lead, I can understand him not being worried by the dark but neither is his Aunt. Did you see the way she stroked the fish in that lagoon?'

'I just hope they can lead us to these goddam aliens, I'm beginning to get the eegie beegies about this.'

'Don't let the Captain hear you say that ... we're supposed to be the elite of the force.'

'And so we are; but I do like to know my enemy, what they look like and are capable of. In this scenario we don't; we're following creatures from outer space, or so we're told. I've been wondering if those films are just a clever hoax.'

'Sshhh, keep moving, we need to catch 'em up.'

Ryuu and Atsuko were in their element. Water. They swam and listened; not only with their ears but with their whole body. Water was a great carrier of information. Ryuu could sense their presence; they were not that far ahead. He could feel grooves in the algae where clawing nails had caught the edges. Atsuko spotted a red feather float pass - they were finally in the right cavern. They had been underground almost two hours now. They put their heads above the water line.

'There's a waterfall ahead, I can hear it. I think we should stop for a drink and breather, before we dehydrate.' Atsuko was ever sensible.

'You're right. Sorry, I didn't mean to push you so hard.' Ryuu had forgotten his aunt was ten years older than him.

'Oh no, it's not too hard, but I think we will need our wits about us when we catch up with them and ... maybe we should have a plan?' Atsuko raised her voice, a fraction above a whisper, into a question.

They reached the pool at the base of the waterfall and surfaced. Another feather, bright blue this time, was caught on the reeds.

'Look,' Atsuko gave the feather to the army divers when they reached them. They're tracker devices worked well. James Elliott clambered down the woodland walk alongside the gushing torrent within a couple of minutes. The waterfall crashing down the other side of the boulders provided a welcome sound barrier. They were free to talk.

'These look too exotic to come from any birds around here. I'll get them identified. How are you two?'

'We're fine, don't worry about us. Worry about them. They're not far ahead, we can feel them.'

James Elliot believed the Japanese Elders, they exuded sincerity and confidence.

'How far? Don't get too close, we want to have time to prepare a trap, we want them alive... if possible.' He added the last two words with some hesitation. He wasn't sure these Invaders would come quietly and he was not prepared to let them run wild taking anyone they wanted.

'Well if Ess is with them and, as we think, he's looking for Atsuko, then I think we should use her as bait.' Ryuu saw nothing irregular about volunteering his aunt in this way.

'Yes, I will do my best to draw him in but will need to be fairly close as his hearing's not that good. We can hear them half a kilometre away and, generally, their hearing is even better than ours, but not Ess. His is very limited, comparatively.' Atsuko shared some of her intimate knowledge of the aliens.

'Hmmm, I think we need to go on quite a way in front of you,' Ryuu spoke his thoughts aloud. 'We don't want them to pick up on a party of people following them ... they are far less likely to think two manOids on their own are after them.'

'I hear what you're saying, and I agree with you, but I don't like it.' Captain Elliot's face was grave. 'This is army work and, whilst we appreciate your help, we are the one's better equipped to deal with any invasion.'

'In normal circumstances I'd agree with you but we have these special powers given to us by the aliens. Atsuko can swim like a dolphin.' The corners of Atsuko's mouth turned up as she bowed her head in acknowledgement of the fact. 'And I'm almost as good, plus, although I cannot see with my eyes, I can see with my other senses, it's almost like having a sixth sense; and, of course, I can understand what they say.'

'Okay. We'll give you a five minute head start but keep your trackers on at all times.'

Atsuko and Ryuu silently dropped back into the water. There was no splash just two circles of ripples gently spreading across the water. The Captain looked down river, there was no sign of them to the naked eye but his Sergeant indicated he had them on screen - they showed as two identical red lines following the flow of the river.

It felt wonderful to be in water. Back in their element. Free to flex their skills in all directions. All too often they had to dumb down their attributes so they were not perceived as freaks. Their bodies synchronised effortlessly and they were half a mile along the river before they heard the army divers drop in. They didn't stop.

Atsuko kept humming 'Ess, Ess, Ess,' in her head, hoping her target would hone in with his sixth sense.

They came up for air near a clump of woodland, off the beaten track. From the water's edge they could see evidence that the Invaders had disturbed the ground here.

'We are getting closer,' Ryuu observed. 'I can sense them in the air.'

Atsuko felt her adrenalin rise, more from excitement than fear.

'I've drawn arrows on the bank so the divers know to keep going and will keep trying to tune into him. Let me know if you hear anything.'

And away they went, back into the water, their mouthed conversation inaudible to the average human ear.

They were aware of kingfishers diving after small fish; ducks and moor hens paddling overhead; eels slithering beneath them. They heard the rain start. They kept going. Then Ryuu heard it: the babble of their language. He put his arm out stopping Atsuko. Finger over his mouth he signalled silence as he slowly put his head above the water line, cupping a hand around his ear. Atsuko looked and listened. In the distance she saw a flock of sheep being herded by a shepherd whistling his dog.

'Grr... grr..... yelp!'

The listeners jumped.

'Laddie, come by, come by, what's up? Aahh...'

'On no, they have them both,' Atsuko screamed internally and felt her body cringing.

'Come on, follow me,' Ryuu signalled; he was already back in the water.

Atsuko drew another arrow, this time with an exclamation mark after it, pointing in the direction of the sheep.

They swam gently, virtually gliding around each bend in the river, ever alert. Ryuu held his hand to his ear and nodded. He could hear them near some rapids.

'Ess,... Ess,... Ess,... Atsuko is with me.'

'Where are you? Who are you? Where is Succo?' The response came in Japanese.

'We are in the river, upstream. We can't come too close. I was on the island. My name is Ryuu. Can you swim to us?' Silently Ryuu exchanged Japanese thoughts with Ess. At the same time he stopped swimming and signalled Atsuko to surface, very quietly. There was no more communication.

'I'm sure it was him.' They lent against the bank and waited.

'It might take him a while to get away. He might not believe you.' Atsuko spoke quietly and at the same time kept calling Ess in her head.

Atsuko drew the name Ess in the mud.

'We're better off in the water, we're quicker swimming than running these days.' Ryuu tried to keep his voice light but there was an edge to it.

'He's here, I sense him.' Ryuu stood stock-still.

Atsuko looked under the water just as Ess swam into view. She waved to Ess and tugged at Ryuu's leg.

Ess held a prodgun and approached them cautiously, looking nervously about him. Atsuko smiled and beckoned again, realising she must look totally different, 59 years older, greying wet hair tied back, her body contained within a wet suit. She surfaced and waited for Ess to do the same. Ryuu was tense. He could feel years of fear, anger and hate rising in him. His smile didn't reach his eyes but he too beckoned and pushed himself to the surface and onto the river bank.

'We need to get him away from here, before the divers catch up.' Atsuko spoke English.

Ryuu looked at Atsuko – was she serious?

'I mean it, we can't let him know we're not alone, he might alert the others.'

Now he understood. He followed Atsuko. His smile almost natural as he watched Ess hop towards them over the rocks.

'Konnichiwa Ess,' Atsuko bowed the traditional greeting. 'It is good to see you again after so many years.' This time she spoke Japanese.

'And you. I knew you would be waiting for me.'

Both Ryuu and Atsuko were taken aback when Ess spoke Japanese out loud, albeit with a clipped accent. Somehow it made him more human.

'This isn't the island is it? Where are we? How did you find me?'

Atsuko's voice warbled with gentle laughter. She found his childlike ignorance and self-centredness both amusing and disgusting at the same time - but kept her response warm. 'We're in a country called Wales and I didn't find you, Jennifer did; Jennifer was also on the island when you came the first time.'

'We hadn't realised so many of you escaped.' Ess paused, he couldn't put his mind to this revelation just yet, he had a much more important matter to address. 'Succo, I've come to take you back with me this time, just as it should have been before. The other citiXens are here to collect specimens of all the creatures on your planet but I'm here just for you.' Ess ventured a smile; he saw no reason to think this would not be acceptable to Succo, after all she'd been waiting for him. He didn't register her as an older woman but as an alien being, a femanOid, which, fortunately, he couldn't smell but could still see and hear – with concentration.

'What's happened to your eye?' Atsuko played for time.

'Oh that, I lost it in another adventure,' Ess announced proudly 'I'm well known for my athletic prowess.'

Atsuko put up a hand to halt the mirth escaping her mouth and bowed her head. 'How did you get away from your fellow citiXens?' she asked.

'Not a problem, they've just caught a manOid specimen and a furry beast, so they're thoroughly amused at the moment.'

Atsuko shuddered inwardly, her heart hardened for the task ahead. Ryuu could hear both the army's divers and the aliens approaching.

'I can see I'm in the way, your two have a lot to talk about. Why don't you take yourselves off into those trees and have a quiet chat and I'll see if I can find us some eels to eat.'

'Yes, why don't we? Would you like to do that Ess?' Atsuko smiled and bowed yet again, knowing that Ess lapped up this token of obeisance.

He just couldn't resist her. 'Of course. Make sure you catch me a big one ... I'm feeling very hungry all of a sudden,' he called in Ryuu's direction, totally oblivious to the fact that they were not here to do his bidding.

Atsuko led him to the trees, trusting that Ryuu had a plan.

Ryuu slipped effortlessly back into the river and swam upstream towards the divers. He didn't have to go far, as promised they were only five minutes behind.

'We've found them and Ess is with Atsuko around the next bend. The Invaders have just caught a shepherd and his dog and are only a few hundred yards further downstream but they've realised that we're behind them and Ess is missing.' He spoke very softly, in English, a language the Invaders did not understand.

'Thanks, we guessed something was happening when you stopped for so long. We will soon have back up.' The Sergeant nodded his instructions to the communications officer who was texting avidly to the main incident unit. The use of texting kept the aliens in the dark. If they'd spoken instructions aloud the enemy would have heard and might have registered they were a fighting force. As it was the aliens simply anticipated there were a few more people upstream - for the picking.

A helicopter flew above their heads following the line of the river.

'What is that?' Ess twitched as he pointed upwards.

'It's what we call a helicopter. It is a machine that flies overhead and can search for lost people. It's probably looking for some wayward canoeists.' Atsuko didn't think her response was that convincing but it kept Ess talking.

'What is canoeists?'

'They are people who paddle small narrow boats in the rivers. They sometimes overturn and get washed downstream.'

'Ha! If they get washed towards my fellow citiXens they'll get a warm welcome,' Ess laughed at his own humour.

Atsuko smiled externally at this witticism, it was not to her taste but her role was to keep Ess chatting and she knew how to do this..... she fed him the lead and he spoke endlessly and passionately about himself, his exploits and plans for the future. She sat, sagely smiling, tilting and nodding her head.

Ryuu could hear their conversation and signalled to the soldiers to keep quiet. He could also hear the aliens; they too were listening in and creeping upstream towards the pair, aiming to capture Atsuko. The soldiers continued with text and coded messages for communication – this silent form of interaction eluded their prey, who, with their arrogance and misconception of human capabilities were as gullible as Ess. They too accepted Atsuko's reason for the flying machine they had seen and heard overhead and had already discounted it as a particularly early and gross form of mechanical flight. The soldiers moved ever closer, underwater. Their diving gear meant they didn't have to come up for air; the river flow masking their particular smell and noise – up to a point. They couldn't stop the tell-tale trail of air bubbles.

Ess was the first; flailing; helpless; caught unawares. His impaired hearing and lack of sense of smell meant he was totally unprepared for their attack until it was too late; he had no way to prevent himself from being taped up and bundled ignominiously into a brown hessian sack.

'Succo, Succo, his plaintive cries rung in her head ... until his mouth was taped. Then only Ryuu heard his mental pleas ... he set his jaw firmly shut.

A Mosaic in Time

Turning her back on the departing sack Atsuko headed for the stream. A tear meandered down the side of her nose - she caught it with her tongue. The saltiness reminded her of all those earlier tears: tears for her own incarceration: tears for the imprisonment, abuse and death of her family and friends: tears of relief when she was reunited with Ryuu. Atusko had shed so many tears throughout her life and still her resilience shone through - she was not about to give up, not yet. There were many more aliens to capture, maim or kill, whatever it took. Whatever happened they could not be allowed to return to their pod and take any other poor souls with them.

'Ma'am, Ma'am, this is no place for you, please wait here.' The soft voice of the solder belied his burly shape. His hand applied gentle pressure to her arm.

'Don't worry about me – I can look after myself – I've been doing so for nearly 80 years. Actually, I can help you.' Atsuko's dark eyes pierced his - there was no doubting her conviction. He let go and gave his attention to the job in hand.

'How's it going up ahead?' He text.

'No report as yet, they are going in under silent cover, using tranquiliser darts rather than bullets, we're the decoy.' The female sergeant knew her stuff, her response brusque. She'd had to fight to survive in this man's world, fighting was her vocation, she enjoyed it. Her body was alive, tuned into every vibration, every manoeuvre and minor transgression. Sergeant Emma Jones tolerated no mistakes from herself and few from her men.

Atsuko re-entered the water seamlessly, not a ripple. She could sense Ryuu, alert and excited, up ahead; the Invaders just beyond him. She gave up a prayer that her brief interaction with the soldier on the river bank did not alert them further. Her fears were groundless; the aliens had mastered basic Japanese - not English –they had no concept of different cultures and nationalities, in their world everyone was virtually cloned to be the ideal citiXen. However, they could sense movement from quite a distance and knew that manOids were approaching them from all sides. Mae, the chieFScout, grouped them into a square on the river bed, like gladiators, waiting for the onslaught. Ryuu wondered what sort of trap these beings might set; they had extensive powers and resources on land, but in water, away from their pod – maybe they were less omnipotent. They had to come up for breath, eventually. There was hope.

Wil, impetuous as ever, fired by youth rather than acumen, was next. He'd broken away from his fellow citiXens to swim along the far edge of the bank, intent on surprising their prey. He didn't realise that whilst 'Oids personally, didn't possess his advanced sense of smell, hearing and sonar, they had equipment that did. He put his head out of the water to take a breath; a well-aimed dart caught him in the neck; his good looks turned sour as he winced and lost muscle control. He sunk into oblivion. It was the same for each of the birdcumdolphin creatures in turn, until only one remained, Mae. She held up her elegant purple feathered arms, in the universal sign of submission, chameleon eyes ablaze and fearful. It was over; for now.

Wil was lucky, he was pulled from the water before his lungs filled with water but his fellow citiXens were less fortunate. They had each remained under water for as long as they could, before coming up for air and being shot, one at a time, as they surfaced. The underwater siege took nearly an hour, there were so many of them determined not to give in. Eighteen aliens died; Mae, Wil, Ess and Woo, the penultimate female shot, survived. The cadavers of the others were taken away for scientific examination; airlifted out of the zone quickly before any press arrived - but not fast enough to go unobserved.

A step behind

The intrepid foursome, plus Dom, followed the river downstream until they reached a waterfall. There they saw footsteps; boot and flipper prints to be precise – they knew they were on the right track but at this point they had to veer away from the river and go through woodland, slightly off trail but still with glimpses of the tumbling water through the trees.

'Hey, can you hear that? Choppers! We're getting closer.' Peter was excited. Dom barked catching his mood.

'Shhh.' Jennifer signalled for them to keep quiet, 'they can hear you from far away.'

And so it was that with a lot of face pulling and gesticulation the friends carried on, in animated silence. That was when they saw it, the procession with the shepherd and his dog, caught in nets, unconscious and swinging from side to side as they were carried on poles by masked birdmen deeper into the woods.

Jenny gasped; her hand clasped her mouth, her eyes wide open and child-like; the horror of her parents' capture re-lived. She was back there, peering through her grandma's skirt. Her parents and the others wincing as they were poked with prodguns; her father, his arm about her beautiful mother, trying to offer what protection he could.

'We must help them.'

'We're with you on that Jen,' Luke spoke for all of them. Dom sniffed the air and curled his lip, revealing white canines ready for action.

They followed at a distance. The aliens, unable to differentiate the smell of their hunters from that of their captives, suspected nothing.

Then Luke's arm shot up. He silently pointed. He could see their quarry reflected in a mirror.

'That's the pod - it looks just like on the film, the one I watched with Ryuu on the island, except it is hidden in trees not caves.' Jennifer whispered, awestruck.

'Actually it is more camouflaged than hidden,' Peter favoured accuracy. 'The mirrored sides reflect its environment ... an asset which is probably more effective in darker surroundings than this.'

'Yes, that's why we didn't see it in the Well.'

'Snap!' Viv and Jen spoke at the same time - still mindful to keep their voices low.

'What are we going to do? Yes ... I know the question is obvious but someone has to ask it.' The ever pragmatic Viv piped in.

Peter responded, 'Whatever we do we must stop them entering the pod.'

'I have an idea.' All eyes focused on Luke.

Fortunately the aliens had stopped to talk to each other and possibly their colleagues within the pod. There seemed to be a dispute about what to do with their smelly captives, especially the poor collie.

'Keep out of sight and walk quickly, we need to get ahead of them, between them and the pod.' As he said this and urged the others forward Luke pulled his flare pack from his rucksack. He no longer talked but relied on sign language. They got the idea. Peter produced a laser flare from his inside pocket. Luke wanted to start a fire between the aliens and their pod. It was risky. It would delay the birdmen from reaching the pod and, hopefully, it would be quickly spotted by the Armed Forces. Luke was relying on them seeing it and coming to their aid - before the shepherd and his dog disappeared into the mirrored chasm.

'Yes!' 'Yes!' 'Yes!' 'Yes!' They couldn't contain their exuberance. They each threw a flare at the same time and the fire had taken hold; the aliens were pulling back from the flames. Peter shone his laser into the eyes of the Invaders - just as the chopper approached ... then another... and another.

'Go! Go! Go!' Luke cheered the paratroopers on. The troopers didn't bother with tranquilisers this time. They used real bullets.

The four fell silent. It was one thing to watch people being killed in films, it was another to watch it in person. The cries of pain, the moaning, the smell of urine and blood; yes, the aliens bled blood, they were not so different from their human captives and captors. Their prodguns were useless against a sustained attack from the sky. Soon the troopers were on the ground, their targets floored. They untangled the shepherd and his dog from the nets, both too groggy to know what was going on.

'I feel sick.'

'I know what you mean Jen, feel a tad queasy myself.' Viv couldn't pull her eyes away, even though she found the sight of so much carnage nauseating.

'At least it was all over quickly for them.' Luke tried to assuage the horror enacted before them.

'You're right Luke. They died more humanely than my parents, with less pain and indignity thrust upon them, but that doesn't make it right. I keep thinking of the words of Donovan's song ... you know... Universal Soldier .... he's fighting for me and you. We are all responsible for every death our forces cause, even if it is for our own protection.'

Her friends were silent – each lost in their individual thoughts.

'Sorry, I didn't mean to be so downbeat ... obviously I'm glad we've saved the shepherd and his dog but the cost was high ... even if it wasn't of our making.'

Luke and Viv each put an arm around Jennifer's shoulders.

'We actually agree with you Jen, but when your back's against the wall you have to make a stand.'

'Yes, I know. Funny, I choose not to eat meat or fish because I couldn't kill an animal for food but, I realise now, I could kill another being to protect myself and my loved ones - if we were under attack.'

'Look, look! The pod is moving.'

Peter pointed to where they could see the tail end of the Pod as it purred beneath the roots of the trees.

'Oh no you don't!' They heard a soldier shout out as he threw a grenade after it. Others also threw their grenades but, whilst they hit their target and caused a huge explosion and fireball, they did not break the surface.

'They must have one almighty headache - whoever's in that pod.' Viv's innate humour could not be kept down for long.

'I don't think they'll be back in a hurry.' Peter was almost flippant in his relief.

'That's if they get away, I'm sure the army will track them wherever they go.' Luke was more optimistic.

'I don't think they'll get them,' Jen was less convinced, 'I think once they're underground they'll find their way to the sea and then on to wherever their planet is.'

'They might not live on another planet; they might live in an underworld Atlantis,' voiced Viv, the dreamer, the secret author.

Jen shuddered. 'Oh Viv, don't say that, it would be awful to think they were so close.'

'I know, but if the combined forces of various countries can't find a plane when it goes down in the sea how will they find a pod that is made of an unknown material and reflects its surroundings.'

'You should be a science fiction writer' laughed Peter, 'with your imagination you would enthral your readers.'

'Or scare them witless!' Jen lifted her mood and laughed with her friends.

Dom took time out to sniff the air and growled, loudly this time.

The fire was soon under control but no matter how hard they searched or how sophisticated their equipment – the combined armed forces of four nations never found the pod. And no one gave a thought to the worms.

The end?

kaRRak lingo and meaning

aDvisor – consultant
aPHidLink - across space communication link

background - -unobserved area
bio connections - physical links
blueWater - -sea
blueWorld - Earth
brainBox - brain
breeDers - studs/parents
breeDin - breeding
breedKWarters - married quarters
breedinPair - married couple
breedinPartners - potential mates
breedinPermit - marriage licence
breedinStock - egg/sperm providers
brethren - people
brethren - person
breWen - children
breWeen - child
breWn – born
buBBle - encase in an oxygen sack

camRa - camera
citiXen - citizen
citiXenScout - hunter

citicAPsule - enclosed town

chiLLocker - freezer

cocKRoach – cockroach

coMMa - multi-functional communication device

coMMandant – Commandant

coMMon gOOd - everyone's wellbeing

coMMunity wardens - police officers

coUNcil - government

coupling - marriage

courtiNChambers - meeting rooms

dOns - decision makers

dWellers – inhabitants

echOSonar - sonar system

eGGlings - confused bi-products of cross insemination

eXploratory - exploratory

eXpired - dead

eXplorers - explorers

eXtremeKlub - extreme sports club

femanOid - female human

fisHPop - breathing pellet

flyTScouts - airborne scouts

flyin Locusts! - expletive

fodder - food source

forum - discussion group

fRend - friend

growth - expansion

isoblution unit - quarantine unit

kaRRak - Karrak home state

keePers - guards

knowAll - scientist

labCell - observation room

labRat - laboratory specimen

lingOPop - language pellet

lodge - family home

manOids - humans/men

manure - fertilizer

masQ - mask

medic - doctor

mediCAid - nurse

mediCUnit – surgery

minions - large quantity of inferior beings

mission - mission

mistakes - errors

mooNRing - 1 day

mothRworm - data receiving unit

nestBox - bunk

noNer - loner

nYa - no/not

odDBrew - mis-fit

Oid - slang for manOid

OidBeats - derogatory slang for heart beats of lesser life forms

oZone - ozone

paSSion - key focus

phYto-knowAlls - botanists

Pip - pill

Pop - pellet

prep-sKool - primary education

pOd - pod, transporter

prodgun - futuristic tazer

programmed - programmed

sanBag - poo bag

satellite aPHid - orbiting space-craft

sCent - odour

sibling - brother or sister

sonSon - grandson

soSHal - social

soSHally - socially

sQWad - team

sQWark - news

stupor - kill

stupORize - render lifeless

suNRing - 1 year

tAg - seize

talker - interpreter

talK-up - insert lingOPop

titanium - titanium

teCHno - technical wizard

toxin - toxin

travelPip - sleeping pill

trawliNnets - barbed nets

tunnels - caverns

understanding - betrothal

wacky – fantastic

webbed - encased in neoprene strapping

wingBeat - 6 seconds

worKaid - slave

worKstat - work station/unit

worMCamras - Genetically modified worms

worMRoom - makeshift depot

yo - yes

Printed in Great Britain
by Amazon